SUPERVILLAINS ANONYMOUS

By Lexie Dunne

SUPERVILLAINS ANONYMOUS

LEXIE DUNNE

HARPER

VOYAGER
IMPULSE

An Imprint of HarperCollinsPublishers

This is a work of fiction. Names, characters, places, and incidents are products of the author's imagination or are used fictitiously and are not to be construed as real. Any resemblance to actual events, locales, organizations, or persons, living or dead, is entirely coincidental.

EPub Edition JUNE 2015 ISBN: 9780062369130

Print Edition ISBN: 9780062369147

10 9 8 7 6 5 4 3 2 1

To those who screamed, tweeted, or hit me upside the head
with the book after that cliffhanger (hi, Mom!):
Sorry not sorry.
Hugs and kisses,
Lexie

ACKNOWLEDGMENTS

Shout-out to my personal superheroes:

First off, thank you to Tyler and Ariel Henderson and DJ Elson, for being my fight coordinators and ensuring I could beat Gail up real good. Erica Lilly and daroos, you are the best designated drinkers a writer could hope for, and I owe you so much for that motivation. My sanity crew, who listened to me whine for hours, are some of the loveliest people I know: Kathleen Kayembe, Sharon, and my sister. Grace Viray, Karen Valenzuela, Samantha Brody, and Miriam Weiss: I could not have asked for better cheerleaders. And, as always, Maximus "C. C." Powers—I was not kidding when I said couldn't have written this book without you. Or at least it wouldn't have nearly so many Vicki scenes, so truly, you are a gift to the world.

To all of my internet friends: you're weird. And I love you. Yes, even you.

My deepest gratitude goes out to the Rebeccas: my agent, Rebecca Strauss, who knew just when to send the "Um, are you okay?" e-mails, and my editor, Rebecca Lucash, who cheerfully researched robotic sharks and rabbit punches.

And finally, to Mom and Dad: thanks for not putting me up for adoption after I almost accidentally burned down the house. Just think how much egg there would be on your face if this book goes on to win a Nobel Prize. Just kidding, I love you both.

CHAPTER ONE

When the person throwing the book at you has superpowers, the book moves supernaturally fast. I learned this when, less than a day after I'd been unceremoniously accused of being an accessory to murder, I stood in court, officially charged with the crime.

Actually, stood was a bit of a stretch. Swayed was a little closer to the truth. I was fortunate to be upright at all, thanks to a recent three-story drop headfirst into a mall fountain. A normal human wouldn't have survived. I was a little luckier due to some enhancements that had made me more than human, but even then, the drop had been a bit much for me. Everything hurt: my ribs, my throat, my head, even the backs of my knees.

None of that changed the fact that I was chained up in the middle of a secret underground courtroom facing a panel of men, and they'd just declared me guilty of helping kill the closest thing I'd ever had to a best friend.

Who hadn't even been dead a *day*.

There were five of them—or six. Possibly seven. Definitely not more than eight. My vision swam in and out, so details were a little difficult. Five or six men, each face grayer than the last, each haircut worse than the next, all of them sitting at a table at the head of the wood-paneled chamber. They were lit from above by yellow spotlights that cast their ghoulish features into deep shadow. They'd been speaking for either one minute or ten, but their words had floated in the air, incomprehensible.

One word punched through the haze of agony now: "Guilty."

I tried to look up. It upset my balance, so I tipped forward instead, and the guard who'd been pulling me around all—what was it? Morning? Evening?—day jerked me back upright.

I tried not to throw up on his shoes.

As I stared at the floor, words cut through the dizziness, clear as a bell rung right by my head. "Gail Godwin, for the crime of accessory to the murder of Class B Hero Angélica Rocha by the Class B Supervillain Chelsea So-Called, you are hereby sentenced to serve thirty years in Detmer Maximum Security Prison."

I forced my aching head up and looked at the man at the end of the table, the only one I recognized. I knew him. We'd only met formally once, but it had left an impression. The second time I'd seen him, he'd arrested me. And now he had convicted me of murder. I looked up in the blue eyes of Eddie Davenport, CEO of the largest company in the world. The light fell in a perfect halo over his blond hair. I squinted at him, and I said, "What the *hell*?"

Or at least I tried to. What came out was, "I don't like these potatoes. Can I have them scrambled instead?"

And I passed out cold.

Overall, not very inspiring last words. Luckily, they turned out not to be my last.

I'd heard of Detmer Maximum Security Prison.

Even if I hadn't been Hostage Girl, I would have. It was the place they threw all the supervillains who had committed terrible crimes against society. The woman who tried to take over New York City with radioactive gerbils, the idiot in San Jose who had tried to boil the Pacific. They all ended up in Detmer. And usually, they ended up breaking out of Detmer.

Unfortunately for me, I was usually the villains' first stop after they escaped. It's a little difficult being in the *Guinness Book of World Records* under "Kidnapped Most Frequently," but for four years, that had been my life. Some of it had to do with proximity, I figured, since Detmer wasn't that far from Chicago. Simple, really. Escape prison, kidnap Hostage Girl, get your name on the news and a quick fight with Blaze. I'd even made it convenient for them by never trying to fight it.

I never thought I would actually end up in Detmer, though.

Detmer was for supervillains.

I'm many things, but I'm *not* a villain.

Davenport Industries, which ran most of the world and anything related to superpowered individuals, had not received that memo. I woke up in a prison transport vehicle, my eyes practically crossed from the pain of a metal harness pressing against what had to be at least one broken rib. When I politely tried to scream and let the driver know, a syringe became involved. Which was why I stood now in a line with six other women, hands cuffed in front of me as they marched us down a long hallway that smelled like lemon Pledge, and everything seemed pleasant and disconnected. Just a handy side effect of the fact that I was tripping balls from whatever they'd plunged into my neck.

A chain kept me attached to the woman in front of me. A second chain attached me to the woman behind me, and so it went. Guards in gunmetal gray uniforms walked alongside, fingering the triggers on their stun batons so that sparks rained down onto the tiles.

I frowned at the handcuffs wrapped around my wrists. I didn't like them. I didn't know why, but I didn't like them. I wanted them off.

"Stop fidgeting," one of the guards told me, sending out a new shower of sparks.

I blinked at him and wondered why my left eye wouldn't point straight.

After the hallway, we were led into a room with

drains set in the floor. Medical equipment, a woman in a white lab coat, another woman in scrubs, and a new set of guards awaited us.

"Face forward."

I started to turn the wrong way. The woman next to me rolled her eyes. They moved along the line, undoing the chains and cuffs. When she got to me, the woman in the lab coat—Dr. Kehoe, it said in pretty blue stitching above the pocket—frowned. "What's wrong with her?"

"Reusabital. Driver says she got a little quippy."

"That's probably true," I said. "I have, like, backtalked pretty much every villain this side of the Mississippi."

Dr. Kehoe frowned and held her hand out for her tablet. "Godwin," she said, reading the screen. "Gail Godwin. Look at you. That much Reusabital would turn an elephant into Sleeping Beauty, and you, you're just a bit drunk."

"Don't think I am. Drunk feels nicer than this. Plus, I don't remember any tequila."

"Uh-huh." The assistant undid my handcuffs and moved on to the woman next to me.

"*Salud* to you, too," I said, and looked forward again. This time it was my right eye that felt off. That was going to be a problem eventually.

I kept squinting as they ordered us to strip out of the orange jumpsuits. Some of the women hesitated, but I kicked off the clothes easily enough. Modesty was for people who hadn't been given Mobium and therefore didn't have my rather amazing muscles. Those were a pretty new addition to my life, which was why I was proud to show them off. I felt a little less proud when I realized how cold the room was, and that the woman next to me had a fantastic tattoo of Edvard Munch's *The Scream* across her upper arm, which definitely put my muscles to shame.

Dr. Kehoe and the nurse in scrubs moved up the line of us. It took me a couple of women to realize that they were cataloging birthmarks, scars, and tattoos with the tablet. Dr. Kehoe dictated to her assistant, asking for origins on tattoos and scars. With the first few women, this took a couple of minutes at most. Motorcycle accidents, the occasional knife fight, chemical burns. Easy stuff.

When they reached me, they both stopped and stared.

"Hmm," Dr. Kehoe said. I tilted my head back to look at her. "We'll start from the top. This scar on your hairline?"

I rubbed it with my fingers. "Dr. Laboritorium was trying to perform brain-wave experiments on me. The helmet cut into my head, but don't worry, Blaze saved me and knocked him out."

"And this scar on your temple?"

"TongueTwister hit me with a rock when he called up a dirt devil. I was in the hospital for like a week."

"The scar below it?"

"Can't remember. That might be Queen Bae knocking me out with a Swarovski honeycomb. Diamonds are definitely not Girl's best friend." I grinned at my own joke though it had been nearly a year since I'd called myself by my own terrible nickname.

"What else could it be?" Dr. Kehoe asked. Her assistant's fingers were flying over the tablet as she desperately tried to keep up.

"Might've been Lady Danger. She has Great Danes, you know. Big ones. Scary teeth." I waved my fingers in front of my mouth in approximation of fangs before I touched my forehead again. "Wait, no, this scar? This scar is definitely from that time the Saratoga Kid visited Chicago and wanted a hostage to present to his new bride at Niagara Falls. Sorry. I get them all mixed up."

Dr. Kehoe sighed. The other women in the line were openly goggling at me now. "Just how many of these scars do you have, Godwin?"

I shrugged. "I lost count years ago. There've been a lot of villains. They're dumb, and they leave marks." I turned to look at the other women in the line with me. "No offense."

"None taken," Scream Tattoo Lady said dryly.

"Why don't we move her to the end, Dr. Kehoe?" the assistant said. "We have a schedule."

"Good point."

So I waited, cooling my heels while Dr. Kehoe and her assistant moved down the line. Each woman was handed a box at the end and they were shuffled together through a door that led into the prison. I didn't like that door. It did funny things to my stomach.

Finally, Dr. Kehoe approached me with a sigh. "Let's get this over with, shall we?"

An hour later, my throat was dry and I wasn't feeling so pleasantly drunk anymore. "Yes," I said, answering Dr. Kehoe's question as she looked at the bottom of my foot and the tiny scar that ran along the seam of my instep. "I was dangled over an active volcano by Melodrama Madam. I really don't like to remember that one."

"All done," she said. "You can put your foot down. You can collect your box and your bunk assignment. Where's she going?" The last was directed at her harried-looking assistant.

"She's going in with the Villain Syndrome patients," her assistant said. She paused and looked at the screen again. "Is that right? She's not tagged for VS herself. Oh, and *that's* even stranger. Her doctor from Davenport's requesting access to her."

I felt my spirits inexplicably soar. My doctor from Davenport was a woman named Kiki, and while I wasn't sure she'd be able to help me, as she hadn't stopped my arrest, I had some questions. Maybe she could answer them.

"That's certainly not going to fly," Dr. Kehoe said, looking at the tablet as she crushed all of my hopes. "Send the denial straight to Dr. Cooper. We look after our own in Detmer. Are you ready to go to prison, Godwin?"

"No," I said.

"Too bad."

I was handed a box full of clothes and given an opportunity to pull them on: a green tunic-style shirt, black pants, new black shoes that were surprisingly comfortable. Less comfortable was the needle pushed into the part of my shoulder that met my neck. I only protested a little, though it made my entire arm feel sore. I felt a spurt of nerves in my middle as I was escorted to the door that would take me into the confines of Detmer Maximum Security Prison.

I stepped through.

By some counts, I had been kidnapped over two hundred times by more than fifty villains in a four-year period. I had been mentioned by news media so often that I had my own tag on the Domino, nobody remembered what my real name was, and the sight of my face alone had been enough to send people to sidewalks on the other side of the street to avoid being in my potential blast radius. There had been political cartoons, tourist T-shirts, and little plaques around businesses near my apartment talking about various attacks. What I'm saying is I probably clocked in over a thousand hours in the company in supervillains during my tenure as Hostage Girl.

And not a single one of those jerks had seen fit to mention that Detmer Maximum Security Prison was, in essence, a day spa.

Bewildered from the drug and by the bamboo floors, fluting music, and papyrus wall hangings, I followed a guard—"Oh, no, we're called monitors here! Please, call me Tabitha!"—away from the processing area. Detmer was open and airy. There wasn't a ninety-degree angle to be found in the entire place. I was shown the recreation areas, a giant cafeteria that looked more like a five-star dining lounge, the most high-class gym I had ever seen (the chrome was blinding), and several lounges that looked like they had sprung fully formed from the pages of a designer magazine.

"Detmer was, of course, designed with the comfort of its guests in mind," Tabitha said in a bright, plasticky voice as she bustled along. I followed in her wake in a drugged haze. There was a feeling niggling at the back of my mind, like I *should* protest this, like if only my thoughts would work together I would be angry beyond belief. Mostly I was mystified. Maybe everything had just been one prolonged nightmare. Perhaps I hadn't seen a shopping mall ripped to shreds by a man with earthquake abilities, and I wasn't wrongfully in prison for assisting in the murder of my trainer.

Maybe polka-dotted camels would show up and start dancing the marimba around the next corner.

"Guests are free to wander around the complex as they choose. There are no mandatory mealtimes or lights out, which you might find in *other* facilities." Other prisons, I realized hazily. She was talking about places where people who had committed crimes were held and punished, not other spas.

"And if you ever have any questions, feel free to ask me or one of the other monitors." Tabitha redefined perky. If she stopped smiling, the Elder Gods would probably descend upon the world and feast on the entrails of the living. "That's what we're here for!"

I blinked dumbly at her.

"You must be tired!" Tabitha led me down a new hallway, one lined with glass doors at even intervals. The track lighting along the ceiling made everything appear soothing. "These are the living quarters. You've been housed with the Villain Syndrome patients."

"Huh," I said now. Did I need to be alarmed about that? Villains with VS were the most terrifying kind: they truly believe they were committing acts of good—usually through colossal destruction and loss of life. Come to think of that, this was probably worrying, yeah. I scratched my nose and nodded. "'Kay."

"Do you have any questions for me?" Tabitha asked.

I thought about that for longer than usual. "When is dinner?"

"Very soon. You'll find a schedule inside, and it has all of the movies playing in the cinema. We're very lucky to have the newest releases. Here we are: room 407! That's you!" She stopped in front of one of the glass doors, identical to the rest. "Only you and your roommate can enter your room—and the monitors, of course, but we hardly count!—so you'll have all the privacy you need."

I looked at it. "With a glass door," I said.

Tabitha's smile grew strained at the edges. "In you go. The Reusabital should be wearing off now, which is good. We don't believe in any restraints, medical or otherwise, in this complex."

"In prison," I said, tone never changing.

Tabitha chuckled, like I'd said something extremely amusing. "Enjoy your nap."

I put my palm on the little panel beside the door and watched it slide open. Apparently, Detmer worked just like Davenport. There was probably some irony in there somewhere.

With Tabitha gone, the world seemed a little less plastic. My thoughts began to connect in logical fashion once again as I stepped into my cell. I was in prison. I wasn't supposed to be in prison. I was in my room in Detmer, which was actually like some kind of demonic day spa, and Angélica—

My breath hitched as everything finally broke. Every emotion under the sun slammed into me at once: fury at the injustice, grief so sharp that it felt like it was cutting into every exposed inch of my skin, confusion and anger and sadness. My hands began to shake. I clenched them into fists, but it didn't help. Everything built and built, the pressure growing behind my temples until it finally happened: I screamed.

I screamed and I kept screaming even though my throat felt raw and ripped to shreds. What felt like hours ago to me, I'd had everything: I'd been happy, shopping for new clothes at the mall with friends. And now, I was in prison for a crime committed by an *actual* supervillain, and every time I tried to point that out, they drugged me. My friend was dead because of a hit she'd taken for me. The scream went on and on until I couldn't breathe. I dropped to my knees and hiccuped as tears spilled. I finally did what the drug had been keeping me from doing: I broke down and sobbed.

At some point, I must have crawled over to the bunk beds along the wall and climbed onto the bottom bunk. My eyes were swollen from crying, and my throat ached, as I stared at the underside of the bunk above me.

I was in prison.

I didn't even *know* Chelsea, the woman they'd claimed I had helped kill Angélica. We'd met a grand total of twice, and both times, she'd been doing her damndest to kill me. Unluckily for her, I'd had a run-in with a mad scientist who had dosed me with some kind of super-element. The Mobium in my body made me faster and stronger, quicker to heal, and more perceptive. It sped up my metabolism to frightening levels, which was why my stomach currently felt like it was trying to digest itself. But the most important thing it had done had been to enable me to survive Chelsea's powers, which was why the first time she'd tried to kill me (in a bank, while I'd been trying to meet with a journalist associate of mine), she had been unsuccessful.

The second time, my superhero trainer had knocked me out of the way, and Chelsea had unloaded a full blast into her. I'd watched Angélica seize and die in a hospital bed while I'd been fighting off my own injuries and unable to help her.

I rolled over onto my side and felt another set of hot tears leak out of my eyes.

Why did Davenport believe I knew Chelsea? Why would they *ever* think I would do anything to Angélica? I liked her. Sure, she'd spent most of our acquaintance attempting to put me on the floor, but she had been genuine and kind, and fiercely hilarious. A tear dripped onto the bridge of my nose and onto the feather pillow under my head.

"Do you plan on knocking that off anytime soon?"

I flailed, which was a mistake because pain exploded up and down my side. Angélica's lessons kicked in: in an instant I was halfway across the room, on the balls of my feet with my hands held in loose fists in front of me.

The woman who'd spoken, who had to be seventy if she was a day, stared at me, utterly unimpressed. She found me so uninspiring that I almost wanted to apologize for my very existence. She leaned one shoulder against the wall and raised a single silver eyebrow.

"Who are you?" I asked, wiping at the tears so they wouldn't hamper my vision.

"Your new roommate. I'm tired of listening to you snivel." With surprising spryness for a seventy-year-old, she crossed over and pulled herself easily onto the top bunk. Her legs dangled over the side. "Name's Rita."

I eyed her warily for a second. The sniveling comment had made my ears burn, but I didn't see the point in alienating my roommate right away. "Gail," I said. "I'm Gail."

"You smell like fresh meat." Rita actually sniffed the air. "Hell, you're still shiny. What'd they get you for?"

I swallowed hard. "They say I helped kill somebody."

"Only helped? Underachiever, I see."

"Yeah, thank you for your opinion," I said. "I'll cherish it always."

Rita tilted her head and considered me. It didn't escape my notice that she hadn't volunteered what she'd done to get her locked up. "So that's how it's going to be," she said.

"How what's going to be?"

Rita hopped down off of the bed, landing lightly on the toes of her orthopedic sneakers. She wore an outfit similar to mine. What her arms lacked in tattoos, they made up for in sheer muscle tone. She was only a little taller than me, and her skin was sun-worn and withered like an old nut. But her eyes were bright and hard.

I tightened my fists as the hair rose on the back of my spine. Every sense tingled.

"Hurt yourself, did you?" she asked instead of answering my question. "You're leaning a little."

I raised my chin. "What's it to you?"

"Looks like you hurt yourself right here," she said, and delivered a short, sharp-knuckled punch to the side of my rib cage.

I immediately dropped to one knee with my hand over my abdomen, air hissing between my teeth. I hadn't even seen her *move*. "What the hell was that for?"

"You're new," she said, leaning over and twisting

her head so she could meet my eye. I had to bite down hard on every instinct I'd ever possessed, all of which were screaming at me to lunge at her face and blind her. Angélica had warned me time and again not to attack in anger. Rita might be old, but she was fast, and she was strong. "You seem stubborn, which means you probably won't learn quickly. That's fine. The only one you're hurting is yourself."

"What is your problem?"

Rita's smile was so cold, it dropped the ambient temperature a couple of degrees. "With you? There is no problem. But there are rules here, and you will follow them. As my new cellmate, you represent me." She grabbed my chin hard enough that I swear I heard my jaw creak. "You will not embarrass me, child."

I hissed out a breath. "Screw you, old bat."

Nothing changed behind those flat blue eyes. "Oh, you're precious. I should—"

I punched her. Because I was in pain and still a little dizzy, it wasn't the precise, devastating punch Angélica would have wanted, but I struck Rita's wrist, knocking her hand away from my chin. I dropped onto my elbow to try and spin and kick her legs out from under her. She leapt nimbly out of the way. Though I expected her to kick me in the abdomen, where I was vulnerable, she did something else entirely: she started clapping.

"So you *do* have some fight in you," she said, bringing her hands together hard enough that the sound hurt my ears. It felt like an explosion in the tiny white space of our cell. "Good."

SUPERVILLAINS ANONYMOUS 17

I climbed to my feet. "Stay away from me. I'm innocent, but that doesn't mean I'm taking any crap from you."

"We're going to have so much fun together." She toyed with the hem of her shirt for a second, and I noticed that all of us had DETMER stamped on the bottom of our shirts, as if we would ever forget where we were. She inclined her head like a queen dismissing her subject and strolled right out of the room.

I stared after her. Great. I'd been wrongfully thrown in prison, my friend was dead, and my roommate was a psychopath. When was this nightmare going to end? And could it get any worse?

Fate really had it out for me, apparently. Two seconds after that disastrous thought crossed my brain, I saw movement in the hallway outside. A flash of green walked past, and back, like the person had seen something and needed to double-check. Just like that, there was only glass separating me from the yellow bug eyes of one Razor X, who had personally kidnapped me seventeen times (a record). He stared at me through the glass in utter puzzlement.

When he removed the silver helmet he'd always worn, I realized I'd gotten something very wrong about Razor X: she was not a dude. Strawberry blonde hair spilled over her shoulders. The bug eyes looked even creepier without her helmet.

She reached up and knocked on the door. I stumbled back until I was pressed up against the wall. All of my old enemies were in this prison, and the only thing between them and me, I realized with a horrible feeling of dread, was a glass door.

"Crap, crap, crap, crap," I said under my breath, like a mantra. She couldn't get in, but I felt like a zoo creature, trapped in the room while she stared. I took a deep breath, gave her my best glare, and went to sit on the bed. Surprise crossed her face (maybe; it was hard to tell with the huge yellow eyes) before she shrugged and walked away.

I put my head down and stared at my own lap, at the black pants and the edge of my shirt, with my name on the bottom hem. GODWIN stared back at me. No longer Hostage Girl, Girl, or Gail. Now I was going by my last name.

Rita's shirt had said DETMER in the same place.

I'd assumed that it had been the name of the prison. It was, but I had forgotten one fact: Kurt Davenport, founder of Davenport Industries and the original Raptor himself, had built Detmer Prison. He'd named it after his wife, the very first prisoner.

His wife Rita Detmer.

My cellmate wasn't just any random supervillain.

My cellmate was the very *first* supervillain.

I was rooming with Fearless herself.

I stared at the wall. I stared at the ceiling. I thought about Angélica, and about Chelsea, and that weird secretive council chamber. About stripping naked in front of a complete stranger and having my scars cataloged like library books. How I was in prison with at least fifty people who had ample reason to hate me.

How I couldn't stay in my room forever, not with the way my stomach was beginning to hurt from lack of food.

Thinking about that, I did the only thing I could: I crawled under the covers, pulled them over my head, and stayed there, shaking, until I fell asleep.

CHAPTER TWO

Hunger woke me.

Sometime during the nap, it had migrated from being a pressing concern to an outright distraction. The minute I opened my eyes, my stomach growled. My hands trembled. I could feel my vision blurring, which only made me feel sicker. Angélica had warned me about what would happen if I didn't take care of my incredibly fast metabolism. My body required fuel to fight off leukemia, which was a side effect of the Mobium. I wasn't allowed to ever let it get this bad. I needed to eat, or I would become incredibly ill.

But eating meant walking to the dining room that Perky Tabitha had pointed out. Beyond the door to my cell lay at least fifty sources of highly individualized terror.

"You're strong now," I told myself as I fumbled my way out of bed and to the door. It didn't do a thing to stop my knees from shaking. "You can take them. You're not Hostage Girl anymore."

My hand hovered by the panel. I watched my fingertips quiver and bit my lip hard.

If Angélica were there, she would have made some mocking comment, or called me something insulting in Portuguese. I could practically hear her voice right then and there, so strong that I had to squeeze my eyes shut. I took a deep breath and pushed the button. The door slid open, inviting a gust of lavender-scented air.

The hallway beyond my room was empty, which made sense when I leaned back to check the schedule. Dinner had been going on for a solid twenty minutes, so I would be walking into a meal already well in session.

I'd survived high school. I knew what that meant. It couldn't be helped, though. If I didn't eat, the bruised ribs and throat wouldn't heal, and my condition would only worsen.

At least the Mobium ensured I would be able to find the dining room again. After a lifetime of forever getting lost, being able to find a place as long as I'd been there already was a godsend. As I walked off to enjoy what could possibly be my last meal, I worried. Prison food was supposed to be the worst of the worst, wasn't it?

I smelled lobster thermidor before I even reached the dining room.

"Good evening, mademoiselle." A tuxedoed man stepped in my path and made a little bow. "If you would be so kind as to follow me, please?"

Well, he didn't *look* like any supervillain I'd ever faced. Taking a deep breath, I followed him into the dining room, which was lit by candlelight. Placing open flame around the world's most dangerous supervillains seemed like a prodigiously bad idea to me, but I did have to admit it was really pretty with the way it flickered and reflected off the snowy white tablecloths. Seated at the tables were several people I recognized and quite a few I didn't. Their casual Detmer uniforms seemed out of place with the silver dishes and fancy centerpieces, but I couldn't deny that the food was what drew my attention. Lobster thermidor, a beef dish that smelled positively delectable, and something done with cod that made me salivate. Waiters whisked about with dome-covered platters, bowing obsequiously.

I *felt* the atmosphere in the room change as I followed the maître d'. Villains at various tables turned their faces to follow me. The candlelight made their eyes seem beady and calculating.

Halfway across the room, the inevitable happened: one of them recognized me.

Venus von Trapp practically leapt out of her seat. It had been a couple years since she'd snatched me out of Union Station, and she no longer wore her lily-pad couture, but I recognized her right away. I flexed my wrists automatically. She'd once suspended me eighty feet in the air with the help of a few giant vines.

"*Hostage Girl?*" she asked, her eyes so wide, I could see her unnatural red irises clearly even in the low light. "*Dionaea muscipula*, is that *you?*"

"I don't go by that anymore," I said, sneaking looks at the other diner at her table. My stomach sank farther when I saw the fangs of the pale woman sitting next to her abandoned seat.

"Don't tell me you've joined the *corps mal*," Venus said, shaking her head, so that the vines and leaves that made up her hair clattered against each other.

"With the trash they let in?" I said. "Not damn likely."

It occurred to me that sassing the woman who'd once turned me green for two weeks was a bad plan. But Venus waved an impatient hand and turned to the maître d'. "She'll sit with us, Pierre."

"Very good, madam." He whisked himself away, leaving me in the den of my enemies. Literally, it appeared.

"You were always the easiest way to get a good dime in here," Venus said, and my jaw dropped open a little. "It was like the best-kept secret. But if you're in here now, guess we'll have to find some other way."

"Hostage Girl's been off-limits for nearly a year, Ven," Lady Danger said. Without her Victorian dress, she seemed like an entirely different person. But she still had the beehive hairdo. Luckily, she did *not* have the genetically modified Great Danes on either side of her chair (I checked). "Hello, Girl. You're looking well."

I didn't tell her to go to hell though it was a very near thing.

"Have a seat. They'll bring out the first course for

you. You're a little behind, but no worries. Do be sure to try the beef."

I sat only because it was growing too painful to stand. "Hold it," I said as I reached for the bread basket and began tearing a roll to pieces. "You all *wanted* to come to Detmer? That's why you were always kidnapping me?"

"Well, yes." Lady Danger passed me the butter. "You were our favorite, too. You did make things so much easier for us, dear."

Venus nodded enthusiastically. "And Blaze was never cruel about taking people down. I always thought you were rather cute together. How's he doing?"

"You *turned me green*," I said, the words finally exploding out of me.

Venus paused with her wineglass hovering from one of her hair-vines. "Yes," she said, like she wasn't sure why I would be upset. "And wasn't the photosynthesis great? I keep trying to convince Lady D to give it a shot, but alas, no luck. Did you not like it? And I tried to get Blaze's shade just right. I thought you would appreciate that supportive little touch."

Photosynthesis had not, in fact, been all that great, and being able to understand plants had been even worse. I hadn't been able to eat a salad for over a year without feeling like a cannibal. Even worse had been the fact that the Domino had gleefully turned their entire page green in my honor. Lady Danger gave me a sympathetic look as though she understood how I felt completely and did not actually find the idea of communing with plants all that interesting herself. The last thing I wanted was sympathy from a woman who'd attacked me with giant, terrifying dogs.

So I pushed my palm into my forehead as a waitress brought over another breadbasket, a menu, and a wineglass for me. "What the *hell* is going on? What is even happening?"

"Dinner," Lady Danger said. "It happens every day. Today's is actually exceptionally good. I really must send my compliments to the chef."

"No—not dinner." I picked up the menu and stared angrily at it, as though I could channel all of my frustration into it. If I could, it probably would have spontaneously combusted, and I would never have known that the fourth course was blackened fish tacos with tropical fruit salad and chipotle lime corn relish. Those sounded really good, actually. I focused past the hunger. "Not dinner," I said again. "This whole place. Detmer. You guys are supervillains."

"Well, I wouldn't go that far," Venus said. "I mean, it's a compliment, but really we're lower tier at best, and—"

"Super. Villains. Eating the nicest food I have ever seen in my life. I passed a massage parlor on the way here with a twenty-four-hour therapist on staff. There are *candles*." I reached forward and flicked the long taper. "I don't understand. Where are the bars? And the hideous orange jumpsuits, and, and . . ." My voice broke.

Lady Danger and Venus exchanged a look. "Girl," Venus said. She cut into her filet mignon and waved a juicy bit of steak at the end of her fork. There was not a single vegetable on her plate. "You're among several hundred of the most dangerous criminals the world has ever known. Within this room we have, collectively, the talents to blow the world up twenty-seven times over, rebuild it from the ashes, and blow that up four times. For fun."

"If you ever wanted to keep one group content, this would be the one, I daresay," Lady Danger said.

Venus swallowed her steak. "Life isn't all oranges and lemons here, though. We can't leave, and you can't get fresh seafood that's worthy of the talents of Mr. Kanezachi this far inland."

"Though he tries, the dear," Lady Danger said.

"Who is that?" I asked.

"Our sushi chef," Lady Danger said, dabbing daintily at her fanged mouth with a napkin. "Do try not to escape before Thursday. We share him with the men's side of the prison, and he won't be back until then. You simply *must* try the Damselfish in Distress roll. I think it's named after you. Isn't that a gas?"

I cradled my face in my hands and seriously considered moaning. They had a sushi chef. They were the *bad guys*, and Davenport apparently paid for them to have a man come in on alternating days and prepare fresh sushi. Fresh sushi named after me. While I'd been languishing in and out of the hospital for *years*, sticking to a job I hated because the health care was just that good, the very people tormenting me had landed right in the lap of luxury.

"Have you decided, mademoiselle?" I heard a waitress at my elbow.

Without opening my eyes, I reached out and pointed at the menu. It didn't matter. I'd hardly taste it on the way down. My body needed the fuel, and it wasn't like it mattered. Nothing mattered anymore.

"I must say, we're delighted to have you here, Girl," Lady Danger asked. "You'll be a good addition. Who's your roommate, if you don't mind me asking?"

"Rita," I said, raising my head.

Both women stopped midchew.

"I take it that's bad," I said.

"They put you in with *Rita*?" Lady Danger shook her head regretfully, as if to say *It was nice to kidnap you, but you're not long for this earth*. "Oh dear. Rita can be a bit . . . tempestuous."

"Yeah," I said, thinking of her lightning punch to my injured side. "We've met."

"I'm sure it won't be too bad." Lady Danger gave me an encouraging smile. It really was a shame she'd gone the way of evil. She would have made an excellent grandmother, provided you liked big, scary dogs.

"Wait," Venus said. "We still don't know what you did, do we? How did you end up in here? What sort of crime does a Hostage Girl commit?"

"Nothing." I ripped a roll in half. "I did nothing."

"Everybody in here's done something, girl. You can tell us. We won't judge. Remember: you're among villains now."

"Davenport thinks I helped somebody. I didn't, and

I have no idea why they think I would, and it sucks because the woman who *actually* did it is getting away, and I'm stuck here."

"Who was it? That you helped, I mean," Venus asked.

"Her name is Chelsea."

"Chelsea what?"

"That's it. Just Chelsea."

Lady Danger frowned. "That's not a very villainous name. Are you sure she's actually a villain?"

"She killed my friend." My voice was dull. I felt the hot threat of tears pricking against my eyelids, but I clenched my right fist so hard my nails nearly punctured the skin. "I didn't have a damned thing to do with it. But hey, it's not like they gave me a chance to *say* that during their creepy underground council meeting before they bundled me off to the Detmer Day Spa."

"Oh, Detmer Day Spa. I like that one."

"And their little underground council *is* creepy," Venus said.

I opened my mouth to agree, and it occurred to me: they were supervillains. I did not want to agree with supervillains.

"Your first course," the waiter said, putting a plate in front of me. I stared at the asparagus tips that had been wrapped in some kind of meat and drizzled with a dark sauce. It smelled like the first good thing to happen in over twenty-four hours.

"Ooh, good choice," Lady Danger said. "Make sure you really savor that, and—"

I finished the course in three bites.

"Or not. I must say, it strikes me that you were a bit softer-looking the last time I saw you. More to chew on, as it were."

The scar from her Great Danes twinged. I glared at her and returned to rummaging through the bread basket.

Apparently, that was all Lady Danger really needed to know that I was not going to join her Victorian circle of best friendship, for she turned back to Venus von Trapp with a little *what can you do about it?* shrug. They immediately launched back into the discussion I'd interrupted, which appeared to be about the sexual proclivities of a villain I'd never heard of.

While they speculated, I kept my head down. Anger brewed in my chest, but I was so tired that it felt like a feeble flame as opposed to the forest fire I knew it could become. I felt sick. Whether this was from the fact that my body was doing its best to repair itself or from finding out the truth about Detmer, I had no idea. I had so many questions and no idea whom to ask about them. Where had they taken Angélica's body? My friends had to know by now what had happened, but were they being told the truth? About how she had stepped in the way of a hit meant for me? Or how she'd had a seizure and died, and it was my fault?

The waiters brought me one course after another. I slurped gazpacho, wolfed down a Caesar salad, and swallowed the meat course almost whole. It was, hands down, the finest food I'd ever had in my life.

It tasted like ash on my tongue.

It was during the fish tacos that I spotted the door. My table was near the edge of the room. About thirty feet away in my direct line of sight stood a door that I thought led to the kitchen, at first. Waiters disappeared in and out of it with covered dishes fairly often. Every time a blue light next to the door blinked. Since I never saw any of them flash an access badge at a scanner, I had to assume it worked by proximity.

Midbite, I saw the door open fully. Through it, I could see all the way down a long hallway, to a court-yard beyond. A delivery truck idled right there by the door.

I stared until the door closed. The food had already given me a little more energy and a little more response from my limbs. How many villains had I known that had escaped this very prison? It couldn't be *that* difficult, really. Surely, they didn't expect me to start causing trouble in the first day . . .

I scooted my chair back, and I didn't think. I just took off, walking as fast as I could without attracting attention, making a beeline for that door—

Something hit me in the lower back, on the right side. Starbursts of pain exploded behind my eyes. I gasped and started to topple forward, only to have somebody grab me by the arm and yank me back up-right. This, naturally, did not do any wonders for my already sore rib cage.

"Mademoiselle." The woman who held me up now

was a waitress with a starched white shirt and a square face. "Ms. Detmer sends her compliments and requests that you join her at her table."

Like hell I would. I goggled at my attacker. "Did you just *hit* me?"

She gave me an affronted look. "I'm sure I have no idea what you mean. I have not touched you, save to spare you an unfortunate rendezvous with the floor."

Maybe she had a point. It hadn't felt like a fist striking my back. It had felt smaller, like a pebble, but the pain was a sharp, biting one. My brain caught up with the rest of me. "Oh, no," I said. "No way. I'm not going near that lunatic unless I absolutely have to, and I don't have to do that now."

"Girl." Lady Danger looked rather pale, even for a woman who willingly modeled herself after a vampire. "Girl, if Rita's asking for you, you need to go."

"We're just looking out for you here," Venus added.

"Why? You never have before."

"Mademoiselle?" the waitress asked, her voice a silky-smooth command over steel. "The table is right this way, if you please."

It appeared I didn't have a choice. I shot a glare over my shoulder at the door, as though it had somehow caused all of this. When I looked back to push myself to my feet, I saw something small and white on the ground. Frowning, I picked it up and followed the waitress to the new table, where Rita sat like a queen on her throne.

"Thank you, Carlotta," she said to the waitress, holding out a hand. The denomination on the bill she passed over made me gape.

Apparently, this prison came equipped with ATMs. It figured.

"Sit," Rita said.

I lifted my chin and stayed standing, my hands on the back of the empty chair. Rita shrugged. She held out her hand. "Tic tac?" she asked.

I eyed the little pill-shaped white mints. How had she done that? I'd heard of pinpoint accuracy, but this was ridiculous. I tossed the one she'd pelted me with on the table between us. "I think I've had enough of those today, thanks."

"Suit yourself." She tucked the mints back in her pocket.

Since my torso was actively throbbing again, I finally took a seat and reached for the bread basket. "I could've made it, you know."

"You go out through that door, the implant in your neck delivers the largest dose of Reusabital you've ever tasted, and trust me, even *your* body won't like that." She caught my look of surprise. "You think I don't know every last detail about you, Girlie? I know *everything*. I know about your mother, I know your father—"

"Then you're ahead of me there," I said.

She gave me the most regal look I had ever seen. "If you're done interrupting me."

"For the moment, or permanently?"

"If you're so determined to escape, at least learn the

lay of the land before you blindly run into something that kills you." Rita expertly used one mussel shell to pluck the meat from a second, and popped that between her lips. "You lack foresight. Nobody escapes Detmer Prison."

"Tell that to the twenty or so villains that kidnapped me right after getting out of here."

"Girlie, look around. Do you *really* think people want to leave? Gourmet dining, free alcohol, an Olympic swimming pool. Free cable." Rita snorted and pulled out a cigarette. The waitress who had fetched me discreetly showed up with a light, and Rita sucked in a puff of nicotine. "Prisoners don't escape. They get kicked out. And I can see that look in your eye. Don't even bother. According to the idiots in charge, you're not a small-time career supervillain, you're potentially a mastermind—though I've seen no evidence of that myself. You're in here for the long haul."

My jaw tightened. "I didn't do what they said I did. Somebody else did."

"Doesn't matter. They think you did, and they're the ones that make the rules." Rita took a long drag and blew a smoke ring. "Welcome to life with the Davenports."

"You'd know about that," I said.

She smiled. "So you *do* know who I am. I was a bit worried that whatever they did to you in that mall, it killed a few brain cells. Good thing to know there *is* a brain in there."

"Why do you care?" I asked. "I'm nothing to you.

I'm not a hero, I'm not a villain. At the most, all I've ever been is a hostage. So why do you even care? It's less effort to just ignore me and let me go about my business. If I break my own neck escaping, that means nothing to you."

"Or does it?" Rita tapped ash off of the cigarette and sucked in a long drag. "I told you earlier, Girlie. Inside this prison, you represent me, and you'll act accordingly."

"Why?" I asked.

Rita gave me a look that made my blood run cold. It wasn't a threatening look or even a sneer, but it was an expression I'd seen before. HypoThermos had worn the same expression when he'd tried to dose an entire wing of the hospital with small pox. To save them from their own immune systems, he'd claimed. King Killer's face had positively overflowed with the same look when he'd tried to turn Chicago's rail system to rubble. After all, he'd told me, people complained about it so much, he was just doing them a favor.

I remembered, on my very first day at Davenport, my mentor Vicki explaining Villain Syndrome to me. The desire to save the day at all costs, no matter the body count. It usually involved *a lot* of rubble and an unhealthy fixation. With everything that had happened to me, it hadn't really occurred to me that things could get even worse, but in that moment, I understood. Rita's Villain Syndrome had fixated on something.

And I had a horrible feeling that something was me.

CHAPTER THREE

The problem with discovering your roommate has a terrifying disease that focused on you: it doesn't lead to quality sleep. I tossed and turned half the night, hoping it was all a nightmare. I woke up to Rita poking my side. "We're going to be late."

I shoved her hand away. "Late for *what*? I thought this place was basically the Elysian fields."

"For work. Move your tiny superhero ass. Elysian fields. Pah." She walked off, rolling her eyes.

I sat up and looked owlishly around our room. As tired as I was, I was loath to emerge from the two-thousand-thread-count sheets. It had been like being cradled softly by a cloud in my sleep.

Wait, had she said *work*? We were in the fanciest place on the planet, surrounded by criminals who had essentially blackmailed Davenport into handing over Michelin-rated sushi chefs and all of the fine accoutrements of life. And they expected us to work? What could they possibly expect a group of supervillains to do for employment? In the end, curiosity dragged me out of the bed. I stumbled to the sink, brushed my teeth, washed my face, and tried not to look at myself in the mirror. The bruises were in their final stages of healing, and that color always made me feel ill.

"When I said move your ass, that was not secret code for 'take forever and make us *both* late,' you know," Rita said from the door.

I yawned and pulled on a shirt. "After you, sunshine."

I trailed after her since there was no way I was ever letting her walk behind me. We passed the dining room, which made my stomach rumble hopefully for breakfast, but Rita only collected two boxes from a table stacked with them. "Don't sulk," she said. "It's a croissant day. They're delicious even if you'll have to eat them at your desk."

"What *desk*?"

Rita, as expected, did not answer me. We stepped into a crowd all heading in the same direction. They gave her—and by default me—a wide berth, as we headed down a hallway that hadn't been part of Perky Tabitha's orientation. I spotted Lady Danger and resignedly returned her little wave. At least Rita's presence was scaring off any of the actual villains who hated me from attempting to track me down and get revenge. I had, I realized, become a flunky to the very first supervillain.

It figured. It really did.

"Hey, Rita," I said, lengthening my stride to catch up. "I have a question."

"Of course you do."

"Do I get a phone call?"

"Who would you be calling? That caped boyfriend of yours?"

"He doesn't wear a cape." I hadn't seen Guy since he'd kissed me and flown off to save Naomi Gunn, the reporter I'd been meeting at the mall that had been destroyed. I'd talked to him on the phone afterward, but we'd been cut off. And I needed to warn him that Chelsea was after him.

Rita sneered. "Didn't anybody ever tell you not to waste your time dating superheroes?"

"Weren't you married to the very first superhero?"

"What of it?"

We turned a corner and Detmer High Security Prison shifted from a day spa to a very posh office building. Glass walls exhibited offices with mahogany desks, rolling chairs with actual lumbar support, and some of the finest computers I had ever seen.

I actually stopped in the middle of the hallway to stare.

Rita reached back, hauling me easily into motion. "What did I say about not embarrassing me?"

"Yeah, I'm going to level with you, I'm not very good at listening to people, no matter how terrifying I find them. What is all of this? Why are there *offices*?" Ahead of us in the hallway, inmates—guests, Perky

Tabitha's voice reminded me—filed in through a set of double doors and filtered their way to the cubicles. The doors faced another set, through which I could see male prisoners filing in. My stomach dropped. "But I need to know: do I get that phone call?"

"Talk to a guard."

"Fine, I will," I said, and stopped dead in my tracks when I saw the middle-aged man who entered among the throng of other prisoners.

He looked like an accountant. He wasn't particularly tall, but he was a little round and his comb-over had only grown more severe in the two years since I'd last seen him. My brain whispered at me to *run*, to get away *right now*, but I couldn't move. It was like my feet had been bolted to the ground.

Razor X had scared me the day before. Encounters with Razor X usually ended in pain and tears, after all.

My one encounter with this man, with Shock Value, had ended in a crater in the middle of Naperville.

I saw the moment he spotted me, his eyes narrowing behind the smudged lenses of his glasses. And just like that, I was back in the bottom of a silo that had been turned into a labyrinth, trying desperately to scream and warn Blaze about the razor blades. His face went from blandly pleasant to a mask of fury and rage. He let out a yell and charged through the crowd, right at me. I couldn't do anything but watch him loom larger and larger, hands stretched out to choke me.

Rita stepped into Shock Value's path and calmly clotheslined him. She barely even seemed to move, but in the next second, she was holding him up by the throat. While hovering three feet off the ground. She looked down into Shock Value's rapidly purpling face without a single expression of violence or anger in her eyes, and in that moment, I understood what made Rita Detmer so dangerous.

"And just what, pray tell, do you think you're doing?" she asked, her tone almost bored.

Shock Value garbled something and tried to break free of her grip, Velcro shoes kicking uselessly at the air.

Rita merely tightened her grip. "No, I think *you* misunderstand," she said, her tone never changing. "It doesn't matter what happened between you and Miss Godwin, or that she is the reason you're in here. She's mine now. Get me?"

Shock Value made a high-pitched wheeze.

"Thought so," Rita said, and threw him against the wall so hard, I heard the metal clang. He lay in a motionless heap.

Rita, on the other hand, drifted back to the ground. Tucking her breakfast under her arm, she pulled a handkerchief out of her pocket. She wiped her hand clean, meticulously. "Any questions?" she asked the gathered crowd.

Unsurprisingly, nobody had any. People hurried past Shock Value's prone body, keeping their heads down so they wouldn't have to meet Rita's eye or look at me. Rita sniffed and turned to me.

"Why did you do that?" I asked, dual feelings of dread and relief rising through me.

She shrugged. "You cry enough as it is."

"Thanks, I guess," I said, my voice frosty.

She started walking toward the offices again, completely blasé about the fact that she had maybe just killed a man. "At least you bothered to say thank you. My last roommate wasn't so circumspect."

I really, really didn't want to know what happened to her last roommate.

"Somebody'll be along to show you to your cubicle. Toodle-oo," Rita said, as we walked past a receptionist. I checked to make sure it wasn't the same receptionist from my old job at Mirror Reality. But even though *I* might think Portia McPeak was the worst, the justice system didn't seem to believe she belonged in prison. The receptionist was a young man with spiky blue hair that matched the spikes protruding from his wrists and elbows.

"Wait," I said before Rita could walk off. "What do we even do here?"

"Girlie, we're supervillains. What else would we do?" She pointed up.

The sign hung from the ceiling. internal revenue service, headquarters.

"Oh, that is *not* good," I said, and Rita cackled as she walked off.

A second later, a new figure rounded the corner, and I wanted to sigh. I'd already faced my worst-nightmare villain that morning, so of course it made sense that they would send my most frequent villain to apparently turn me into an IRS agent. "You're not here to attack me, are you? Rita doesn't take kindly to that sort of thing, and she's scarier than you, no offense."

Razor X, however, gave me a hurt look through her face shield. It was weird seeing her without her little cape though apparently the bulbous purple helmet was allowed in the prison. Maybe it helped her breathe.

"How could you?" she asked.

"Huh?"

"*I* was supposed to be your archnemesis, but you went and got yourself another one. I'm so offended. Did all of our time together mean nothing to you?"

She'd dosed me with so many painful concoctions of her own making so many times, I'd lost count. I didn't want to give her any sort of loyalty. I wanted to give her a punch in the face. "What are you talking about? You're a villain!"

"Oh, come on. That hardly means anything if you don't kill people. You were going to develop powers sooner or later, so I was perfectly positioned to be your personal archnemesis. I had it all worked out, but apparently you went and found *Chelsea*. Yeah, Lady Danger and Venus-von-Shut-Your-Trapp told me all about it. Ugh. She doesn't even have a real villain name."

"What is even happening?" I asked the ceiling.

"You're my cubicle mate, so we'll always have that, I guess." Razor X flopped petulantly into a desk chair. "We could've been great, Girl."

"Gail." I dropped into the other chair. "You want to be my nemesis, get my damn name right."

"Fine. You can call me Raze."

"I didn't pick my archnemesis. She killed a good friend of mine," I said, setting my breakfast on the desk and lining the box up neatly against the edge. Focusing on the precise movements helped. Otherwise, I really would hit something. Chelsea was out there, free, and Angélica was *dead*. I breathed deep and looked over my shoulder at Raze. "Whereas you only managed to give me a headache more than a dozen times. Why didn't you ever learn a new trick?"

"Because the old one was funny. Why mess with perfection?"

There was no arguing with that, and frankly, I was too worn-out to try. So instead, I poked through the box of food. In addition to a croissant, there was a little tube of juice, a pat of butter shaped like a rose, half an orange, and some spreadable cheese. It would last me maybe an hour if I was lucky, but it was all I had, so I finished it all. Finally, I turned my attention to the computer.

It occurred to me that I did not have a degree in accounting, tax law, or anything numeric in nature. Also, I wasn't evil, so I really didn't know how to be an IRS agent. "Uh, what am I supposed to be doing?"

"Pretty much whatever you want. Ruin as many lives as you like. But I should warn you, they keep an eye on that." Raze's voice made it clear that she thought it was totally lame that she couldn't just destroy thousands of people's livelihoods. "You should probably do actual work to keep it balanced. I don't know. I mostly just play Solitaire."

"Prison," I said, staring bleakly at the screen. "It's office work."

"Yeah, right. Like real office computers have actual Solitaire on them these days."

I poked around through the computer, trying to figure out what I could and couldn't do. All types of communication seemed to be forbidden. I couldn't reach any of the messenger boards, and even the Domino was blocked. So I'd been handed a computer, but it was useless.

"What's she like?" Raze asked, breaking the silence.

"Who?" I asked.

"Your other nemesis." Raze's voice held all of the hurt of a kid accidentally forgotten after school. "She has a stupid name."

"She killed my friend and she did her best to kill me. Trust me, I'd rather you were my archnemesis," I said, paging through the files available to me.

"You really mean that?"

Though I was about to open my mouth to say that of course I did because Razor X hadn't actually managed to do any *lasting* harm, it occurred to me that maybe pissing off my cubicle mate was probably not the wisest policy. "Yeah," I said instead. "I mean that."

"That's the nicest thing anybody's ever said to me." She spun back around to play Solitaire again.

"Great," I said under my breath. "That's not gonna come back to bite me in the ass at all."

"Miss Godwin?" One of the guards appeared. It wasn't Perky Tabitha, but it could have been a close relation. She had the same one-sudden-move-away-from-running-for-my-life smile. "Your boyfriend's here to see you."

My heart leapt. I was on my feet so fast that Raze shook her head at me, but I didn't care. Guy had finally made it out to the prison. Finally, I would start to get some answers. I followed my new guard out of the office, through all of the places I'd already visited, and finally into a little hallway near Processing. She dropped me off with two guards who were wearing the same blue-gray uniforms I recognized from the transport van.

"Check her implant," one said, and the other pushed down hard on the side of my neck, where I had a little bump in my shoulder. I swiped at his hand, but he'd already pulled it back. "Still active?"

"Affirmative."

"Thanks." The first guard held up a set of handcuffs, which automatically made my stomach jump. But if it meant seeing Guy . . . I held up my wrists. "You will be granted fifteen minutes to meet with your visitor. Any talk about what happens inside these walls will be grounds for immediate removal of both you and the visitor from the area and subsequent removal of all visiting privileges. Is this understood?"

"I can't . . . talk about anything at Detmer?" I asked, squinting at him.

Instead of giving me a simple yes or no answer, he repeated the entire spiel.

"Fine, fine," I said, hoping to stop a third repeat of the speech. "Understood. I won't talk about Detmer."

"You will be under constant watch the entire time," my guard said, taking me by the elbow and leading me through a vault door into the visitor's area.

The bamboo floors and pristine walls were immediately replaced by scuffed linoleum and plaster. Several low tables were spaced throughout the room. A guard was posted at every window, with several weapons on display. I swallowed hard. The windows and doors probably all contained the taser that would incapacitate me easily if Rita was to be believed. I could see blue sky beyond, beating down hard over what looked like a barren, empty field. August in northern Illinois had struck hard, it appeared.

I forgot all about that when my eyes fell on the tall man with green eyes sitting at one of the tables.

"Hey, babe," Jeremy Collins said. "Miss me?"

CHAPTER FOUR

I stared at him, mouth bobbing silently. There had been a time where I could call Jeremy Collins my boyfriend, but those days were long past. He'd dumped me in a hospital room after an attack from the very same villain I'd just left in my cubicle. That sort of thing tended to fester though I'd forgiven him after finding out that he was being held underground in a superhero complex for his own protection. It was a little hard to hate the guy whose life had been screwed up due to his association with you.

I stepped forward because he might be my ex, but he was still the most familiar thing I'd seen since coming to Detmer. Abruptly, a lump formed in my throat. I shut my eyes.

"Oh god," he said, and I heard him scrambling to his feet. "Don't do that. *Please* don't do that. If Gu—if he finds out that I made you cry, he'll probably drop the nice-guy act and kick my ass. Don't do that."

"What the hell is going on?" I asked, opening my eyes. The tears were still a threat, but it was mitigated for now. "Why are *you* here?" And where was Guy, my actual boyfriend?

"Here, give me a hug," he said, stepping forward. I stepped into his arms, which proved awkward because my hands were still cuffed. "Sorry," he whispered. "He was going to come—in uniform. But he and Vicki got word that Chelsea had been spotted, so we thought I could sneak in. We needed to see you."

"Thanks. I'm glad you're here."

"Consider me an official liaison, willing to pass on any messages. But don't ask me to kiss him for you. You know how I feel about redheads."

I couldn't help it. The joke was stupid, but it made me laugh, or at least let out a hiccupy sob. It made sense for Jeremy to show up in Guy's place. We were in public, and my physical appearance might have changed, but I was still recognizable as Hostage Girl. And if Hostage Girl were ever seen in public with a well-built, tall man, suspicions about his identity would automatically be raised. People needed to keep thinking Blaze was Jeremy Collins, which meant that Guy Bookman and Gail Godwin were only ex-coworkers and nothing more.

"You love redheads," I said, stepping back and swiping covertly at my eyes.

He wrinkled his nose at me. "Sure, the redheaded *women*. But—uh, I would never be unfaithful to you, babe. You have my undying love and devotion for all time."

"You are really terrible at faking this," I said, and I finally really looked at him. I'd always teased him for how much time he put into his appearance, but his clothing was disheveled, his hair a mess, and there were bruise-like circles under his eyes. A thick bandage was wrapped around his right hand, which made me wince. No video games for a while for him. He also smelled like he hadn't showered in a couple of days. Not quite rank yet, but sometimes having enhanced senses wasn't the nicest.

From the way he was eyeing me, though, I guess I looked about the same.

"What the hell have they done to you?" he asked. "Are you okay?"

"For the most part. These injuries are all from the fight in the mall." I looked at the guards posted all around the room and took a seat at the table, trying not to let it bother me that they weren't even hiding their open interest in Jeremy and me. "I have a question."

"What is it? I'll answer anything I can."

"*What the hell is going on?*"

"I don't know. None of us know."

I leaned forward onto my elbows. "They think I'm helping *Chelsea*. The woman's tried to kill me every time she sees me, and they think I'm working with her. They didn't even need to present any evidence.

Just wham, bam, guilty, and now I'm in prison, dealing with—"

One of the guards coughed, loudly.

"—everything," I said, glaring at the guard. Right. Not allowed to talk about Detmer. Have to hide the fact that we took society's most dangerous criminals, coddled them, and gave them unlimited rein to run our country's taxes. "Why on earth do they think any of this? It's ridiculous! And Angélica—" My voice broke a little. Since another sob seemed imminent, I bit down hard on my lower lip. "Angélica, she—"

Jeremy cautiously reached out and covered my cuffed hands with his own. The bandage felt scratchy against my skin. "It's rough," he said. "How are you holding up?"

"I'm, you know, dealing and—you don't think I had anything to do with that, do you? And G—he doesn't, right?" It was suddenly, wholly vital that they know I would never hurt Angélica.

"No way. You love—you loved Angélica. We all did."

"Even you?"

"I mean, I didn't know her as well as you." Jeremy shifted uncomfortably in his seat. "The few times I talked to her, though, I liked her. She was scary, but she had your back at the end of the day, and you could tell, you know?"

I could only nod. He'd described Angélica to a tee.

"And nobody in our group thinks you would ever work with Chelsea. We know you better than that, Girl. Gail." Jeremy squeezed my hands once and drew his own back. When he picked up his water, I could see little tremors shaking across its surface. "But they have evidence."

"That's not possible," I said, sitting up straight.

"They have—"

"Jeremy," I said, "that's not possible. That can't be possible because I have never and I will never work with Chelsea. Ergo, there is no possible evidence that they could pull out—"

"They have text messages," Jeremy said in a rush. When I stared at him, not comprehending, he set the water cup down and picked it up. "They say they're between you and Chelsea. From—from the time you were missing. They were from your old phone, and they sound just like you."

"I lost that phone," I said slowly. "When Mobius kidnapped me in the coffee shop. It vanished, and I was—I was unconscious. There is no possible way I could have—"

"None of us think you did it," Jeremy said. "We know you, Gail, and we're doing everything we can to clear your name. But . . ." He scrunched his eyes shut, taking a deep breath like he was bracing himself. "But you *were* kind of missing for nearly three weeks, and nobody saw you or had any idea of your whereabouts. They haven't found this doctor you claim gave you your powers—"

"I don't know where he is!" My memories from the place where Dr. Mobius had kept me were annoyingly vague. I remembered escaping with him from *something*, and of being hit by a van and waking up in an ambulance, but I hadn't known where he had been holding me or anything else about the escape. My body had been acclimating to the Mobium, and now I suspected he might have sedated me, but I had no way of being sure. What I did know was that there was no way I could have sent text messages in that state.

"And . . ." Jeremy cringed again. "You did kind of drop back on the grid the same day Chelsea first attacked."

"That was a coincidence. You have to believe me, that was a total coincidence. I'm—I'm being framed." I had to take a deep breath. When that did nothing, I took another and another until I was nearly hyperventilating. It had been at the back of my mind the whole time. Somebody was framing me, somebody was setting me up. But now there was *evidence*, and I couldn't think or focus.

Why was this happening to me?

"Yeah, we're pretty sure you're being torpedoed," Jeremy said.

I threw myself against the back of the seat, a bad move since it made discomfort sing up and down the length of my spine. It helped with the shock, a little. "So their reasoning is, what? That Chelsea and I were secretly in cahoots? That we planned that attack at the bank together so I could infiltrate the Davenport complex as a spy?"

"Basically. And according to the briefing, you were alone with Chelsea after Gu—Bla—after *I* flew off with that reporter chick, so theoretically you could have worked together and planned to take Angélica down. Because maybe she was onto something about you."

"I would never do that, Jeremy," I said, my voice rising. Chelsea had been unconscious on the floor when Blaze had left the fight to get Naomi to safety. I'd run off to help Angélica fight the last of Chelsea's little group of misfit thugs. I have no idea when we could have been working together at all, given that the building had been falling down around all of us. "I wouldn't, okay! I just—that's not me, I didn't do *any* of that—"

"Gail, calm down." Jeremy cast a nervous look over his shoulder at the guards. "Please, calm down before they start something. We're going to get you out of here. We are. We're going to get to the bottom of this and find out who's setting you up, and I promise you, there's a redhead in our life who will probably pulverize whoever it is."

"None of it makes any *sense*," I said. "The only one who hates me that much is—well, there are a lot of people who hate me that much, but they're all in here with me. Is it Chelsea? Is Chelsea setting me up? And why?"

"I don't know. But you're not going to be in here long, okay? And you're not alone. The others wanted me to tell you that."

But I *was* alone. They could offer their emotional support through the conduit of my ex-boyfriend all they liked, but at the end of the day, I was the one Eddie Davenport and that weird council of old men had decided to screw over. *I* was the one wearing a prison uniform and handcuffs.

I wanted to put my head down and cry. I bit my lower lip hard enough to draw blood, but it forced the tears and the panic back.

"Tweedle-Dee and Tweedle-Jane," Jeremy said, and I realized he was talking about Guy and Vicki Burroughs, our friends, "they think it's Chelsea, and you know them. They're on the case, and they're invested. They won't let anything get in their way. So it's going to be okay."

I forced a nod and swallowed hard. "Thanks, Jer. And thanks for being here."

"I know you wish it was somebody else," he said, giving me a hesitant smile.

"Yes," I said, "but you're not terrible."

"Such high words of praise." He shook his head. "I'm sorry I don't have more to tell you. We're still working out the details, and it's all happened so fast. But the minute I know more, I'll come back."

I could only nod at that.

"So." He folded his arms over the table and leaned in. "How's the food in there?"

"I can't talk about it." Though my stomach was rumbling, the croissant a distant memory. "I'm sorry. I don't want either of us to get tackled by any of these guards."

"We could take 'em," Jeremy said.

I wanted to smile at that. At times, his confidence could be weirdly like Guy's whenever Guy wore the Blaze mask. It was also incredibly familiar, and—

Blaze.

"Oh god," I said, breathing the words out. "I completely forgot."

"Forgot what?"

"Naomi. Is she okay?" The last time I'd seen my reporter acquaintance, Guy had been carting her off to the hospital. "Chelsea didn't kill her, did she? She's not hurt?"

"We don't know." Jeremy crushed the empty styrofoam cup, refusing to meet my eye.

"What do you mean, you don't know? Wasn't she with Gu—with you?" After all, I'd talked to Guy on the phone right before the crap had hit the fan with Angélica and Eddie Davenport at the hospital. Naomi had been hit by one of Chelsea's sting-ray blasts, but she'd been breathing.

"That's the other thing. Davenport took her."

"What do you mean *took* her?"

"We have no idea where she is, and they're not telling us a damn thing, that's what I mean. How is she even connected? What did Chelsea want with her?"

"She wanted to know how to hurt Blaze and War Hammer," I said.

Jeremy snorted, spinning the pieces of the cup on the table with his good thumb. "Good luck with that. They're pretty indestructible."

"I'm worried she may have found something. Please, warn th—please be careful." I grabbed Jeremy's wrist, trying to communicate with a significant look that he should let Sam and Guy know immediately that Chelsea was after them in particular.

"Okay," Jeremy said. He looked around the visitor's room again, his eyes stopping to rest on my prison tunic. They cut down to the giant GODWIN stamped on the hem. In my prison shoes and my uniform, sans makeup and with my hair barely brushed, I must have looked every inch a prisoner. "How the hell did this happen? How did it get this bad? You're in *prison*."

"Yeah, trust me, didn't miss that memo. We need to get Chelsea. And by which I mean, *you* need to get Chelsea." I let my head fall forward from exhaustion. "I don't think I'm getting out of here anytime soon. Detmer's really bizarre, and I've been dealing with—"

"Inmate Godwin!" My guard from outside snapped into action, striding toward us. "Do I need to remind you of the rules?"

"Hey, man," Jeremy said, pushing himself halfway up from the table, "we're not breaking your stupid rules, so back o—"

The guard hit him with the nightstick. Or at least I thought it was a nightstick until Jeremy's eyes rolled back into his head. He convulsed, fingers wrapped around the edge of the table. For one horrifying second, I wasn't in the visitor's area, but in a hospital room miles away, watching Angélica's eyes roll as she seized.

Jeremy cried out and snapped me back to reality. I lunged forward and hooked a foot behind the guard's knee. A single jerk sent him toppling.

Jeremy curled in around the table with a gasp at the same time the guard hit the ground. I backed away, senses kicking into the hyperactive mode that brought every detail of the room into painful clarity. The whir of the fan blades overhead echoed like an approaching locomotive. The dust spread by those same blades seemed to hang impossibly on the air for an eternity of a second. At the same time, I noticed every bead of sweat on the foreheads of the three guards all racing toward me at once.

"Whoa!" Time slowed back to normal as I dropped to my knees, holding my hands up with my palms out. "Sorry! Reflex, I swear. I didn't mean to."

"This visit's over." My guard climbed to his feet and hauled me to mine. He waved irritably at the coughing Jeremy. "Get him out of here. You were warned, Godwin."

"It was an accident," I said, straining to look over my shoulder at Jeremy as they hauled us in opposite directions. He looked dazed, his eyes glassy. "I didn't mean to—"

"Wave bye to your boyfriend."

"Gail!" Jeremy, at the visitor's entrance, turned and tried to run my way though I had no idea why. "I'll be back as soon as I can, okay?"

The guard shoving me forward scoffed under his breath. "Wouldn't bet on it," he said to his buddy.

I got one last look at Jeremy's pained face as he was shoved unceremoniously through the visitor's door.

The guard holding me by my wrists leaned around me to tap three times on the riveted metal door leading back into Detmer. As it opened, I cast one final look at the visitor's room.

Right as Kiki stepped in from the opposite door.

I stumbled. Had she come with Jeremy? She'd been the last person I had seen before Eddie and his goons had dragged me off to my tribunal, and she was a close friend of Angélica's.

Kiki met my eye across the room. For a second, there was a brief flare of recognition. She backed up into the hallway behind her.

"Huh?" I asked.

"Keep walking, Godwin," the guard said, and slammed the door shut behind us.

I looked back at the door. "I think I have another visitor. My friend—"

"Nice try. She's your problem now," the guard said, addressing Perky Tabitha, who'd appeared like a giddy phantom. "Visiting privileges revoked for a week."

"Hey!" I said.

"Wanna make it two?"

I bit my lip again hard, before I said something about his mustache that I would later regret. When he took off the handcuffs, my shoulders relaxed. I followed Tabitha, letting her lead me back to the offices. So Kiki hadn't come to see me. But what was she doing here? Who would she possibly be meeting at Detmer? Maybe she had another patient who had crossed the evil line. After all, if she was there to see me, she probably would have brought her boyfriend and my other doctor, Lemuel Cooper, along.

Either way, I had bigger things to worry about. I was being framed. Somebody had gone so far as to plant evidence. Text messages between Chelsea and me, set in the weeks of my life I couldn't remember and therefore couldn't completely refute.

For a sick moment, I wondered.

Had I been working with Chelsea? Was it some subliminal thing? What if a psychic had managed to break my natural mental shield, and I really had somehow set Angélica in Chelsea's path? When I considered how crazy the rest of my life could be, it didn't sound *that* far-fetched.

But I also had a gut feeling that I would somehow know if I'd been working with Chelsea. My brain had never been that subtle.

So. Somebody was setting me up.

Great.

Back in my cubicle, there was a gift basket of freshly baked danishes on my desk. Since Raze was pretending not to notice my every moment, I picked through them until I had found all the thumbtacks. With Raze watching me and sulking, I took a big bite of the first one.

"Spoilsport," she said, turning back to her monitor in a huff.

At least the danishes made me feel better, or at least less hungry. Everything else, that pretty much sucked.

I wanted to put my head down on my desk and stay there until the nightmare was over.

They had text messages. From *my* phone.

How was that even possible unless . . . had Dr. Mobius set me up? After all, he'd vanished off the face of the earth after I had escaped from his lair in the suburbs. But why would he do that? Was he so angry that I'd escaped that he was getting his revenge by letting me go to prison for the murder of my friend? There were so many more direct ways to get revenge, and, frankly, I hadn't exactly pictured him as the "thinks ahead" type.

So who was it?

I looked up at the creak of Rita's crepe-soled shoe. She had a pleasant look on her face, but the skin on the back of my neck began to prickle.

"Let's take a walk," she told me.

"I've still got some work to do," I said, though there was no way in hell I was doing any tax forms.

Rita's hand clamped down on my shoulder. "Wasn't asking."

Well, when she put it that way.

We left the offices, heading back into the women's side of the prison. Through the glass in the parallel hallways, I saw workers looking at us warily, which only made the pit in my stomach grow. Rita's body language was loose and calm, but there was a tic in her jaw that I didn't like.

"So you had a visitor," she said.

"Yes." We were near the gym now. "My boyfriend."

She snorted. "The Collins boy."

Great. The world's first supervillain knew my ex's name.

"Last I checked, you weren't in charge of who's allowed to see me," I said, raising my chin.

She made a "hmm" noise. The skin on the back of her hand was wrinkled and liver-spotted, and none of that eased my suspicions as she palmed open the door to the gym and gestured for me to precede her. "Heard you gave the guards some trouble," she said.

"I'm not fond of watching my friends get tasered. Draw your own conclusions."

"What did I tell you yesterday?"

"Before or after you hit me with a tic ta—"

Something blurred at the edge of my vision, and I was on the floor, my left arm screaming in pain. I rolled by instinct. Rita's foot stomped down. The soles of her shoes might be soft, but I doubted that mattered when she was doing her best to break my elbow. I propped myself up on my good arm, trying to pivot my weight so I could sweep Rita's feet out from under her. If I could knock her to the floor, I'd have a better advantage.

She jumped over me.

I rolled out of the way of a second kick, and rolled again. My back slammed into a wall, giving me a nanosecond to fill a flush of dread. I blocked the next kick with my forearms, curling up to protect my middle. Rita's hand snaked down and grabbed me by the injured left arm. She wrenched me to my feet and raised an eyebrow when I tried to scratch at her face. In addition to being humiliating, it asked *Are you done yet?*

I tried to knock her hand away, but it was like trying to fight a wall. "What the *hell* is your problem?"

"I told you not to embarrass me. Did you think that doesn't include petty scuffles with guards?" She shook me like a rag doll. My teeth clicked together. "Embarrassing."

"I was protecting my friend."

"In here, you represent me." She cuffed me upside the head.

It wasn't a hard blow, but I still saw stars. "No, I don't. I won't be the center of your sick obsession. You're insane."

"Obviously." She released me with a flick of her fingers, and it still sent me reeling back. I backed up even farther, out of range. "How do you think I got here?"

"Stay the hell away from me," I said, panting as I braced myself against the wall. "I have enough problems without getting your crazy all over me."

Rita cocked her head, considering. When she nodded, I felt a chill in the air, but she only spun on her heel and started to walk away. "No can do, my young friend. Somebody really needs to teach you how to fight," she called over her shoulder.

"Somebody already did," I said, my throat burning. I clutched my left arm, which still throbbed. "She died."

"They all do, in the end," Rita said. She gave a flippant wave, like she couldn't be bothered to deal with it, and left me alone in the gym.

CHAPTER FIVE

Unfortunately, Rita meant every word. Somebody really did need to instruct me in the martial arts, never mind that Angélica already had. And in Rita's opinion, the best fighter in Detmer was . . . Rita.

Her lessons were nothing like Angélica's. My trainer had taken time to break down each lesson into fundamental building blocks. Every kick started with core power and balance. Every punch was explained in great detail. She had instructed me patiently, humor lacing her voice as she walked me through every new move.

Rita preferred the Socratic method. And by Socratic method, I mean Rita preferred to beat the hell out of me whenever she felt I wasn't paying attention. Angélica and Rita were the same size, but Rita was stronger, faster, and she could fly. Angélica's could alter her velocity, but only when she was in motion. She couldn't go from standing on one side of me to standing on the other, for example. Rita suffered no such drawbacks.

Rita fought *mean*. Her lessons weren't limited to the gym.

Attacks came at any time. During dinner, over steak tartar. On my way to the shower. *In* the shower (I was a little perturbed that not a single guard came to my rescue after I screamed). At work. At the water-cooler. In our cell. Movement in the corner of my eye was the only warning before I usually ended up on the floor in pain. She liked to target my knees and ankles. Her favorite trick involved pepper, my eyes, and if I wasn't fast enough to block a handful of condiments to the face, several hours of burning red eyes.

I didn't dare approach a single guard. I could see sympathy in their eyes whenever I walked by, but nobody was going to say a thing. Even the other in-mates avoided my eyes. I had to figure they were just grateful Rita's desire to "help" had been focused on somebody else. The only good side effect of the con-stant attacks was that they distracted me from driving myself crazy trying to figure out who could have set me up. With no way of contacting anybody outside the prison, no escape plan, and no chances.

Three days after Jeremy's visit, I ducked a cloud of salt to the face.

Rita kept walking, hands in her pockets.

"*Why?*" I asked. It had been the third time that day.

Rita just kept walking, hands in her pockets. The guards on the other side of the corridor pretended not to notice. They looked a little frazzled—the veal the night before had been a little gamy, leading me to witness my first supervillain meltdown. Rolexes had been produced to placate the angriest of the offenders, and our time watching C-SPAN had been extended for the evening.

Supervillains apparently love C-SPAN. As Raze helpfully put it, it was the greatest puppet show on earth.

"Are you coming?" Rita asked, turning to look at me over her shoulder.

"Coming where?" I wiped salt off my face.

"Your form offends me. You need work."

"I don't have a choice, do I?"

"Girlie, everybody's got a choice." Rita considered this for a second, and brightened as much as she ever did. "Yours just happen to suck."

I saw two options: I could go to the gym and let Rita beat on me until she grew bored, or I could turn her down, and she'd beat on me anyway. With a sigh, I fell into step behind her. How long was this Villain Syndrome fixation going to last?

"You're like a mystery wrapped in a riddle and smothered with crazy sauce," I said glumly.

"I don't think I've ever been called a burrito before." Rita clicked her tongue. "That's a new one. Creative."

I absolutely was not going to thank her for a compliment on my insult.

"Makes me almost wish I could keep you," Rita said.

"What did you just say?"

Instead of answering me, Rita cuffed me upside the head. The blow connected because, in my surprise, I didn't block in time.

"What did I *tell* you?" she said as I reeled back, ears ringing like steel bells. "You keep letting me get these easy hits in. It's pathetic. One confusing statement and bam, you're down. Amateurish."

"You caught me off guard!"

"Off guard means dead." She grabbed my ear like she actually *was* a violent old schoolmarm. "You allow somebody to get the drop on you, it's over. How do you not understand this? Merciful heavens, they really grow them thick these days. When I was your age—"

"You rode a triceratops to school?"

Rita tried to cuff me again. I blocked her and wrestled her off my ear. "I am trying to *heal*," I said, stepping back. "What part of that do *you* not understand? My health is practically *the only thing* I have. Stop hitting me!"

Rita harrumphed. "Fight me off for once, and it won't be a problem."

"You're a psychopath."

"They never proved that, actually."

We entered one of the sparring rooms. Rita swung, trying to drive me back with a haymaker.

The first lesson Angélica had put me through at Davenport had been the doorway test. Open the door, receive fist to the face. I'd been suspicious of doorways ever since, so Rita's fist met nothing but air. I threw myself to the side and did a handspring away to avoid the kick aimed at the center of my back.

She set in on me from above, dive-bombing me and flying out of my range. These surprise ambushes were one of her favorite tactics, and I had no idea why. I just focused on fighting her off, blocking the flurries of hard punches and sudden kicks. When she dove at me for the fifth time, I dodged another cloud of pepper, knocked back her right cross, and she hit me in the face with something out of a little purple squirt bottle.

My face erupted into flame.

I stumbled back as what felt like fire ants crawled into my eyes. Tears welled up. "What the—what *is* that?" I asked, reaching for my face to wipe my eyes clear.

Rita's talons grasped my wrists. "Wouldn't do that if I were you," she said cheerfully. "Capsaicin hurts even worse when you get it everywhere."

"Capsai—you *pepper-sprayed* me?" It felt—and smelled—like somebody had poured straight bourbon right onto my eyeballs and lit a match. I yanked my arms out of her grip, mouth wide open as I tried to suck in gasping breaths. My nose was streaming even more than my eyes, but I didn't dare touch that either. My throat had begun to ache just like the rest of my face. I sniffled miserably, which only made things worse. "*Why?* Why would you do this?"

"Eh," Rita said.

I needed to find the exit. I needed to go stick my

head into the coldest bucket of ice water imaginable. But when I tried to squeeze my eyes open a millimeter, it felt like napalm applied directly to my corneas. I stumbled toward what I hoped was the door.

Rita had other ideas. She cuffed me upside the head yet again.

"Hey!" I swiped blindly and met nothing but air, of course. "Knock it off!"

"Make me." She tagged my shoulder this time, hard enough to bruise.

"What the—I can't even *see* you."

"You've got other senses." I could practically hear her shrug. Her voice was coming from somewhere behind me. "Something wrong with those?"

Considering I couldn't see or smell a damn thing but the capsaicin? I turned angrily in her direction. "What," I said as calmly as possible, "will it take to get you to leave me alone?"

"Hit me."

With pleasure, I thought, fury growing and making my ears burn. Irritation raging through my eyes, nose, and throat, but it seemed to lessen when I focused. I had to take her down with one good hit. One hit, then I could go pound my head into a wall and knock myself unconscious.

She tagged me a few more times, all taunting hits. My knees, my thigh. My elbow. Nothing designed to take me out, but they stung. I clipped her once as she flew by. Patience had been the first thing Angélica had tried to teach me, and I used it now, gritting my teeth, keeping my stance ready.

I heard her flying, just a *whisp* to my left. I put everything I had into the spin-kick. The blade of my foot connected with a grimly satisfying *crunch*, and then Rita's curse filled the air. I forced my eyes open again, just a sliver. They hurt, but it was a tolerable pain compared to the agony of before.

Rita skidded to a stop a few feet away. Blood gushed from her nose and over her hand.

"You deserved that," I said.

"Go wash your face, you're an unseemly mess, and I'm tired of looking at you."

"Same goes," I said, limping toward the door.

"I'd use milk unless you want to be up all night crying. Or will you be doing that anyway?"

"Screw you," I said, stalking to the door. She didn't stop me.

By the time I made it to the cafeteria to request the biggest container of milk they had, my eyes barely hurt anymore. They were still a frightening shade of red, though. It appeared the Mobium hadn't liked the capsaicin any more than the rest of me had.

My eyes were still red and irritated, but I could blink freely by the time Raze came to find me for dinner. She studied my face for a minute. "Rita?" she asked.

"Who *else* would pepper-spray me in the face in the

middle of a sparring match?" I asked, and immediately her face fell. "I mean besides you, obviously."

"Sometimes I feel like you don't respect me as a villain."

"Trust me, you're a great villain." I sighed and pulled up my shirt to show off a purplish scar just above the waistband of my stretchy prison uniform pants. "See this?"

"Looks nasty."

"All you."

"Really?" Raze blinked a few times in quick succession, which always looked a bit creepy thanks to her overlarge eyes. "I did that?"

"Three years ago. That time you kidnapped me in Wrigleyville, remember? You hit me with that blast-ray gun. Hurt for *weeks*."

"You always know how to cheer me up." Raze hummed the rest of the way to the dining room, even skipping a couple of steps. "I miss that gun, though."

"I'm sure you'll create a newer, scarier one the minute you get out of here."

"Thanks, Girl. It's nice that you have that kind of faith in me. Want to go to the bar for dinner instead of the dining room? I heard they're doing fondue."

I thought about it. Detmer did indeed have a bar, but since I was still banned from alcohol—it had been Angélica's rule and in my mind, she was the only one that could lift it—I'd only been once. It was a beautiful bar, equipped with a pleasure garden and a waterfall and everything. You just had to cross through three security checkpoints and four separate vault doors to reach it. And as good as fondue sounded, I really just wanted a big meal. Picking up the cheese pot and slurping it all down sounded like a *faux pas* that even the villains wouldn't be willing to overlook.

"Can we not?" I asked. "I don't really want to go through all of the rigmarole. Maybe tomorrow?"

Raze pouted. "I like fondue," she said, but she went back to humming and skipping.

The call of fondue was apparently a strong one, as the dining room was mostly empty. It made me grateful I'd chosen to skip the bar. I could feel the malaise growing every day that passed without any word from the outside about what had happened. I didn't know what was going on with my friends, I didn't have the first idea how to find out who had framed me, and with Rita's constant bullying, I felt helpless and useless.

The last thing I wanted was to be surrounded by the drunk and the evil.

"Ooh," Raze said, as we sat down at what was becoming our usual table. She reached for the centerpiece, broke the white rose off at the stem, and tossed the whole bud in her mouth. She chewed with her mouth gaping open as usual, but I'd made my peace with that already.

"Don't let Venus catch you doing that," I said as I studied the menu. Venus von Trapp's all-meat diet freaked me out a little bit, but it wasn't as terrifying as the look on her face if you dared to eat a vegetable in her presence. I was beginning to wonder if Lady Danger's vampiric pallor wasn't intentional.

"Duh," Raze said. She picked up the other rose and held it out. "Want?"

I stared at the flower. For four years of waking up in the hospital, there had been a similar white rose on my bedside every time. This one lacked the green ribbon Guy had always wrapped around the stem, though.

I missed him.

"No, that's okay. You eat it," I said.

She bit it off the stem. "Fanks," she said, her mouth full. She chewed and swallowed. "Hey, have you picked a color yet?"

"For what?"

"For your hero outfit, duh. I was thinking we could coordinate. Not too matchy-matchy or anything, but just complementing each other, you know? I know I've got the yellow and the purple right now, but you look like you have a yellow undertone to your skin, so maybe that's not a good combination for you. What do you think about—oh, you could be green like your boy, and maybe we could do a green-and-pink thing?"

"Raze," I said. "What are you talking about? I'm in here for a long time. At this rate, there will never be a 'hero outfit.' I'm not getting out of here."

"Not with that attitude, you're not." Raze snorted, and when the waiter came over, she waved at him. "My usual, Carmichael, and she'll take one of everything on the menu."

"Hey," I said, but it wasn't far from my order. I shook my head. "Yeah, I guess what she said."

"You're going to have to stop being so passive if we're going to be enemies on the outside," Raze said, frowning in disapproval. "Well, what do you think?"

"About what?"

She rolled her eyes at how slow I was being. "The green and pink. I'm willing to change it over and go for something in that general ballpark, even if it *does* mean paying homage to your weird boyf—oh, hey, Tabitha."

Guards didn't normally come into the dining room. I had to figure they were happiest when we were all eating, as we were the waitstaff's responsibility then. Proving me right, Tabitha's smile was stretched to its fullest, terror-filled capacity right then. "Razor," she said, giving Raze a little nod. "Gail, I wanted to let you know that there's been a temporary lift on your ban from having visitors."

I immediately perked up. "Is Blaze here?"

"Your doctor from Davenport has been granted permission to visit you, because of the severity of your medical condition."

Confusion and defeat hit at the same time. The severity of my medical condition? I'd healed up surprisingly well from that fight in the mall. In fact, I would have been better if only Rita wasn't beating on me the whole time. The first couple of nights had been a little worrying, as I knew that I had to keep myself reasonably fit to beat back the leukemia. But that was over now, wasn't it?

And the fact that it wasn't Guy coming to see me was crushing, but I swallowed hard past that.

"Kiki's coming back?" I asked, as she was one of my physicians at Davenport.

Tabitha's headshake was tight and controlled, as though she feared the consequences of ever having to use it. "The memo I was handed lists a Dr. Cooper. I'm sorry. He'll be here first thing in the morning. I'll come to collect you."

"Thank you," I said, and Tabitha practically ran out of the dining room. I turned back to Raze. "How many antacids do you think she takes every day?"

"How come you've got a doctor? Are you sick?"

"Well, I got pepper-sprayed today, so there's always that." With a renewed appetite, I dug into the appetizers that Carmichael the waiter brought over. I would have preferred one of my friends, but surely Cooper would have news, and maybe he could shine a light on some of the mysteries surrounding my imprisonment. I looked up and caught Raze frowning. "Don't worry, I'm not that sick. If Rita's Villain Syndrome fixation doesn't kill me, I'll be alive to be your archnemesis. Maybe. And we'll meet up after a battle and have a drink or something."

"If you say so. But Mind the Boom's expensive, you'll have to buy."

"Deal," I said, though I had no idea what Mind the

Boom was. I didn't care. Tomorrow, I would have a visitor, and I would finally have some answers. Then I could start focusing on a strategy to get myself out of Detmer, no matter how long it took.

It turned out the answer to that was "not long at all" because hours later, I woke up in the semidarkness to find Rita standing over my bunk with a ghoulish smile.

"Time to go, Girlie," she said, and grabbed the front of my tunic.

CHAPTER SIX

Rita jerked me upright before my eyes were even fully open. I didn't even get a chance to flail before we were airborne.

I'd been flying before. When your personal super-hero is a flying type and regularly snatches you from above vats of acid, volcanoes, and robotically modified sharks, you grow accustomed to the feeling of flight. But Blaze had never grabbed me by the shirt and taken off like a shot. Not like Rita did now.

My head snapped back on my neck, my stomach dropped, and we were aloft. I couldn't shout. Rita bulleted through the air, through our open cell door, and down the hall. My body flew like a rag doll.

The prison just *blurred* right by.

"Hope you weren't planning on sleeping much tonight," Rita called.

"What possible reason can your shriveled little

mind have for wanting to train in the middle of the night?" I shouted, trying to struggle free.

"Who said anything about training?" Rita said, yanking me around a corner, and I realized it: we had streaked right by the gym nearly three turns before. We were heading into some part of the prison I had never visited before.

"Stop struggling! You crash into a wall at this speed, even you won't survive it."

Well, when she put it that way. I fought the force to raise my arms and lock my hands around Rita's wrist. Outside of the main area where all of the inmates lived, Detmer looked a great deal more like what you would expect from a maximum security prison. Cinder-block walls and flickering lights dashed past as we flew.

"Solitary!" Rita said, her voice one tiny step away from a cackle. "You don't want to meet any of these yahoos."

We whipped around another corner, my body snapping behind her like a Gail-shaped flag. Abruptly, Rita dropped to ground, skidding the last few feet on her old-lady corrective shoes. I saw the ground rushing toward my face and instinctively curled, rolling until I slammed into a wall. It knocked the breath out of me.

"Graceful," said a new voice, and I looked up to see Raze standing over me. She sighed and pulled me to my feet even as I coughed and looked around. Rita had chucked me to the ground at the end of a long, dimly lit hallway.

Still coughing, I looked from her to Rita. "Either one of you feel like telling me what's going on?"

"You'll catch on soon enough," Rita said.

I looked at my supposed archnemesis. Raze's helmet had been buffed to a high shine, its silly little antennae bobbing with every move. She'd fashioned a little half cape out of prison shirts that had been cut up and untidily sewn together. It should have looked absurd, but it instantly brought to mind the half dozen attacks she had relentlessly laid on me on the way home from work. Several weapons had been clipped to the waistband of her pants. A gun-shaped firearm looked like it had been composed of cannibalized bits of her IRS work computer and a couple of the silver forks from the dining room. How she'd lifted the latter, I had no idea, as the serving staff watched over their cutlery like hawks. Another device looked like she had stolen one of the showerheads to make it work. What it sprayed, I *really* did not want to know.

I had a strong feeling I was about to find out, though.

"Cool, huh?" she said, noticing where my gaze rested. "I didn't have much time to whip 'em up, but they're going to be impressive. Hold still."

She pulled out what looked like a set of metal pincers with deathly sharp tips.

I instantly backed up. "What are those?"

"It'll only hurt for a second, I promise."

"Get away from me, I am serious—"

Arms wrapped around me from behind, squeezing tight. When I struggled, Rita looped an arm around my neck instead. My vision started going dark almost immediately. "Hold still," she said, her voice wavering in and out like a bad radio. "You're making things unnecessarily difficult, per usual."

In response, I gurgled. The choke hold had left me too weak to do anything, though, so when Raze dug the pincers into the flesh where my shoulder met my neck, I gritted my teeth through the pain. Rita's arm muffled my scream.

"Got it." Raze held up a bloody bit of metal, and Rita let me go, letting me stagger into the wall.

I clutched my shoulder. "What did you just yank out of me?"

"Your tracker. You're welcome."

"*What?*"

Rita checked her watch as I put pressure on the wound on my shoulder. Why weren't they removing their own trackers? It was obvious to anybody with eyes that this was some kind of prison break, and while I wasn't sure *why* it was happening, I wasn't going to turn down the opportunity. But even I could see there were several things not adding up.

"One minute," Rita said. "I nearly forgot: did you get it?"

"Tabitha says you owe her." Raze reached under her half cape and pulled out a little radio, which she passed to Rita. "Double the usual fee for the last-minute nature, you understand."

"She's getting greedy," Rita said with a sigh.

"Tabitha?" I asked. "Perky Tabitha who never stops

smiling like we're going to kill her at any second gave you a radio?"

"Never underestimate the value of capitalism," Rita said. I held still while she clipped a two-way radio to my collar, luckily avoiding the bleeding shoulder. Maybe that was my value in this escape. I was supposed to be the lookout.

"Did you guys already take your trackers out?" I asked, looking from one face to the other.

Rita snorted. "Razor? Fifteen seconds."

"Got it." Raze patted me on the bad shoulder, and I winced, sucking air through my teeth. "I may be helping you now, but remember me when you get out. Best enemies forever, right?"

And she pulled out the ray-gun-looking thing with one hand and the shower-nozzle gun with the other and nodded to Rita. The older woman grabbed my shirtfront again, bunching it in her fist.

"Hold on, Girlie," she said. She grabbed the push bar on the door in front of her, crumpling it with her free hand. "Go!"

Like a shot, she took off, knocking the door off its hinges. Raze rolled through at the same time. We'd broken into some kind of break room, from what I could see, with a table full of guards sitting in the middle. In an instant, the air was full of smoke and beams of red light from Raze. I was too busy flying after Rita, gripping her wrist in a death grip and trying not to scream.

We broke out of that room in a shower of glass

and concrete, and a second later, night air, warm and humid, hit my face. We appeared to be flying through what looked like some kind of Japanese garden. Well-manicured lawns whipped by, silvery in the light from the streetlamps overhead. It was the first time I had been outside since they'd hauled me out of the transport van and through the front doors. If it weren't for the actual terror clogging my throat, my spirits would probably have been lifting. Ever since I'd been dosed with Mobium, outdoors had been a thing other people experienced, not me.

And Detmer looked beautiful from the air. We jetted by a beautiful fountain that could have come straight out of Rome itself, a fountain that I imagined would flare up with gold in the middle of the day. It was almost far more expansive than even I had suspected, given how fast we were rocketing through the air. A fence, at least five stories high, rose in the distance. With my enhanced sight, I could see every glint on every barb in the wire atop it.

We were aiming straight at those, actually.

That was not good.

"Rita!" I said, tugging as best I could on her wrist. "Rita, there's a—Rita, *fence*! Fence, Rita!"

"I see it."

She didn't actually *do* anything about it, though. The fence zoomed closer and closer to us, and I pictured us being cut to bloody ribbons straight through that barbed wire. Or just me, actually, because I suspected Rita would probably just laugh off being sliced to death.

I really, really did not want to die at the hand of lunatic, I thought, squeezing my eyes shut.

But the razory death never came. Instead, Rita jerked to a stop once more, and I felt myself swing around. She'd stopped in midair and was dangling me a bare six inches from the sharp blades of the fence.

It took me a second to catch my breath, looking at those blades.

"So," she said, "this is as far as I take you, Girlie-Girl."

"*What?*" I snapped my gaze back to her. "You're not coming with me?"

"You think I want to extend my sentence by breaking free of this place?" She scoffed. "I've got better things to do. You, on the other hand, have a job, and I expect you to do it the same way you do everything else. Try not to screw it up *too* badly, though. I have people depending on you."

"You're crazy," I said, and it wasn't a revelation or anything, but it certainly felt more pressing when she was holding me up by the shirt fifty feet in the air. "You're absolutely nuts."

"Obviously." She jerked her head. "City's that way. You don't have much time."

"What do you even want me to do? And why *me?*" I asked, struggling to get out of her grip. But say what you will about Detmer prison, their clothing manufacturing was top-notch. The shirt was easily supporting my extra-dense weight, and Rita had a steely grip.

Rita's face briefly took on a faraway look, but she

was completely there, evil and beady, when she looked at me again. "I may be a villain," she said, "but I've got a family, too. Ciao, Hostage Girl. Good luck figuring it all out."

"Wait," I tried to say.

Rita, however, wasn't in the mood to listen. She grabbed the back of my shirt with her other hand, spun sharply in midair, and flung me like a fish at Pike Market. My stomach in my throat, I flew right over the fence, missing the barbed wire by a millimeter—*thanks*, Rita—and hurtling into the free space beyond the prison fence. For a second, there was nothing but weightlessness as I flew.

And then I dropped.

Angélica had taught me how to fall during one of our very first lessons together. Muscle memory snapped into place. I saw the ground speeding toward me in crystal-clear detail, the individual blades of grass, the pinpoint dewdrops on each. My muscles relaxed. I swung my legs around so that I was feet-first rather than headfirst. When I hit the ground, I landed easily on the balls of my feet, redirecting the momentum so that I rolled forward into a crouch.

I immediately sprang to my feet and whipped around, looking for Rita.

She was gone.

I looked around, expecting her to be standing somewhere just behind me so she could attack me. But I saw nothing but the forest clearing around me, full of trees and birdsong. I was completely alone.

From the prison, invisible thanks to the distance, my hearing picked up/warning klaxons and I realized that I was standing outside the prison fence. Entirely without my consent, I had just broken out of prison. All I had was the clothes on my back, some superpowers that weren't actually that impressive in the grand scheme of things, and the radio my psycho roommate had put on my collar.

My psychotic roommate who seemed to have some kind of plan for me in mind.

Oh, god. If I was caught, Rita wasn't going to be happy. And I'd seen what happened to people who'd displeased Rita. With that in mind, I started to run.

I'd been a hostage over fifty times. Time to become a fugitive instead.

I knew where Detmer was only because we'd passed it on a school trip in the sixth grade. Thanks to the Mobium, my memory had become a strange beast, able to guide me through any place as long as I'd been there at least once. I sprinted through the forest. The first time the radio on my shoulder chirped, I jumped so high I accidentally clipped a branch with the top of my head, knocking me completely off step. It wasn't Raze or Rita, though, but the guards.

They were doing a bed check, I realized. In the actual chaos, they had no idea yet if anybody had broken out.

I ran on.

I had been running for nearly half an hour—something I could only tell because I'd taken up distance running at Davenport and had learned to judge distances by how hungry I felt—when they first said my name. "Anybody seen Godwin?" came over the radio, and the negatives started flowing in.

"Tracker puts her inside, but bed's empty."

"Somebody make sure Fearless hasn't killed her, will ya?"

I didn't have a plan. But that wasn't unusual, really. Plans were generally things that happened to other people. Better, more prepared people. I needed to get on pavement soon, though, as they could easily track me with all of the scent and footsteps I was leaving.

I veered left when I heard the sound of cars. The forest turned into a residential area, so I slowed my run to a jog, trying to look like I was out for a leisurely run at three in the morning. Every car that passed made me tense, but for the most part, people seemed completely uninterested in the woman running alone through a town right next to the most dangerous prison on earth. Granted, it probably took a special kind of person to live in this town in the first place, really, so maybe I shouldn't have been surprised.

I made it to the highway and stared in dismay at the very first sign I saw.

DO NOT PICK UP HITCHHIKERS.

THEY ARE VILLAINS AND VERY EVIL.

"Of course," I said, slinking back into the brush. "Of *course* it would be that sign."

I jogged on, keeping the highway in sight as best I could. This route would eventually take me up to Chicago though what I would do once I arrived, I had no idea. Chicago was familiar, though. Chicago was home.

For once, luck seemed to be on my side. About ten miles north of the prison, I stumbled onto a train yard, nearly tripping over the tracks. The scream of a freight-train horn made me look up and over to realize that one was just beginning its slumberous journey north to Chicago. I didn't think: I ran as hard as I could, launching myself at the side of the car and gripping the railing along the top. I hauled myself over, dropped into the rusty divot made by time and weather, and lay flat on my stomach. For several seconds, I waited for the train to stop, for somebody to shout that they had a stowaway.

The train chugged on. Relieved, I let my forehead rest against the disgusting, dirty metal for a second.

What was I possibly going to do now?

Clinging to a train in the middle of the night at least gave me time to think as I chugged my way north. No amount of turning Rita's cryptic remarks over in my head made them make any sense, though. Rita's two children were Eddie Davenport, the man who had thrown me in prison, and Jessica Davenport. Given that Jessica Davenport had taken up her father's superhero mantle and nobody on the planet knew that the Raptor was actually a middle-aged woman with two kids, I had a feeling she could take care of herself. So why would Rita think they needed help? And why would she think I would help them after I'd been thrown into prison for a crime I hadn't committed based on the barest, made-up evidence.

Maybe it was one of her grandchildren she wanted me to save. But why couldn't she just have *said* that?

And now that I was out of prison, I didn't want to help Rita. I needed to clear my name and stay out of Detmer forever. Which meant finding Chelsea and getting to the bottom of my own frame-up.

"Gee," I said though I was completely alone, pushing my forehead into the cold metal underneath me, "and just when I thought life was getting boring."

I stayed vigilant, worrying about tunnels that might cut me in half. More and more, I began to recognize landmarks. We came into Chicago from the south, and it took me a little while to figure out the train was heading farther north, tracking up the west side. When the Lake finally came into sight, near a dirty, run-down part of the city, I readied myself, took a deep breath, and leapt before I could think about it. I landed lightly on the balls of my feet and ducked behind a transformer box to wait for the rest of the train to pass.

The minute it had trundled out of sight, I peeked out from behind the box and carefully turned the volume down on the radio on my shoulder. It had regularly spit out updates on my manhunt, which had been both unnerving and something of a relief. They were sure I had turned south, possibly going to Miami.

Blaze's territory was Miami. It made a certain amount of sense.

The buildings around me were worn by age and neglect, windows broken and occasionally covered with plywood. I wouldn't have been surprised to come across at least three drug deals as I trotted along, but I tried not to think about that. Before the Mobium, this area would have scared me. Now, it just made me wary. Guns could still kill me, but any human I came across, I had a chance of being stronger and faster.

The only problem, really, was that it was dark, and even my night vision sometimes wasn't enough. As I passed a building where the windows were entirely boarded up, I tripped over a broken bottle and stumbled forward.

It saved me from a giant headache.

After all, when somebody behind me tried to punch me in the back of the head, they missed.

Mostly.

CHAPTER SEVEN

The fist still clipped the top of my head, and I still saw stars.

Thanks to Rita's constant ambushes, instinct took over. I kicked backward, my heel driving into something solid right before hands locked around my ankle. At this, I did look back.

The Raptor and I gazed at each other for a split second. *She* was probably shocked that I'd dodged the fist to the head in the first place. *I* was shocked to be facing New York City's number one superhero. She was the Raptor. Her logo and her silhouette belonged on cereal boxes and soft-drink ads, not on the person holding onto my foot or punching me. But no, that was really her. I was really facing off against the Raptor.

I looked at her, and I did the only thing available to me: I yelped.

She twisted my foot. Luckily, I went with it, flipping over easily and yanking free. I scrambled to my feet and ran. No direction, no idea of where to go, just *away*. The Raptor was the best, and the Raptor was after me. I was not going to survive this. Good god was I not going to survive this.

I heard a hissing sound. Something skittered across the pavement in front of me. Sparks flew everywhere, crackling like demented toy poppers. I yelped again, swerving to try and avoid them. Another hiss, another set of bright, tiny explosions in my path. My only option was to let the Raptor catch me or duck into the building to my right.

When I turned to look back, all I saw was the grenade launcher she held.

"Shit!" I threw myself into the open door, tripping and rolling to my feet. Afterimages from the sparks made it difficult to see, but if the smell was anything to go by, I really didn't want to see much anyway. I took off down a hallway, looking for an exit.

A *thud* made me look up in time to see a black canister go flying past. Over fifty different villains over the years, you can bet your ass I recognized that sucker. I was midshout, an arm flung over my eyes, when the flashbang exploded.

The percussive wave hit like Angélica at full velocity: a battering ram intent on liquefying every bone in my spine. I hit the wall with my shoulder blades. Every noise had been replaced by a high-pitched whine. I charged forward, stumbling but mostly in one piece. It scared me not to hear anything that might give me a clue about my environment, but time wasn't a luxury I had available, and neither was my hearing.

The old building had several floors, most of the windows were boarded up. It was dark—and currently silent—as a tomb. I hit a dead end and spun on my heel. Something dark crossed my vision. I threw myself to the side. Raptor's fist breezed past my left ear. I blocked the follow-up punch to the gut with crossed arms.

The melee that followed was almost too fast to follow. She aimed for every vulnerable area on my body while I did my best to block and dodge. It only took half a second before everything started to feel oddly familiar, like she was an opponent I'd fought before. I never had. I'd met Jessica Davenport once in an elevator, but that didn't explain that she ducked when I expected her to, returned with the disorienting open-handed strike that I anticipated and dodged. We weren't evenly matched. She had armor and years of fighting experience, while all I had was blind panic.

She kicked me, hard, right in the midsection—and vanished as I doubled over.

A second later, a canister landed at my feet and gas spewed everywhere. I froze up as the smell hit me. Pepper spray *again*? This was *really* not my week. I covered my nose and mouth with my hand and raced down the hallway, every muscle tense.

I had to get away from the gas. Which meant going up.

I'd seen a horror movie before. I knew this was a bad idea.

But as I really, really did not want to experience the amount of snot pepper spray produced ever again, I raced for the staircase, taking the steps three at a time. There was a miraculously open window at the top that I could see. A one-story drop? That was nothing. I aimed for it, eyes streaming, ears ringing.

The floor shook as something hit the wall in front of me. I stumbled to a stop and gawked at the window, now covered by a net. Instinct made me turn and drop into a crouch on the stairs. A second bolt flew over my head, a net exploding all over the exposed wooden panels behind me.

Raptor, who had appeared at the bottom of the stairs, raised the net gun again. I leapt up, grabbed the banister, and hauled myself over, landing in the hallway in an uncoordinated pile. I scrambled for the next flight because I could hear her footsteps right behind me. On the next floor, I had to dodge a tranquilizer dart. When I tried to race back down, yet another net blocked my way, covering the opening to the stairs. Taking a chance, I jumped on that both feet first. It bounced me right over the banister and back onto the landing, right into Raptor.

She blocked my leading strike. I tried for an upper-cut and dodged the cross that I somehow *knew* would follow.

A bright light like a camera flash seared my corneas. I cried out, my strike going wide, and when I blinked, Raptor had disappeared. I wheeled around. Noises were beginning to break through the ringing in my ears, but I couldn't hear anything that would tell me where she'd gone. I couldn't get through the net, the windows were boarded up, and the second I tried a doorway, she'd get the drop on me.

She'd trapped me yet again. My choices were to go up or to surrender.

My ears picked up a *whip* of noise, and something slammed into my shins. I toppled forward, hitting the ground hard with my elbows. A glance down told me there was a rope wrapped tight around my legs, tying them together. Crap. Just how many toys did the woman have? This was beyond ridiculous. I yanked hard at the rope. It cut into my thumbs, but I heard the groan as the rope protested.

It snapped with a satisfying noise. Unfortunately, the minute I jumped to my feet, I found myself face-to-face with a gun barrel.

It wasn't a regular pistol, but it was still gun-shaped, it was still large and threatening, and it was pointed directly between my eyes. My throat dry, chest still heaving from my exposure to the gas, I looked past the muzzle and at Raptor's mask. Jessica's chin and mouth were exposed. It swooped over her nose in a beaklike point. The entire ensemble wasn't black, like I'd always thought, but a dark bronze.

Jessica Davenport's eyes were the same as Eddie's. The same as Rita's.

"You know," I said as I realized why the fight had felt so *weird*, "you fight just like your mom."

Raptor's eyes widened for a split second. I ducked, and she pulled the trigger.

I heard the kick of the gun going off, and my left shoulder felt like a steel trap had sprung around it, ripping into the muscle and bone. It knocked me back and to the side, so that her next blast missed. I leapt into another room, kicking the door shut behind me. Raptor kept shooting.

The room wasn't large, and thanks to the boarded-up windows, it was dark. A perfect trap, I realized instantly. All she had to do was throw in some knockout gas, and I was down for the count. I spotted a gaping, eaten-away hole in the ceiling and ran hard at the corner of the room, kicking off one wall and then the next to give me the height I needed. Grabbing the edge of the hole with both hands was sheer agony, tearing a scream from my throat as I hauled myself up and free. Outside! At last!

Now I just had to scale the side of the building with one good arm while being pursued by a psychotic superhero with more gizmos than a toy store. Right. Easy. At least in my inevitable death, I'd see Angélica again. She'd wallop me upside the head for going into the death trap of a building in the first place.

When I ran to the edge of the building, though, I got my first break: it was over the water. I could leap off and survive. Probably. I climbed onto the lip of the roof, took a deep breath, and jumped.

Something caught the back of my shirt.

I was yanked backward, flying through the air once again. Raptor, weirdly enough, hadn't put any superstrength into it, so I landed four feet away and bounced. Every movement drove a new spike of pain into my shoulder. She swooped in on me. I saw her fist coming and rolled, rolling again and again. I blocked kick after kick as best as I could, grunting whenever one landed and spread a starburst of white-hot pain.

And then she kicked my shoulder.

I felt the agony all the way to my toes. My body arched up. It felt like my entire existence was sucked right into one point in my shoulder. And when I opened my eyes, I saw Raptor's fist hurtling straight at my face.

I blinked and, just like that, I was two feet away. Her fist plowed into the rooftop.

I gawked at her.

She gawked back at me.

My brain helpfully pointed out that now would be a good time to run even though my entire body felt paralyzed from the pain throbbing in a spiral from my shoulder. I scrambled to my feet, made it two steps—and was hit by the worst headache I'd ever experienced. Every blast of pain juice from Raze, every concussion from any supervillain I'd ever faced, none of those had anything on the pressure suddenly building behind my forehead.

I dropped to my knees, clawing at my temples. I had to relieve the pressure building up behind my eyes before my head exploded. I had to do *something*.

A rope wrapped around my middle. It trapped my

arms, jerking them down and pinning them to my sides so that I was completely immobile. When Raptor hauled me to my feet, I swayed. My head felt like it weighed three hundred pounds. I whimpered as she stepped close, one gloved hand pulling something blue and spidery from my shoulder. Instantly, the pain where my neck and shoulder met vanished. It still felt like somebody was trying to poke an ice pick through my eye socket, but I could at least focus again.

"Huh," the Raptor said, looking at the filament wires dangling in her hand. Her voice modulator made her sound like a man who'd been chain-smoking since infancy. "You've got quite a high pain tolerance."

"I don't see why we had to find that out the hard way." I kept swaying. Every hit she'd landed was not-so-politely making itself known, and my shoulder throbbed particularly hard in rhythm with my head. "I'm not your enemy. I didn't do what everybody thinks I did. You have to believe me."

"Doesn't matter. I'm taking you back."

"I don't know Chelsea. You have to give me a fair trial, or hear my side of the story, or—"

Raptor slapped something over my mouth. It felt rubbery and sticky, and it made the bottom half of my face freeze up altogether. Another gag. Great. This was just like dealing with the villains all over again. Hell, from where I stood, trussed up like a Thanksgiving turkey, there wasn't a difference.

"I hate the talkers," she said, looking down to fiddle with her belt. She paused, hand automatically going to her ear. She'd evidently received some kind of radio message, but with my ears still ringing, I couldn't hear it. Whatever they were telling her, though, made her frown. "Looks like you'll have to wait."

I made a questioning noise through the gag.

"School bus of orphans dangling from a bridge," she said, looking annoyed. If I hadn't known she was Jessica, I wouldn't have been able to tell that the Raptor was, in fact, a woman. No wonder nobody outside the superhero community knew. "It shouldn't take long. You stay here."

And just where did she expect me to go with my arms tied up like this? It wasn't like I could actually jump into the water without drowning.

She fiddled with her belt again, and my body locked up. I stood there like a shell-shocked statue, unable to move. "That should keep you from 'porting again."

I would have asked her what she'd been smoking if I could. She thought I'd teleported? I'd just been running up stairs. The Mobium made me fast, but not 'porting fast. And 'porting, that was done by professionals, not Class C chumps who couldn't stay out of trouble. But it wasn't like I could *say* that, between the paralysis and the gag. All I could do was watch her run to the side of the wall and throw herself over, her cape extended.

So now I was stuck in a bad part of the city, completely unable to move or talk, and waiting for the world's most sadistic superhero to come take me back to prison.

This had been a fun adventure. I was ready for it to be over now.

Despite the ringing, my ears picked up the sound of something landing on the rooftop behind me. Oh, that was really, really not good. I had a lot of enemies and even fewer friends, and none of them knew I would be escaping. Even *I* didn't know. The hero that stepped into view, though, was mostly an ally. I recognized the battered bronze breastplate over the purple-and-gold mail. The black mask under the pointed helmet, the sturdy boots that were decorated at the ankles with silly little bronze wings.

Not that I would ever tell Sam Bookman that I'd always found his War Hammer costume silly. He'd saved my life a few times. Of course, it had probably just been to help his brother out. Very few of us knew Blaze and War Hammer were related.

He stepped in front of me. Thanks to our height difference, I had no choice but to stare forward straight into the breastplate.

Sam did the unexpected. He leaned forward so his face was even with mine, pulled off the helmet, and then the mask while I stood there in frozen silence.

The hair that spilled out of the mask was not blond, but a dark, very familiar red. And his eyes weren't blue. My heart knocked against my sternum, hard.

Guy Bookman looked into my eyes, and said, "I swear, I leave you alone for *one minute*."

CHAPTER EIGHT

I didn't answer. I probably couldn't have even if I'd been physically capable. Seeing him there, his face in front of me, suddenly made everything feel tremendously real in a way it hadn't seemed all week. It was like there had been a plastic film holding everything back, a necessary one, but now it had dissolved completely. Every emotion I'd been suppressing returned at once. Guy was here. Something was finally right.

A lump formed in my throat. I felt a tear slip down my cheek.

"Oh." Guy's face switched from worry to outright alarm. He rubbed the tear away with his thumb and jerked his hand back, like he wasn't sure he was allowed to touch me. "That was a joke, I swear! This is why I should leave the humor to you, obviously, but—um. I'll have you out of there as soon as I can. I swear. Are you hurt?"

I kind of wanted to glare at him for that.

"Right, can't move. Sorry." After he pulled the gag off me, wrinkling his nose as he tossed it away, he bent to get a look at the rope wrapped around me. I couldn't see what he was doing, but thankfully, he kept talking. "This is her newest model. Electric shocks, shouldn't be damaging, but it will temporarily paralyze you. It's going to take her a few minutes to find out there are no schoolchildren on that bridge, but we need to move fast. Uh . . . oh, here's the triggering mechanism. It should—"

The rope begin to constrict. A second later, he cursed. When he fiddled with something else, the rope constricted faster. Mildly uncomfortable became out-right painful.

"There goes that plan," he said, and I felt his fingers wedge between my midsection and the rope. He grunted, jaw clenched, and jerked his hand as hard as he could. With the sound of a metal cable snapping, I was suddenly free. I fell forward before I could stop myself.

"Whoa!" Guy caught me, holding me up by my upper arms. "Sorry, I should have warned you that—"

I jumped at him, holding on as tight as I could. Guy was here. He had found me. Everything was going to be okay. I scrunched my eyes closed and breathed in. The edges of his armor, so unfamiliar, dug against my forehead, but I didn't care. I had to fight against breaking down in tears right on the spot.

He hugged me in return, rubbing my back. "It's okay," he said. "Are you okay? You're not hurt?"

"She got a couple hits in. I'll be okay." Though I really wanted to hold on forever, I sniffled and took a step back. "How are you here? Not complaining, mind you. But . . ."

"I got wind that there was trouble at the prison, and I knew you had to be involved."

"In my defense, I actually didn't have anything to do with any of that. I really was minding my own business."

"And that's how I *really* knew it had to be you. Raptor always goes after the fugitives, so I just knew I had to track *her*, and I'd find you. Let's go. I've got a place we can hide while we figure out what to do."

"Guy?"

"Yeah?" He'd stepped back to pull on the mask and the helmet, but he paused to look at me.

"Thank you," was all I could say. "For coming to save me."

"Always." His mask hid his smile when he pulled it over his face. "Piggyback, or do you want me to carry you?"

With the way my shoulder throbbed, there was no chance I would be able to hold on. "I'm okay with being carried."

"Just like old times." Helmet secured, Guy picked me up as though I weighed nothing (which I knew was definitely not the case), holding me cradled against him. Before he took off, he looked down at me and said the three most beautiful words I'd ever heard.

"I brought food."

"My hero," I said, absolutely meaning it, and he took off from the roof.

By the time he landed, my heart had begun to calm. Adrenaline from the escape, from the run, from the carnival-house-of-horrors fight with Raptor—all of that drained away, leaving me sluggish and leaden. The sweat had cooled thanks to the brisk flight, and the sun was beginning to peel the edges of the night sky back, revealing pearly pinks and yellows. I rested my head against Guy's shoulder and barely kept my eyes open during the flight.

Guy landed on the rooftop of a building in West Lawn.

"One of Sam's safe houses. We kept it off Davenport's radar." He leaned forward a little, and I couldn't read his expression behind the mask, but he seemed to be squinting. "And you don't really care, do you? You just want food."

"I *am* really happy to see you," I said, my voice only partly rueful. I didn't want him to put me down though he did. Instantly, I started to sway.

He laughed, holding my elbow to keep me upright. "I'm happy to see you, too."

There were many reasons to like Guy Bookman. He was charming in an unexpected way (mostly out of social awkwardness), he was kind, and he'd pulled me out of more than one burning building. But the number one contender at the moment was that the minute we walked into Sam's safe house—it figured Sam would keep an entire penthouse as a place to hide—I could smell the aroma of glorious food. There was a veritable feast laid out on the table. And it wasn't fussy, fancy food like Detmer had insisted on serving. These were hearty dishes full of carbs and protein.

I nearly had to wipe up the drool.

"I'm starving, too," Guy said, already peeling out of the various pieces of Sam's armor. "Don't wait for me, help yourself."

"Did you have this all just waiting?" I asked, as it was a crazy amount of food, even for me. The lasagna I forked onto my plate was cold, but I didn't care.

"I figured you'd be hungry. Sorry it's not warm."

"Sorry it's not warm? Guy, this is amazing. Do you *see* all of this food? I could cry." I could still barely keep my eyes open, but I dug in with gusto, cradling my bad arm and shoulder in front of me. I could feel Guy's concern as he dished out a plate for himself, but I kept eating until the edge of hunger had been dulled. After that, I looked at Guy, really looked at him. Like Jeremy, he had dark circles under his eyes. They stood out more prominently, thanks to his redhead complexion. His hair was stuck down at weird angles from the helmet. I had only just grown used to seeing him partially unmasked as Blaze, so it was a bit of a readjustment to see him sitting there in the chain mail.

"So," I said as I reached for a glass of water, "prison really changes a woman."

He looked up in alarm.

"Or maybe it's you that's changed. I can't tell. Because when I went to prison, I could have sworn you were Blaze, not War Hammer."

"Oh." Guy's shoulders visibly relaxed. "Blaze and Plain Jane can't be anywhere near where you're escaping, but they'll be a little more lenient toward War Hammer. And Sam owed me one, so . . ."

"Sam's wearing the green?" I asked. "Isn't he, um . . ."

"A lot bigger than me?" Guy shook his head, clearly amused. "You can say it. I know I'm a beanpole. He's not wearing my uniform. Last I heard, he was whiling his time away at a dive bar in Queens."

"Blaze has the night off?"

"Blaze is probably busy saving somebody in Miami as we speak." Guy drained his water glass and pushed his empty plate away. "It's probably a good thing Vicki's so tall. Not that it matters. All most people will see is a green streak flying by."

I choked a little. "V—*Vicki* is out there being Blaze right now?"

"My reputation will be in tatters when I get back to it."

He probably had a point. Victoria Burroughs, supermodel by day, superhero by night, wasn't exactly known for her reverence, foresight, or ability to avoid massive amounts of property damage in her fights. She paid for some of it—now that I knew Plain Jane was actually one of the highest-grossing supermodels in the world, everything made a lot more sense—and was apparently insured by Davenport Industries, but that didn't change the fact that Plain Jane liked her rubble.

Blaze was usually a little more circumspect.

"Wait, then who's being Plain Jane?"

"Plain Jane is apparently taking the night off, and Victoria Burroughs is at home watching one of those fashion reality shows. Jeremy's probably tearing his hair out by now running her social media. It's not perfect, but honestly, at this point, it's the best we can do on such short notice."

I thought about that. My boyfriend had taken his brother's costume, let my mentor take his, and now my ex was pretending to be a supermodel on Twitter. And that wasn't even the strangest thing I'd witnessed that day, let alone in life.

"I'm so sorry," Guy said, the words seeming to burst out of him. I lifted my head in alarm. "I'm sorry I wasn't able to come see you—we were so close to tracking Chelsea down and getting the truth out of her. And I know you don't really like Jeremy—"

"No," I said. "No, it was good to see a familiar face. And it helped to hear that you didn't think I did it."

"Of course not." Guy gave me a puzzled look. "None of us believed that for a second. We're trying to get to the bottom of who sent those text messages—"

I couldn't help it: I yawned. I tried to stifle it behind my hand, but the combination of the food hitting my belly and the fear and terror from the fight bleeding away proved a little too much. I was safe, my body recognized that, and now I needed to crash. I winced. "Sorry."

"Don't be. You're tired," Guy said, pushing himself to his feet. "Of course you are, you escaped prison today."

"With the help of my best enemy forever," I said.

"Come again?"

"I'll have to explain it later, you wouldn't believe me if I tried right now." I yawned again. "Sorry. Sorry—I just—"

"I'll let you get some sleep. We can talk about everything in the morning." Guy looked over his shoulder, where early sunlight was starting to creep across the floorboards through the floor-to-ceiling windows. "Or afternoon, technically. There's only one bed, but it has to be more comfortable than what you had in prison."

"You'd be surprised," I said, following him out of the dining room and down the hall. We passed a library and a den before Guy pushed open the door to the master suite. I ignored most of the furniture though it looked expensive. I had eyes only for the king-sized bed.

"I'll stay up and keep watch," Guy said. "Just, you know, to make sure there's no trouble."

"Really? Because you look like you haven't slept in a few days." I yawned and winced. "Wow, that was more blunt than I meant it to be. I'm sorry. I mean—"

"No, no, you have a point. It's been . . . a long week." He pushed his hands through his hair.

"Bed's plenty big enough if you don't want to fold yourself onto that couch."

Guy paused, his eyes darting up to meet mine. "Are you sure?"

I wiggled a hand. If I were any less exhausted, I would probably feel a little more awkward about it. Guy and I had barely even kissed, and that had been in the heat of the moment in battle. Sleeping together—even if it was just actual sleeping—that was kind of a biggish step. On the other hand, we'd spent nearly four years in the weirdest relationship where we regularly faced stark odds and horrifying danger together, all without really talking.

Normal had never really defined us.

"Yes," I said. "I'm sure. Though I'm kind of covered in pepper spray, still. Which could cause problems."

"Right," Guy said, as if he'd only just remembered something. "Stay put." He disappeared down the hallway and returned less than thirty seconds later with a Victoria's Secret bag.

"Let me guess," I said, looking at it. "Vicki."

"It's regular clothes. She didn't feel you'd be enjoying the . . . orange jumpsuit. And she has about fifty of these bags. She uses them for everything."

"Gee, I wonder why. Detmer wasn't exactly a jumpsuit kind of place, but god am I glad to get out of these clothes," I said, taking the bag from him. "I can probably stay upright long enough for a quick shower if there's a bathroom."

"Through there. I'll, uh—you know what? I'll go put away the food."

In the bathroom, I stripped out of the Detmer clothing and stepped under a scalding-hot shower spray. The water felt like it was slicing open wounds on my skin, pounding down on my injured shoulder and all of the bruises from my fights with Rita and the Raptor. I closed my eyes until the pain began to fade, and the heat relaxed the muscles still tensed from the fight. After I'd soaked long enough, I turned the water off, toweled off, and opened the bag Vicki had packed. I grimaced a little at the tank top, as my shoulder was a mass of black and purple, but it couldn't be helped.

"All clear," I called once I'd dressed.

When he reappeared, he wore athletic shorts and a Chicago Bulls T-shirt. "Sam's," he said by way of explanation. "Um, do you have a side of the bed you prefer or—okay, that works."

I lifted my chin from where I'd flopped onto the side nearest me. "Sorry. Sleepy."

"Don't apologize. I'm just glad you're here, and you're safe." I could see the way his eyes lingered on my shoulder.

"Mm. Me too. I'm glad you came for me." I didn't bother with the covers. I felt him rustling around and settling in, then a long, soft sigh. Keeping my eyes closed, on the very cusp of sleep, I reached across the expanse in the middle of the bed, hand outstretched. A moment later, his fingers laced through mine.

I fell asleep holding on.

CHAPTER NINE

When I woke up, I smelled pancakes. Angélica felt like being nice today, evidently, if she was making more than just eggs or peanut butter on toast. Pancakes were reserved for special training days, and . . .

My eyes snapped open. In a horrible, crashing moment, I remembered that Angélica was gone. For a moment, things had been okay. I'd been back at Davenport, listening to my trainer cook breakfast as she prepared for another day of prepping me for superheroism. Those moments, the ones where I temporarily forgot she was gone, those were the worst. Everything might have been okay for a time, but reality inevitably returned. Every time it did, its edges cut sharper.

I sat up and pushed my legs over the side of the bed, fighting to breathe until equilibrium returned. The other half of the bed was empty—which explained how the pancakes were being made—so I had a moment to myself. It was the first time in what felt like forever that I really had been alone and safe.

My head still hurt, and it took me a moment to realize why that was strange. Mobium usually got rid of headaches first. Other aches and pains took a little longer to heal. Frowning, I headed into the bathroom and pulled the strap of the tank top aside. The bruising on my shoulder had faded to an ugly green color. Attractive.

Angélica might not have been there, but there *was* a visitor. Sitting at the table, holding a cup of coffee as she paged through a fashion magazine, was one of the most famous faces on the planet.

Or two of the most famous faces on the planet, really. Most of the world didn't know that Victoria Burroughs, supermodel, put on a very ugly black-and-white mask and became Plain Jane, superhero, every night. Right now, her uniform was a great deal more green than usual. I really, really wasn't sure how I felt, seeing Blaze's outfit on somebody else.

She eyed me up and down. "It's okay. You're not the person I've made question their sexuality."

I had to laugh. "Hi, Vicki."

Vicki swooped across the room. Her hug practically squeezed all of the air from my lungs. "Thank god you're okay," she said. "You know prison's not great for the skin tone. And I really didn't know how we were gonna keep your boy from razing the place to the ground to get you back. How's life as a fugitive?"

"Oh, you know how it goes. I thought life was getting a little boring, so I thought I'd see what being a fugitive feels like." I hugged her back, looking over her shoulder as I did so. Guy, flipping pancakes at the range, gave me a little wave, grinning and rolling his eyes. "I'm glad to see you. Um, how are you? Are you okay? Last time I saw you—"

"Pfft, Konrad was hardly a challenge. I handled him." Vicki waved a hand. The villain she called 'hardly a challenge' had leveled an entire shopping mall with his earthquake powers. This probably said more about Vicki than anything else. "And hey, now there are pancakes, and that's nothing to shake a stick at."

She had a point: the pancakes did smell amazingly, sinfully good. I wished there wasn't a pain sitting behind the bridge of my nose so I could enjoy them more.

"There's coffee," Guy said, "and I got the tea that you used to keep stocked in your desk at the office."

"You went through her desk?" Vicki asked, plopping back down at the table. "That's adorable in a stalkery sort of way."

"Uh." Guy gave me a panicked look. "It was just to get a file, I swear. And it was only the once."

Since reminders that I'd worked with Guy for years and had never noticed a lot of things about him made me uncomfortable, I stepped forward to pull a tea bag out of the box on the counter. I tilted my head to look up at him. "You weren't the one that kept depleting my chocolate stash, were you?"

"No, that wasn't me. I would never—and you're teasing me again."

"I would never," I said. There were pretty white coffee mugs hanging on a rack, but they were close to the ceiling. Right. Both Sam and Guy were tall. Of course Sam would design his safe house with that mind. "Good morning. Or afternoon, I think."

He flipped a pancake, raising his eyebrows. "Sleep all right?"

"Better than I have in a while. How long was I out?"

"Nearly twelve hours." He smiled as he reached up and grabbed a mug, holding it out to me. "Is that what you were looking for? You could have asked."

"Looking pitiful worked just as well, in the end."

"So, Gail," Vicki asked, making me look over. "Just how *was* life in the clink, anyway?"

I sat at the table and considered everything that had happened. Telling them the truth about Detmer, when I knew how they both felt about the men and women who committed evil deeds upon their cities, didn't seem like a great idea. And I really, really did not want to explain that our country's tax infrastructure was being run by the most evil people on the planet. I forced a smile and poured water from the kettle into the mug. "It was okay. You just have to take the biggest con in the yard out on the first day, and everybody listens to you after that."

"Did you really?" Vicki looked inordinately fascinated.

"Sadly, no. Only one guy tried to pick a fight with me."

"You beat his ass like I taught you?" Vicki asked.

For a second, awkwardness reigned, like all three of us were expecting a fourth member of our party to snort at her and ask exactly *who* had taught me how to beat somebody up, again? It sat on the air, almost a palpable thing.

"I didn't get a chance." I played with the string of my tea bag, watching the color swirl and seep into the water. "So, do you two have *any* idea who wanted me to go to jail? Because I've been turning it over and over, and I'm just coming up blank."

"We've been looking," Vicki said. She tossed her magazine to the side, blowing out a breath. "Those texts were pretty damning and—don't give me that look, I know you didn't send them. But they're out there. You're sure nobody had your phone?"

"How would I know? I had it when Dr. Mobius knocked me out in that coffee shop, and when I woke up, it was gone."

Guy put a platter of scrambled eggs with cheese on the table. "We'll keep looking. But right now, the only way to clear your name is to find Chelsea and make her tell us what the hell is going on. The problem is . . ."

"It's like she went *poof*," Vicki said, scowling. "Whoever she is, she's great at hiding—and being a pain in my ass. She was spotted at Avery Science Labs a couple days ago, but by the time we got there, she was gone."

"Did she take anything?"

"We'll let you know when they finish clearing the rubble." Vicki's chin firmed as she scooped a good portion of eggs onto her plate and passed the platter to me. "Davenport hid that reporter pet of yours pretty good, but there hasn't even been a whiff of Chelsea looking for her. They're moving her today."

"I thought Jeremy said you guys couldn't find Naomi."

"Davenport was hiding her. But it looks like they're finally keeping her in one place, and guess who's on guard detail." Vicki jabbed her own breastbone with her thumb. "Been awhile since I've had to do that."

Guy gave her a smile. "Bring a magazine."

Vicki saluted him.

Guy carried a plate of pancakes to the table and set them near me. My stomach roiled rather than rumbled, and I blinked. Why was the food making me feel ill? It looked so good. I swallowed down the nausea and speared a small mountain onto my plate. To distract myself, I asked, "There's a lot they didn't tell me in prison. Like, I have no idea about anything that's happened, or what really went down at the mall."

Vicki seemed more than happy to fill me in. After the fight at the mall, she said, she dropped Konrad the Earthquake Man off at one of the holding facilities and went back to headquarters to find Davenport in absolute chaos. The news that I had been arrested and convicted shortly afterward had been almost as shocking as Angélica's death.

"Guy kind of lost it," she said in an aside to me, speaking quickly to cover the fact that her voice had hitched on Angélica's name.

Guy gave her an aggrieved look. "I'm sorry, who was it that punched Jeremy?"

"That was an accident," Vicki said at the same time as I said, "You punched Jeremy?"

"*Accidentally*," Vicki said. "And I wouldn't have if he hadn't stopped me from punching Eddie!"

"Either way, he saved you from ending up in prison right next to Gail," Guy said, frowning. "You know the rules for attacking a Class D."

"Eddie's enough of an asshole to enforce it." Vicki rolled her eyes. She turned to me. "Eddie gave us the news. I didn't take it well."

"And by not taking it well," Guy said, cutting a pancake into small pieces, "she means she tried to punch the CEO of Davenport Industries even though she's eighty times stronger than him and would have caused some permanent damage."

"Jeremy blocked my punch before I could do something I would regret. He's lucky I didn't break his hand."

That explained the bandage on Jeremy's hand when he'd come to visit me.

"And I apologized. Jeremy forgave me, so I think everybody else should, too," Vicki said, glaring at Guy.

Guy and I shared a silent look as we chewed. Jeremy would follow Vicki around like a lovesick puppy all day if she let him.

"What happened after Eddie gave you the news?" I asked. I wanted to ask what they had done with Angélica's body. Had they taken her back to her family in

Brazil? Jeremy had mentioned a memorial. It made me sick to think of missing it.

"Guy tried to get you a lawyer," Vicki said, and I pushed Angélica from my thoughts as best I could. "And that's when they told us they'd found your phone, and you'd been working with Chelsea all along. Her spy inside Davenport."

"But *why*?" I asked. "Where did they even find my phone? Who would do this to me? And why would I spy for Chelsea? Even she didn't think I was important."

"She was wrong, obviously," Guy said.

Vicki rested her chin on her hands. "Aw," she said.

I ignored her. "What I mean is that Chelsea never gave a damn about me, and so there's no reason she'd set me up to take the fall for her killing Angélica. So who is it? Davenport? Mobius? And *why*?"

"We're looking into it," Guy said. "And we're looking for Chelsea. We're going to get to the bottom of this. Davenport's got a price on Chelsea's head. They've done a media blitz looking for her, but it's difficult when . . ."

"When nobody but Vicki and I know what she looks like? Yeah." Chelsea had popped up out of nowhere. If I hadn't been visiting Naomi to enlist her help, Chelsea might have slipped beyond Davenport's radar for a long time. But I'd seen her, and Vicki had seen her, and the next time Chelsea had appeared in public, she'd masked up.

"I barely got a good look," Vicki said. "She was all

dusty, you know, from the fight. You and Naomi are really the only ones who know what she truly looks like."

"Why not get Naomi to work with a sketch artist?" I asked. "Or me? I'd be happy to."

"Naomi because she's been in a coma, and you . . . I don't know, actually," Vicki said.

"Wait—*what*?"

"She actually just woke up yesterday," Guy said. "The doctors think she's going to be okay, but she hasn't been up to talking much."

I took a deep breath. I might not know Naomi very well, but I couldn't fight the relief that she was okay. "Maybe she'll know something that will help us catch Chelsea. Hey, did Sam have any idea what she would want with him, or with you?" Naomi had confessed that Chelsea had hired her to look into Blaze and War Hammer.

"He couldn't think of anything." Guy shook his head in bewilderment. "I haven't fought her before. I would've recognized those moves."

"Somebody from your past?" I asked. He had never shared with me how he had gotten his powers or come to Davenport. There were still large parts of Guy Bookman and Blaze that were a mystery to me.

Guy shook his head slowly. "I don't think so. I've tried to put it together, but anybody she could possibly be, they're all dead."

"That's depressing," Vicki said.

Guy gave her the same aggrieved look.

"Okay, point. Comes with the territory. Sometimes I forget because I'm not all tragic like you sob-story types." She shoveled the last of her pancakes into her mouth. "But anywho, that's not important right now. I think your reporter's the key to what's really going on here, Gail. Which would be okay, usually, but they're cracking down on security now, and they won't let Guy *or* me in to see her. Not even when we ask nicely. So that means you."

"Right," I said. "Because if they're not going to let two of the biggest heroes on their roster in to see the patient, granting permission to the convict on the run is definitely something that will happen."

"So don't ask permission."

I goggled at her. "You want me to break Naomi out of a secure Davenport facility?"

"You broke out of Detmer. Shouldn't be a problem for you."

"Wait, wait, hold up." I actually held my hands up in a time-out gesture. "Stop. We need to clarify something here. I did not break myself out of prison."

Both Guy and Vicki paused.

"Rita Detmer, *Fearless* herself, broke me out of prison. She literally flew me to the fence and threw me over with, like, no warning whatsoever. I was not in on this plan at all."

"Why would she do that?" Guy asked at the same time Vicki asked, "Wait, you met *Fearless*?"

"She was my roommate," I said to Vicki before I turned to Guy. "I have no idea. Like, none whatsoever.

She said something about helping her family, but she didn't say why, and you can imagine I have no interest in helping Eddie *or* Jessica Davenport right now, especially since the former threw me in jail and the latter did her best to kill me. But it was like Rita was grooming me, or at least expected me to do *something*, but it's not like she told me what it was, so—wait, why are you looking at each other like that? Share with the non-hero at the table, please."

"Rita Detmer has more family than just Eddie and Jess," Guy said slowly.

I knew that. Jessica had two kids who showed up in the tabloids even though they were barely preteens. And then I remembered: Jess and Eddie had a brother. "Marcus, right? You told me he's dead. His picture's in the Annals and everything." And there had never been a creepier memorial to the fallen heroes—and their families—than the hallway in Davenport Tower full of their portraits.

"Marcus had a daughter," Guy said. "You know her."

"I do?"

"Gail, it's Kiki. Her full name is Kiki Davenport."

I stared for a long moment. And when that didn't filter through the membrane of shock, I stared longer. "Kiki?" I said. "Kiki as in my doctor, Kiki? That Kiki?"

"Yes."

I reeled back in my chair, pointing. "I saw her! In the prison waiting room, when Jeremy came to see me. I saw her, and it completely slipped my mind!

She must have been there to see Rita. Is she in trouble somehow?"

Both Guy and Vicki looked troubled. "I don't know," Guy said. "We can find out. After we get Naomi and track down Chelsea."

That didn't sit right with me, I realized. Sure, I didn't want to go along with Rita's crazy plan, whatever the hell it was, but Kiki was a friend. She made me wary because she had telepathic abilities, and I'd never had a good experience with any of those, but she'd seemed like good people.

But Kiki's grandmother and her father both had Villain Syndrome.

Which explained the looks on Guy's and Vicki's faces right now. "You think Kiki and Rita are working together," I said. "Like, what, they're using me?"

"It's a concern. I can do more research." Guy put his fingertips together for a second before resting both hands flat against the table. He looked at Vicki. "Aren't you going to be late for your shift?"

"Good point." She stood up and peeled out of Guy's uniform, stripping down to her panties and bra. Modesty was not a necessity for her. It made sense, since she'd shown up on billboards in Times Square wearing even less. "I left the blueprints for the checkpoint on the counter. I'd move fast if I were you."

"We'll come up with something," Guy said, putting his hand over his eyes and shaking his head.

"Please don't let me know while you're in there."

Vicki reached into her bag and retrieved a length of black cloth. She tossed her Plain Jane mask on the table and pulled her uniform on up to the waist, pausing to tie her hair back. "I really don't want to pretend fight you."

"Uh, sure," I said, though I really didn't remember agreeing to break Naomi out. But hey, I'd done crazier things in the past forty-eight hours, really. "I'll do my best."

"Thanks. See you afterward." She pulled the rest of her uniform on, tugged the mask over her face, and headed for the window.

We both watched her go for a second, and Guy turned to me with a rueful look. "She's kind of a whirlwind," he said.

"That's the Vicki we know and love," I said. "So I guess I'm busting Naomi out of prison. What the hell, it's not like I had other plans for the day. Two prison breaks in twenty-four hours? That's basically a party in my world."

"And that's the Gail we know and love." Guy gave me another smile and ducked his head to finish his breakfast.

CHAPTER TEN

After Vicki left, Guy caught me up on everything vital I had missed in prison, which was not that much. "I mean, you're important," he said, as we carried the dishes to the sink. Mercifully, the food had cut away the edges of my headache, bringing it down to a dull roar. But I still felt a little weak as I helped with the dishes. "The problem is that Davenport has so much going on . . ."

"The world *should* drop everything for me, though," I said, attempting a feeble joke.

He smiled. "If I had my way, they would. I don't get it. I don't understand why they're targeting you, or even who's doing it."

"Or why I randomly got busted out of prison and had my own protection squad inside."

"I'm glad you had that even if I don't understand why."

"Your guess is as good as mine." I finally gave in to the need and leaned over, resting my forehead against his shoulder since my hands were covered in dishwater. I heard his sigh as he relaxed. "Everything sucks, but I'm glad you're here."

"You're where the party is, don't you know that?" He didn't quite manage to infuse the necessary humor in his voice. "I'm so sorry this is happening to you, Gail."

"And you, too. I know Angélica meant a lot to you."

"It happens." Guy's voice was rough. He turned to finish scrubbing the pan, which bent a little under his fingers. I lifted my head and grabbed the towel to dry my hands. "It's the choice we all make. We know what can happen. And Angélica, I think . . . she would make that choice again."

That didn't help much. A life had been cut short to save mine, and it was the life of somebody I'd admired and respected.

I swallowed. "I think you're right. But how are you handling it? Are you okay?"

"I should be asking you that." Guy bent the pan back into its regular shape, holding it up to the light to inspect it. "You're going through a much rougher time than I am."

"I'm scared. And I'm mad. Vicki's right. We have to get to Naomi. I think she might know how to clear my name, and, even more, she might know why Chelsea is after you and Sam." After all, she'd been the one Chelsea had hired to research Sam's and Guy's powers.

But that didn't mean she belonged in custody any more than I did.

"So we focus on the mission," Guy said, setting the pan down and drying his hands.

"Until all of this is sorted out. But I think we can take a minute." I reached up and grabbed his shirt collar, tugging him down to my level. After Jeremy, I'd given myself the rule of no more tall men for this very reason, but that hardly seemed to matter now. Guy stumbled a tiny bit. I kissed him before he could get his balance or try to pull back.

It wasn't a problem, though. After a second, his arms came around me, and he kissed me back, a lot more slowly. He pulled back first. "Gail," was all he said.

I tilted my head to consider him. "Are you going to turn this red every time I kiss you? Because I have to admit, it's really cute."

He scowled. "It's more than a distinct possibility. At least one of us should enjoy that."

"Aww." I kissed him again, quickly, and stepped back. The headache was almost completely gone now, mercifully, which made things seem a little clearer. "But you're right, there's not much time. We've got to get Naomi out."

"Any ideas on how to do that?"

"I'm not nearly as good at busting people out of prison as Raze and Rita," I said, frowning. I smiled a little. "The one time you need a supervillain, there's not one around to be found, huh?"

"Darn," Guy said, snapping his fingers.

"Yeah, it's a—wait." The idea hit, making me stop midstep and midsentence. Guy, leaning against the counter with his arms across his chest, raised both eyebrows at me as I slowly swiveled to face him. "I think I may have an idea. Can you cause a distraction?"

"What kind of distraction?"

"I need you to be Bl—no, not Blaze. Blaze and Hostage Girl shouldn't be in the same city."

"Hostage Girl?" Guy's eyebrows went up farther.

"Shut up, you know what I mean. I don't have a hero name yet, and that's what they know me by." I waved that off. "War Hammer. I need War Hammer to be real obvious, saving the day. Can you do that? Go fight crime for a while?"

"Of course. What are you going to do?"

I winced. "Maybe it's better if you don't know?"

His chin lowered. "Because you love it so much when we do that to you."

He had a point. "Okay, you're right. No more keeping anybody in the dark. It's just that if I'm going to break into this space, I need to officially think like a villain, you know?"

"Can you do that?"

"No, but I know where to find people that do."

If there was ever was a supervillain bar in Chicago, of course it was in Wicker Park.

Of *course*.

I stared at the little dive bar, partly in frustration, partly in complete understanding. I'd been in this neighborhood a few times—a surprising number of villains kept their little hidey-holes among the clustered apartments, next to the college students and the elderly population. So a supervillain bar located there? Yeah, it made sense.

The little steering wheel you'd find on a pirate ship being mounted above the door? That made less sense—until I stepped inside and realized that Mind the Boom was a pun. Sure, supervillains liked explosives. But apparently they liked their alcohol served in the ambiance of a ship's hold, with fishing nets and styrofoam fish and crabs all over the walls. The floor was composed of driftwood planks, the ancient wooden stools had seen better centuries, and the bartender wore an eye patch. Whether that was an evil thing or a nautical one, I couldn't be sure.

I adjusted the collar of my leather jacket and tried to look like I meant to cause people harm. It's difficult to look like a badass when you're barely five feet tall, but I'd been around enough supervillains that a *screw you* presence was easy to cultivate.

The bartender looked over and frowned. "I haven't seen you in here before," she said.

"I'm new to the evil game." I looked at the line of liquors behind her and tried to think of the most evil drink I knew. "I'll have an Irish car bomb, pl—" I broke off. Supervillains probably didn't order drinks politely.

She eyed me up and down. Guy had found me an

all-black outfit and the leather jacket (I kind of hoped to keep that; it was seriously nice, even though it was swelteringly hot, being July), but I didn't really have any blast rays or anything to recommend me like Raze would have. "What's your beat?"

"My beat? Like, my archnemesis?"

"Sure, either or. I like to get to know the newcomers."

Sorry, Raze, I thought. "Razor X is still in prison. Her beat's open, and I'm eyeing it pretty hard, you know?"

The bartender gave me a strange look. Okay, maybe I needed to stop talking like the mob boss in a forties detective flick. "It's a work in progress," I said, watching her build the Guinness. I glanced over my shoulder, making sure nobody else had come in. Something in the corner caught my eye.

"You like that?" the bartender asked. "It's our wall of fame."

It wasn't until I was right up next to the wall that I really understood what I was seeing. Polaroids had been pinned to the board with brightly colored thumbtacks. Every single one of the Polaroids showed a different grinning villain, some shooting finger guns, others holding up real guns of varying types. Selfies, I realized, which would have been fine if it weren't for one glaringly obvious fact: I was in every one of those pictures. Unconscious, but there.

Belatedly, I saw the text above the pictures: HOSTAGE GIRL WALL OF FAME.

"Are you *kidding* me?" I asked.

"Nope." The bartender smiled and lifted her eye patch when I turned back to her. A bionic eye blinked red. "Aha. I thought it was you. What brings the illustrious Hostage Girl to my humble establishment? Switching sides?"

I remembered that I was supposed to be evil now. "Yes," I said. I might as well tell the truth, so: "Just broke out of Detmer."

"Really?" She finished pouring the Guinness and set it on the bar in front of my stool. "Hard-core."

"Thank you." I sat down and tried not to sulk. "And now I'm looking to hire somebody. I need a supervillain of . . . certain skills."

"What kind? We get all types here." She poured the Bailey's and Jameson into a shot glass and pushed both glasses to me.

I stared at the alcohol with a dawning realization that a) I had not had any alcohol since the Mobium, since Angélica had forbidden me from drinking and, b) I had expressly ordered a drink that required chugging. Chugging something that probably wouldn't react well to the isotope taking over most of my body. Right before I was hoping to break into a secure Davenport facility, a plan that would no doubt require all of my mental faculties and some delicacy besides.

"Drink up, me hearty," the bartender said.

Sorry, Angélica, I thought, and I dropped the shot in and chugged.

The alcohol hit the back of my throat. It didn't burn, thankfully, but I could outright *feel* the effect as I drank. One thing was obvious right away: the Mobium did not approve. It didn't like me poisoning my body in any way. But I swallowed the last of my drink and banged the glass down on the bar. "Tasty."

"Another?"

"I'll hold off. I'm looking for somebody that specializes in extraction or infiltration. Preferably both, but I can work with either."

"What's the pay?"

I named a figure. Guy had given me that much in cash. I knew better than to actually carry it into the bar with me, so I'd hidden it in Sam's car, which I had borrowed from the motor pool under Sam's hideout.

"You'll get some takers," my bartender said, not blinking either her regular or her bionic eye at the sum I'd named. "Speaking of which, here's one right now."

I ducked my head as the ship's bell over the door jangled. The newcomer let out a long, drawn-out breath. "You would not believe it, Sal," she said, heels clicking on the driftwood planks. "Angus is asking me to learn this thing called PowerPoint, and it's *ridiculous*. I don't even know what's going on half the time. This is the worst."

I recognized that voice.

"Like, why do *I* have to learn it, anyway? I mean, in two weeks it's not going to matter. These are going to go back to a person who does real work. So awful."

Shocked, I lifted my head.

The newcomer, who was halfway to the bar, stopped in her tracks. "Girl?" she asked.

"I'm going to need another drink after all," I said to the bartender before I turned fully to look at the newcomer. "Care to tell me how long you've been a villain, Portia?"

CHAPTER ELEVEN

I'd known Portia McPeak for over three years. We'd worked together at Mirror Reality, Inc., which managed several of the top magazines in the company. Or I should say: I worked there, and Portia, like many of my other coworkers, had sat around looking pretty in hopes of luring our boss Angus into giving them a modeling contract instead. Portia fit the mold pretty well. She was svelte and blonde and wouldn't have looked out of place in one of those forties detective movies I had accidentally started imitating.

She was also vain and shallow and not once, not *once* had she ever seen fit to mention she wasn't just a regular Class D human. Never had she even so much as hinted that she would ever have a reason to visit a place like Mind the Boom, but here she was right in front of me.

"What are *you* doing here?" she asked, closing the

distance between us. "I thought you were on, like, the longest vacation ever. Are you done finding yourself now? And what are you wearing? That jacket is seriously cute, but it's, like, July."

"I could ask you the same," I said, and a confused line appeared between Portia's eyebrows. It was pretty much the only line on her face thanks to a rigorous schedule of Botox and cleanses. "Not about the jacket—I mean the bar. What brings you to a supervillain bar, Portia? Have you secretly had powers this whole time? Wait, are *you* a supervillain?"

"Not a villain, per se." Portia sighed like she was the most-put-upon person in the world. "But heroing feels like too much work. And I like this place. These are my people."

"Your—your *people*?" My jaw was about to swing in the breeze. "You do have powers, then?"

"Duh. I wouldn't be here if I didn't." She rolled her eyes. "Sal, can I get my usual? A little harder on the sauce. I get the feeling I'm about to have a headache."

"Got it." Sal fetched the bourbon to start preparing her drink.

I, meanwhile, tried to wrap my brain around the fact that one of my coworkers—the only one who had bothered to reach out to me after I'd vanished off the face of the earth due to the Mobium, depressingly enough—had somehow hidden superpowers from me. The entire time, I'd thought she was simply dumb.

Guess it served me right for believing what they said about blondes.

"What kind of powers do you have?" I asked.

"They're not important."

"Oh, no, I think they're very important," I said. I rested my chin on my hand and *stared*. "Please. Enlighten me."

"It's a little ironic, if you think about it," Portia said. I hadn't even been aware that she knew what that word even meant. "But I turn invisible."

"Come again?" I asked.

Portia sighed and vanished, making me scramble off the stool. I looked around for her before my brain informed me that I could hear her breathing, so she must still be right in front of me. I'd never come across a villain who could disappear that neatly or that completely. With most invisibility powers, there was at least a tiny outline in the air, like a piece of hair floating atop water. But even my enhanced eyes couldn't pick up a thing.

"See?" Portia asked.

"No, I don't," I said. "Which is the point. Wait, why is that ironic?"

Portia reappeared to give me an aggravated look. "Because I want to be a *model*, duh! I *want* to be seen! Look at me. These powers do me absolutely no good. It's the worst."

"No good? I mean, you can turn invisible! Think of everything you could do!"

Portia yawned. "Everything I could do? Have you seen me? I'm gorgeous, Girl. That should be celebrated."

Before I could make any arguments, my brain pointed out that it really was a good thing Portia was so vain. With invisibility powers that strong, she had the ability to walk into any bank vault and simply help herself to the goods within. With a little finesse, she could be the richest woman in the world, and yet . . .

"Yes, you're very pretty," I said, turning back to face the bar again. An idea struck. "Wait! You turn invisible!"

"We, like, just covered that. God. Thank you, Sal." Portia took the Old Fashioned from the bartender with a nod and sipped daintily. "Mm, that's good. Perfect for a long day of dealing with Angus."

I looked at the anchor-shaped clock over the bar. "It's not even five o'clock."

"So?"

"So, I used to be there until ten o'clock most nights and—you know what? Not the point. The point is, you can turn invisible. Can you fool security cameras?"

"I guess. I mean, it's not that hard."

"And can you turn another person invisible with you?"

"Well, of cour—oh no. I see that look. And the answer is no. I don't even want to know what it is you want me to do." Portia knocked back the rest of her drink. "Just because I saved your ass from a couple of villains, that does not make us friends. I only do those kind of favors for friends."

"What are you talking about?"

"It was just a couple times." Portia checked her manicure. "Walking back to the office, maybe I turned you invisible for a second or two so a villain wouldn't see you. It's not a big deal. Like, we had important meetings on those days. Couldn't it wait?"

"With them, hardly ever." How had I not noticed turning invisible? Yet another thing to wrap my mind around. One of my most selfish coworkers not only had some of the coolest powers I'd ever seen—or rather, *hadn't* seen—but she'd also protected me in my true Hostage Girl days? "Portia, my boyfriend is in real danger from a villain, and if I don't get this woman out of where she's being held, I can't help him."

Instantly, Portia's entire demeanor changed. She sat up, eyes bright. "You've got a new boyfriend?"

I started to say that yes, I did, but another idea occurred to me. Sending a silent apology to Jeremy, I shook my head. "More like an old one. Blaze is in trouble. I have to help him."

Portia stared at me with an unreadable expression for a full half minute before: "Yes! I knew it! I *knew* Blaze was Jeremy. Girl, you little sneak, that's excellent news. So you two made up? Damn, you've been busy. You got these now"—she squeezed my upper arm through the jacket—"*and* you made up with the man. I want details. But not, like, boring ones."

"You always thought Jeremy was a jerk," I said, squinting at her.

"But he's *hot*. So he's in trouble?" Portia turned on the barstool to give me her full attention. "I thought he was always helping you out, not the other way around."

This time my silent apology was to both Guy *and* Jeremy. "Completely in trouble. And I need so much help. I would be willing to . . . trade? You help me, I help you."

Portia's eyes narrowed. "How so?"

"Weren't you just saying you need to learn Power-Point?"

"You want me to help you break somebody out of a secure building in exchange for teaching me Power-Point?"

"And whipping up a couple presentations. I know what Angus likes."

"Hmm." Portia tilted her head as she considered this. "You'll be back at work in a couple of weeks. I can just wait and make you do the PowerPoint then. Really, I see no benefit in this for me."

"Portia." I folded my arms over my chest. I'd quit—well, had been let go from—my old job, but Portia was eternally convinced that I was coming back. "I am on the run from Detmer Prison."

"The supervillain prison?" Portia asked. "That's weird, you're a Class D."

I pulled off the leather jacket and flexed. "Look at me. I got these in under two weeks. Does that say Class D to you?"

"I guess not. Why would they throw you in prison? You don't do anything. Like, ever."

The reminder of my past passivity burned. "It's a long story."

"Oh, in that case, I'm not interested."

"Portia," I said.

"What? I'm not."

"So you're not gonna help me? At all?"

"Probably not." Portia waved at Sal the bartender. "I'm going to need another round."

"It's that reporter," I said, blurting it out. "The one you thought sounded really cute on the phone."

Portia swiveled to face me. "Go on."

"Just saying, um, she would be really grateful to anybody who rescues her. And maybe you'll get her number."

"*Is* she cute, though?"

I thought about Naomi Gunn. I wasn't really into women at all, not like Portia, but if I had to rate Naomi, I'd call her hipster cute, I supposed. "Yes," I said. "Very cute."

"I know this is manipulation, but hey, I didn't have any plans tonight." Portia tossed back the next drink that Sal brought over. "So, what are we breaking into? I hope it's interesting."

"Just how much do you know about superheroes?" I asked her.

Luckily, the facility where they were keeping Naomi was actually in the Willis Tower. I had no idea why, not when Guy had originally taken her to New York, but after everything that had happened to me, I wasn't about to look this particular gift horse in the mouth. Vicki had given me the blueprints of the floor layout and a copy of the guards' schedule. How she'd gotten a hold of those, I didn't even want to know.

There were lots of gift-horse mouths I was planning to avoid checking, actually.

We took the car I'd borrowed from Sam's garage because Portia didn't want hers anywhere near the scene of the crime. While I drove, she fixed her makeup in the visor mirror. "Why are you even doing that?" I asked as I switched lanes. "The point is that nobody is going to see you."

"*Now* you understand why my powers suck!"

We parked a couple of blocks away. Luckily, the area was crowded with tourists on their way to see the SkyDeck, so nobody really paid attention to us. Hopefully, we could slip in, snatch Naomi, and get out without anybody being the wiser. I ditched the leather jacket in the backseat of the car and led the way.

"So how does this work?" I asked, as we walked along.

She heaved a gusty sigh, like I had just asked her for the largest favor ever—and technically, I kind of had—and wrapped her bony fingers around my wrist. "Ta-dah," she said.

I looked at her. "You didn't do anything."

Portia gave me her "you're an idiot" look, one I knew for a fact she'd practiced. Wordlessly, she pointed at the mirrored windows on the building behind us. When I turned to look, I jumped. The space where we were standing was empty in the reflection. Not even a shadow was present. Portia let go of my wrist, and I reappeared in the mirror. I couldn't see her anymore, though, not until she wrapped her fingers around my wrist again.

"So that's how it works. Satisfied?" she said, sounding bored.

"We'll have to carry our shoes when we get inside," I said, frowning. "They'll hear your heels."

Portia sighed again. "I should have just stayed at work."

Now there were words I would never hear her say ever again.

They were keeping Naomi in one of the Davenport checkpoints, a set of offices that theoretically belonged to a company called Dartmoor Incorporated. Davenport had several of these areas, Guy had told me earlier. Dalloway International Hospital, where they'd taken Angélica and me after our fight at the mall, that was another checkpoint. These areas had quick access to a 'porting station, medical equipment for a good number of different hero types, and emergency supplies for supervillain attacks on the city. They weren't typically used to hold civilians like Naomi, which was why Vicki had been called in as an extra guard.

"It works out in your favor," Guy had said as he pulled on the War Hammer costume. "This isn't a fortress. It could be easier to break into."

"I sense a 'but' in your voice," I'd said.

"It's a slim chance, but it could be a trap. Either for you or for Chelsea." He'd frowned.

"I promise to do my best to stay out of any traps."

"Good." He'd handed me a little earwig. "I'll be as nearby as I can be without being suspicious. If there's trouble, shout."

I fiddled with this earwig. It felt strange, nestled in my ear canal. My headache had returned and was only growing stronger, but I focused past it. Portia kept her grip on my wrist as we walked up to the front doors of the building, though she seemed to be fiddling with something in her bag.

"What are you doing?" I asked as softly as I could.

"I'm tired of holding your hand. Ah, here we go," she said. She pulled out a little travel container of dental floss.

"Seriously?"

"Have I questioned how your powers work?" She looped the floss around my wrist several times. When she was done, we were connected by several lengths of floss, which seemed both perilous and oddly funny. "Now we're good."

"Right," I said under my breath, trying to still the nerves in my midsection. It occurred to me that I was about to break into a facility owned by the company hunting for me. And I was doing it armed with little more than a flaky blonde and some dental floss. No weapons. Just my wits, which weren't exactly the sharpest after the week I'd had.

We had to wait for someone to exit, so we could both squeeze through the door. Shoes in our hands, we moved past security, into an elevator, and disembarked on the proper floor. We entered a lobby, which was a lush, carpeted affair done up in turquoises and maroons. A receptionist and a security guard sat behind a wide desk, both looking remarkably alert as they studied the computer screens in front of them. I held my breath, waiting for the guard to spot some anomaly on the screen, for the alarms to start.

Portia strolled through without looking at the guard. When we made it past the lobby, she tilted her head imperiously at me.

Remembering the blueprints, I jerked my head to the left.

Past the lobby, the checkpoint reminded me more of a hospital. DARTMOOR INCORPORATED signs were posted everywhere on the walls and on the shirts and badges of the workers walking by. Carpeting gave way to polished linoleum, doors became bland gray metal. Observation windows were cut into the wall, and through them I could see examination rooms. We passed a patient with pretty gnarly burns covering most of his exposed skin, and both Portia and I flinched.

"You brought me to a hospital?" she whispered. "Is this revenge for all the times I refused to visit you in one?"

"Oh, I wish," I whispered back.

Workers in scrubs that I recognized from Davenport Medical strolled past us as we inched along, careful not to make a sound. Every time one came anywhere close to us, I had to fight off a miniature heart attack.

Down the hall, I heard a familiar voice.

I grabbed Portia and yanked her so that we were flush against a wall right as two people came around the corner. If we hadn't moved, they would have crashed into us.

"I mean, I could've gotten it checked out back at the Tower," Jeremy was saying to Vicki in her Plain Jane gear as he walked along, holding up his injured hand. "But I wanted to say hi. You said these guard posts are really boring."

"Isn't that—" Portia whispered.

I elbowed her hard, but not in time.

Vicki quit walking abruptly. "What is it?" Jeremy asked, stopping a couple of steps later.

She held up a hand. The mask moved in our direction. I could see her eyes behind it, but I couldn't deny that right then, that mask was the creepiest thing I had ever seen. Every scratch on its surface seemed to glint in the fluorescent light. Battle scars. A stark reminder that Plain Jane was one of the biggest badasses to ever badass.

Portia and I held still, not even daring to breathe.

"What are you looking at?" Jeremy asked, unaware that Plain Jane's mask was less than a foot away from my face. She had her eyes pointed right at my forehead, which lessened the creepiness somewhat. But still.

"It's Gail," I whispered as softly as I possibly could.

Because I was so close, I saw Vicki's shoulders stiffen. The mask tilted downward the tiniest fraction of an inch. "Duck," she said, voice almost inaudible. I barely pulled Portia down in time. Vicki's arm sailed right over our heads, and I caught the access card that dropped from her fingers.

"What was that?" Jeremy asked when Vicki danced back a couple of steps.

She shrugged. "Just thought I heard something. My ears are still ringing a bit from that fight with the Shockwave Sisters last week."

"Weird. I got some eardrops back at headquarters if you need 'em," Jeremy said, and the two set off again.

The minute they were out of range, Portia rounded on me. "You know *Plain Jane*? What's she like?"

"She'll surprise you," I said, as I really didn't want to confess that Plain Jane was also one of Portia's personal heroes. She always bought a magazine if Victoria Burroughs was on the cover though she claimed not to be a fan.

"Do you know what she looks like under the mask?"

I looked back. Vicki had ears like a cat, but I couldn't tell if she could still hear us. "No," I lied.

"I bet she's hideous. Like, probably covered in burns like that guy we saw back there."

"Oh, absolutely," I said. Right before Vicki and Jeremy turned the corner, she scratched the back of the black covering her hair, middle finger sticking out prominently. It made me grin. I lifted my hand to study the proximity card Vicki had passed to me. She really was amazing. "Let's get moving."

When we reached the door to Naomi's room, I took a deep breath and swiped the card, praying.

Alarms didn't *immediately* start blaring, so I took that as a positive sign.

Less positive was that the room appeared to be empty. I stepped inside, stomach sinking as I took in the vacant, tousled bed. And if I hadn't had the Mobium enhancing my hearing, Naomi truly would have gotten the drop on me.

She leapt blindly out of the corner from behind the door, swinging at empty air. I easily stepped to the side, letting her charge right past.

She whipped around, faltering. "The hell? Is somebody in here?"

"Yes," I said, and she shrieked.

"Wow, she really is hot," Portia whispered.

"Shh," I said, and I wasn't sure which one of them I was addressing.

"Who is that? Who's talking? I can't see you, but I know I'm not crazy. I know I'm not." In the time we'd been apart, Naomi had lost the caged, on-the-run-from-a-supervillain look. She wore a white polo shirt and navy blue trousers. It was an outfit I recognized: I'd worn the same thing during my days as an official trainee at Davenport. I could see the corner of a patch of gauze sticking out from under the collar of the polo shirt. She no longer had her hair in braids, either. It was pulled back into a bushy ponytail at the nape of her neck.

"Naomi, it's me. Gail," I said. I reached out and grabbed her arm since that would let her see Portia and me perfectly.

She only shrieked and jumped back, arms wind-milling.

"What? You should have been able to see us just now," I said.

"Yeah, it only works on two people," Portia said.

I rounded on her. "*What?*"

"Wait—Gail? Hostage Girl?" Naomi looked in confusion at the air to the left of my head. "*That* Gail?"

"Yes. Hold, please," I told her, and I turned back to Portia. "You can only keep two people invisible at one time?"

"Didn't I tell you about this before?"

"I think I would remember if you had!"

"What is going on?" Naomi asked.

"We're breaking you out of here. Or we will once I figure this out." I pinched the bridge of my nose. Of *course* Portia would wait until we were deep in a Davenport facility to let me know there was no way to get three people out at once with her powers. I thought about it, about Vicki's plan. We needed to move quickly, but the priority had to be Naomi. So I sighed. "Okay, I need to get a worker's uniform."

"What?"

"Naomi, I know you can't see her, but this is Portia, a friend of mine. Portia, Naomi. She's going to get you out of here." I looked at Portia. "Is that okay with you, or is there something else you're neglecting to tell me?"

"Nah, that's pretty much it. How are you going to get a uniform?"

"I'll come up with something. Naomi, is there somewhere the cameras can't see?"

"This corner, I think," she said, nodding at where she'd been hiding.

I stepped into the corner and removed the dental floss from my wrist. When I popped back into view, Naomi jumped. "Sorry," I said, massaging my wrist. "Portia, you take her and get out of here as fast as you can. Go back to the car. If I'm not back in ten minutes, take her to your place. I'll come find you."

"Ugh," Portia said.

But Naomi rounded on me. "Tell me what's going on right now, or I'll scream."

"Isn't it obvious? We're staging a prison break." I had a split second of looking into Naomi's stunned face before she vanished. It really was startling to watch it in action. "I'll explain after we get out of here. If we get out of here."

"You'd better," Naomi said.

I reached over and swiped the card at the access reader and the door opened as if on its own accord, which was honestly a little eerie. They walked off, leaving me alone.

Out in the open.

Deep in the heart of a Davenport facility.

CHAPTER TWELVE

I didn't run though I wanted to. After Portia took off with Naomi, I braced myself in the blind spot for a necessary ten seconds, breathing in deep gulps of oxygen. I needed to find a closet, ambush a worker who was about my size, and steal their uniform. At least I had the blueprints memorized. They listed a storage closet not too far from Naomi's cell. I slipped my shoes back on, eased Naomi's door open, and listened.

If even one person recognized me, it was all over.

I couldn't hear anybody coming. Quickly, but not running, I stepped into the hallway. Sweat coated my entire torso and the back of my neck, but I reached the closet without anybody seeing me. I slipped inside, cringing at the way the hinges creaked.

My first stroke of luck hit when I glanced around the closet. I'd found the medical supplies. Right there on the top shelf were several unopened sets of scrubs. Grimacing, I climbed the shelves (they groaned under my weight) to grab a size small. The pants were a little big, but that was honestly the least of my worries. I yanked the top over my black T-shirt and stuffed my old pants on the shelf, out of the way.

As I reached for my shoes, I heard the access card reader beep.

Oh god.

I looked around for a place to hide, but the closet really wasn't that big, and I was right out in the open, barefoot and obviously out of place.

And also a wanted fugitive.

The door handle turned. By instinct, I grabbed the shelf and hauled myself up with all of my strength. It rocketed me over the top and nearly into the ceiling. I didn't stick the landing at all. Instead, I fell in an uncoordinated heap on top of a pile of scrubs wrapped in plastic.

The shelf squeaked in protest as the door opened, and every part of me went still in terror. I didn't dare breathe as somebody stepped in. I couldn't see whoever it was, but I heard them pause, like they weren't sure they had heard something.

I closed my eyes and prayed the shelf wouldn't creak again. A single twitch would set off another squeak, and the jig really would be up.

Millenniums passed while the person stood there, probably looking around. Finally, I heard him or her grab something off a shelf on the other side of the closet. The door opened again, and I was alone. Sweating bullets, but alone.

I slipped my shoes back on and clipped the access card to the collar of the shirt so that I would look at least somewhat official. A peek into the hallway showed that it was mercifully empty. I stepped out, ducked my head, and started to walk. After being shielded by Portia's powers, every echoing step made it just how obvious and out in the open I was now. The first time I heard somebody approach, I stepped to the side of the hallway and ducked down to tie my shoe, hoping they wouldn't linger and see the sweat on the back of my neck.

They didn't. I pushed out a breath and forged on. Every person I passed gave me a tiny panic attack but none of them really looked at me. They only saw the scrubs. I made it all the way to the lobby, worn-out and terrified, where I encountered my next problem: I would have to pass the guard. Which wouldn't be easy. Security guards were trained to recognize everybody in this kind of office environment, and I definitely did not belong.

Luckily, a woman in a messenger delivery cap leaned indolently over the desk, taking up the guard's attention. I could just sneak out, and everything would be okay.

The woman turned, and my vision telescoped right onto her face. Every cell of my body went abruptly, horrifically cold with rage.

I hadn't seen Chelsea since the mall, when she'd

grabbed me by the throat and tossed me headfirst into a fountain three stories below. But I'd daydreamed about seeing her again. The answers I'd demand, the pain I'd inflict.

I never imagined that I would be completely immobilized, thoroughly unable to move. Rage and sickness welled up in my throat. She looked *healthy*, which was the worst part. I'd had the worst week of my life, and Chelsea was as tall and slim and put together as ever.

She glanced idly over her shoulder to case the lobby and must have noticed me, for she turned to give me a second look. Our eyes locked. Recognition flashed in hers. She straightened up and stepped toward me.

It broke through the paralysis. I slapped the emergency button on the wall to my right.

Chelsea stopped, eyes going wide. Alarms began to blare.

The guard, who'd jumped to his feet, looked around and pointed. Not at Chelsea. At me. "Intruder! Godwin's here!"

And he rushed past Chelsea and straight at me.

Oh, *shit*.

I kicked off the wall to avoid the taser prongs he shot at me. I ran for the nearest door, but I wasn't quick enough. It slammed in my face, blocking that escape route. When I whipped around, I saw two things: the guard rushing at me, and Chelsea standing smugly in the middle of the lobby, arms crossed over her chest.

In that suspended moment, her eyebrow went up. *Good one, idiot*, it seemed to say.

I dodged around the guard and ran at her instead. Her hand came up. I prepared for one of her stinging rays, for the agony of the bee stings crawling all over my skin. It would be worth it for one shot at her.

I'd go through much worse to plant my fist in her face.

At the last second, she faltered. Instead of blasting me with a ray, she dropped her hand and screamed. An instant later, my opening punch caught her on the side of the jaw, snapping her head back.

She didn't fight back. She just kept screaming and cowering, tears streaming down her face before she broke into sobs. About to punch her again, I hesitated, and she shouted, "Stop her! This psycho's hurting me!"

It caught me off guard. She was *Chelsea*. She was supposed to try and kick my ass, so what was she doing? I tried to hit her again, but a guard tackled me from behind. As we crashed to the floor, I saw a smirk cross Chelsea's face for a split second.

"You don't understand!" I struggled to kick the guard off me and get back to my feet. "That's *Chelsea*—she's the villain, not me!"

"Ma'am, stop struggling, or we will be forced to subdue you!"

I broke free and ducked forward sharply, throwing a second guard over my shoulder. They'd swarmed in when the alarms had started blaring. When a third guard tried to tackle me, I elbowed him in the face. A fourth hit me from behind like a linebacker. I stayed on my feet, but only just. Chelsea, nearly at the exit, looked over her shoulder and blew me a kiss. Another guard piled on, right as the door from inside the facility burst open and Plain Jane waded into the chaos. I saw her mask sweep sideways, tracking the running people, the pile of guards, and me.

I didn't need to see Vicki's face to understand her confused look.

I pointed, not the easiest with a guard actively trying to force my hands into handcuffs. "Chelsea's here!"

Vicki turned.

Chelsea let loose.

The blast caught Vicki right in the face, yellow-and-green sparks exploding in a shower around her mask. The guards trying to hold me down shouted, and everybody who'd been trying to run for the exit began to scream.

"No!" I shouted as a guard broke free from my pack and charged at Chelsea.

Chelsea hit him with a tiny puff of yellow and green. He dropped to the ground, unconscious.

I broke free, vaulted over the man, and jumped at Chelsea. I had to distract her, I saw. She would overpower any of the guards, so I needed to give them time to get away. When she tried to hit me in the chest, I dodged to the side, leapt for a chair, and used it as a springboard to launch myself. This time when I punched her, she tried to hit back. I'd anticipated that. I twisted to the right, grabbed her wrist, and yanked it behind her. I dove forward in a roll, using my body to flip Chelsea over my back.

She hit the ground face-first, hand extended to level another blast at me. I rolled and leapfrogged at her. I stomped my foot down on her wrist to pin that hand, stretching to grab the other one. If I could hold her down, that would give everybody a chance to clear the room. Most everyone had; when I chanced a look back, the guards were dragging their unconscious fellow toward the door.

The yellow-and-green beam missed my ear by an inch, so bright it left an afterimage.

I tried to stun her with my elbow. We grappled, her trying to force her free hand up, me trying to pin it to the floor.

"Gail!" Guy's voice filled my ear. I jerked back, and Chelsea freed her arm and grabbed my face with her palm. Her fingernails dug into my cheek.

This was, I realized, how I was going to die.

"Gail, there are reports of alarms—"

Chelsea snarled at me, teeth bloody, and let loose. I opened my mouth to scream, closing my eyes.

A second later, I stopped. Nothing hurt. I felt a sensation against the side of my head, but it was like being brushed with something soft and fuzzy. I opened my eyes, wondering if death really had been that instantaneous and the tickling sensation was St. Peter finally welcoming me to the pearly gates.

But no. I was still in the lobby. Everything in my vision undulated with green and yellow, but I could see Chelsea underneath me, through the fog.

Not heaven, then. Closer to hell, actually, but why didn't it hurt?

"Gail—are you okay? I'm on my way." Guy's voice cut out when I didn't answer.

Chelsea pulled her hand back. "What the *hell*?" she asked. I was still crouched over her, one foot holding her hand down, scrabbling to push her arm back. "How did you do that?"

"Your guess is as good as mine," I said, and something exploded to my left.

"Gail, duck!"

I fell sideways, rolling behind a couch. Vicki, mask burned so badly that it was almost entirely black, rushed at my archnemesis, who wasted no time scurrying to safety and firing a blast of green-yellow back.

I tried to push myself to my feet, but suddenly the world tilted right on its axis. The ceiling and walls switched places. I thought *not again*, and started to pass out.

Somebody caught me from behind. I heard Jeremy's voice. "Just me. Please don't hit me. I don't think my pride can take that."

I staggered and tried to remain upright, which wasn't easy since the lobby of the checkpoint now felt like the deck of a storm-tossed ship. I groped for Jeremy's arm, squeezing my eyes shut. It didn't help. And a second later, I felt Jeremy try to pick me up. "No, wait, don't—"

"Oof!" Jeremy cursed. "How much do you *weigh*?"

"You know not to ask me that." I risked seasickness to open my eyes as he dragged me behind a couch. Green-and-yellow blasts flew overhead, warring with the fiery bolts I never saw Plain Jane use much. Thick smoke began to cloud the air. "What is she *doing*? I had her."

"I don't think she saw your little display." Jeremy peered over the couch. "What was that, anyway? It looked like it didn't even hurt you."

"It didn't."

"But it killed Angélica." Jeremy flinched as one of Vicki's bolts went wide, blowing a smoking hole in the wall behind us. "Wasn't she like a superaccelerated healer? How come you can handle that, and she couldn't?"

"I don't know." I was starting to feel like what I didn't know would fill entire galaxies. "You need to get to safety."

"So do you. You're a wanted fugitive, remember?" Jeremy gave me a look, like he couldn't believe I had ever forgotten that. "They're distracted by Miss Sparks-a-Lot over there, but I figure it's only a matter of time before the guards come back for you, too. And you don't look so hot."

"Yeah, I don't feel so hot, either."

"This way." It was difficult to crawl when I felt like the floor was about to tilt up and smack me in the face, but Jeremy kept an arm around my middle, half dragging, half helping me as we headed for the exit. Above us, Chelsea and Vicki did their best to kill each other.

Why hadn't Chelsea's powers affected me the way

they always had? They hadn't hurt, but now I was discombobulated and sick. Why was it different?

Later, I told myself, and kept shuffling for the exit. Just add that question to the pile.

We'd nearly reached the door when something singed the air over my back, nearly blistering my skin through the scrub top. It hit the doors in front of us, splashing liquid flame everywhere. I stared at the molten hot patch in the middle of the doors, the metal glowing red.

Jeremy cursed again. "Vicki's aim is especially terrible today."

We hit the deck again. This time the blast that missed us was yellow and green.

"Chelsea's isn't great, either," I said. I put my hand to my head, hoping that would stabilize things. It did absolutely nothing. "How are we getting out of here?"

"They didn't teach you how to fly in prison, by any chance?"

"That would be too convenient," I said. "Guy's on his way. Maybe he can get us out of here."

Jeremy winced as another beam cut into the wall over our heads. He hadn't really been close to any big fights, I remembered. My villains had always attacked when he was elsewhere. For somebody whom I'd always viewed as incredibly close to this world, he was new to all of this.

"Hey." I nudged him with my shoulder. "You okay?"

"I'll be better if we get out of here without getting our faces melted off."

"Goes without saying." We hid behind the front desk, since it seemed to be the sturdiest piece of furniture in the room. Though it made my vision swam, I reached up and grabbed a paperweight. "Is your aim as good as I remember?"

"I'm insulted you even have to ask."

I tossed him the paperweight, which had a Bears logo in the middle. "Hit the one without the mask, please."

"Very funny."

"Be ready to run. She's not real fond of things being thrown at her."

"I hate villains," Jeremy said under his breath. He held up three fingers and put them down one at a time. On three, he rose to his full height and chucked the paperweight. I grabbed his arm, pulling us away from the desk.

Just in time, too. There was an "Ow!" right before Chelsea's sting-ray powers blew a hole clean through the desk. Jeremy yelped as we hit the ground.

"See?" I said.

"I didn't actually disbelieve you."

We stayed there as Chelsea and Vicki continued to battle. Chelsea's fists glowed green and yellow as she swung again and again, trying to hit Vicki. Vicki occasionally shot bolts of blue fire, but for the most part she seemed to want to keep it to a fistfight. They both flew and jumped, usually crashing into the ceiling tiles or floor in their haste to get away from each other.

"Time for another distraction," I said when Chelsea

landed a punch on Vicki's shoulder that knocked my mentor back a good ten feet.

"We're out of paperweights," Jeremy said, peeking over the couch. He flinched. "How *do* you all tolerate that kind of pain? That looks like it hurts."

I crawled over to one of the end tables covered in magazines. "It doesn't hurt them," I said.

Jeremy looked over at the magazines. "I can guarantee that's not going to, either."

"No." I picked up a coffee table book on Chicago architecture and hoped my dizziness wouldn't throw off my aim terribly. "But it's distracting."

"Wait for my signal." Jeremy checked over the couch "*Now!*"

I jumped up and winged the book like a frisbee. It struck Chelsea's jaw, spinning her around in the air. She turned and zapped it right out of existence. Her other hand, she aimed at me.

Something burst through the wall to my left, sending rubble flying. War Hammer exploded into the room in bronze-and-purple glory. Guy flew at Chelsea, driving her back with both fists. He landed by skidding to a stop and stood there, tall and defiant in the War Hammer uniform. I expected him to hit her again, to finish the fight right then and there.

Instead, he stumbled. "Br—*Brook?*"

CHAPTER THIRTEEN

Chelsea's face contorted into a mask of sheer, ugly hatred. "*You*," she said, and her voice plunged the temperature in the room down several hundred degrees.

Guy took a step back. "H—How?" he asked.

Chelsea raised both hands and opened fire, straight at Guy's chest. The double blast hit him right on the front of his breastplate.

"No!" I lunged forward, but Jeremy grabbed my arm. At the same time, Guy dodged a second ray, dropping into a zigzag pattern. Chelsea's sting rays chewed through the wall and floor as she tried to obliterate Guy. The entire time she screamed like a vengeful fury, her face twisted up in something between rage and sorrow.

Vicki tried to tackle her from behind. Chelsea merely swung around, turning both of those blasts on her. Vicki cried out, crashing to the ground.

"Vicki!" Jeremy let go of me and started running. Luckily, Chelsea's fury seemed to be directed at Guy— or Sam, I realized, she thought he was Sam—for she continued to try and hit him while he flew and dodged. Jeremy raced for Vicki. I followed unsteadily, tripping whenever my vision made the floor tremor and tilt.

Vicki clutched her shoulder and coughed. Fear made me stumble. When I blinked, I saw Angélica in front of me, not Vicki, her face still and bloodless.

Vicki coughed again, and I blinked away the image. She put her hand over the smoking hole in her uniform. "I'm okay," she said. "I'm good. She just clipped me. Damn, she's pissed. I need to help Sam."

"Guy," I said.

Vicki shook her head, which made her sway a little. "Right. Uniform threw me off."

She leapt into the air. Guy hit the window in a flurry of glass shards, and just like that, all three of the fliers were out of the room, leaving Jeremy and me to be soaked by the sprinkler system that inexplicably and belatedly sprang to life several minutes after the fact.

"We need to get out of here," Jeremy said. We stumbled over the rubble from Guy's entrance and out the exit together. "Backup's on its way, and if they see you here—"

"I'm not sure how fast I can go," I said. The dizziness was beginning to subside, but the world sat at a forty-five-degree angle if I moved my head wrong. What the hell was wrong with me? We ran for the exit, and I kicked the door several times, until it broke off its hinges. Jeremy ignored the elevator and pulled me to the stairs instead.

"You don't know who Chelsea—or I should say Brook—is, do you?" Jeremy asked, breathing hard as he kept me from plummeting headfirst down a flight of concrete steps. "Guy knows her."

"Honestly, Jeremy, I think you know more about him than I do," I said.

"You're the one dating him!"

"Yeah, and we were just starting to figure things out before I went to *prison*."

"Well, she's got to be somebody from his past, right?"

"I don't know."

"I bet you anything she's an ex-girlfriend. Nobody else could be that pissed."

"Hey," I said.

"Present company excluded," he said, and I rolled my eyes at him.

Maybe he had a point, though. Chelsea *had* been furious. But an ex? She'd barely paid much attention to Guy at the mall, so Brook or Chelsea or whoever the hell she was, she must be *Sam's* ex. But why hadn't they known who she was right away? It seemed like a super-powered ex-girlfriend should be at the top of your list of possible suspects. Maybe we were wrong.

Jeremy and I hit the bottom level and ran through the crowds on the first floor. We made for a bedraggled and dirty sight, covered in the debris from the fight.

Outside, the three fighters hadn't flown away. They were all suspended in the air above the building, Guy and Vicki working together to try and draw Chelsea's fire. I could see tactics Angélica had described, ones commonly used to try and pull the villain away from the civilians on the ground pointing their phone cameras at the sky. Chelsea, though, was having none of that. She flew at Guy repeatedly, trying to take him out with her rays. Occasionally, she batted at Vicki the way one might an irritating fly.

"Why is nobody running?" Jeremy asked. To prove his point, a bolt of Vicki's fire splashed hot flame on the statue of the globe on the corner. People shrieked and dodged out of the way, but nobody left. "Don't they realize they're in the blast radius?"

"They won't run unless Chelsea starts attacking them outright." A lot of them looked like they were sending updates to the Domino, the website that served as an unofficial authority on all superhero gossip. "It's a little depressing, actually."

Jeremy shielded his eyes to look up. I did the same, even though it made me stumble backward. "I don't know how you guys do it," he said. "I don't—Vi—"

I elbowed him before he could accidentally reveal Plain Jane's alter ego in public. Both of us watched in horror as Chelsea hit Vicki with yet another blast, and our friend flew backward. She crashed into an upper level of the parking garage across the street.

She didn't emerge.

"Shit, she's not getting up." Jeremy raced for the entrance to the garage, dodging back with a yelp when Chelsea's sting ray cut across his path.

I didn't move. Guy was fighting Chelsea on his own. He'd fought worse and more powerful enemies, but none of them had killed Angélica. My heart stayed in my throat. She swooped closer, and I frowned, squinting harder. What was that device in her hand? She wasn't the type to fight with a weapon, but it looked like some kind of taser.

Guy flew at Chelsea again since she was only firing with one hand. He ducked under the beam she shot at him, darting in close, fist raised to deliver what I hoped was a knockout punch.

Chelsea stabbed him with the device in her hand, right in the shoulder. Guy burst into flames.

"No!"

The crowd let out shrieks of terror and awe as green flames engulfed the man they thought was War Hammer. The fire formed a perfectly round fireball so bright that it burned into my retinas. I couldn't look away. My eyes watered, but I couldn't move, couldn't breathe, couldn't think. In the center of the fireball, Guy's entire body went stiff, his head snapping back. I didn't hear him scream, but I saw his mouth open as though he were in an unbearable amount of agony.

Chelsea raised her hand, open-palmed, in horrifying slow motion. She stuck it *right into the fireball*, planted it on Guy's chest, and let loose the full force of her stinging rays.

"No!"

Guy's scream didn't even sound human. It was wrenched from him, like Angélica's had been. He writhed, limbs convulsing. Chelsea jerked her hand back. The fireball abruptly blinked out of existence so that it was just Guy suspended in midair, shaking.

His head abruptly tipped forward, his body went still.

And he began to fall.

Just like that, I was running harder than I ever had before. I couldn't get there in time. I knew that. But I had to. Guy was hurt. If he hit the concrete . . .

That was *not* going to happen.

I shoved a man out of the way and hurdled over a stroller. My legs pistoned. My breath scraped the insides of my throat raw. I pushed myself harder. I pushed off against the pavement, leaping as high as I could—

And somehow I was right there, colliding with him in midair. My momentum sent us both hurtling to the side rather than down. We seemed to fall forever, but I grabbed Guy, rolling to take the force of the landing as we hit the ground. We bounced a few times and finally stopped, rocks from the pavement digging into my back. I groaned, clutching hard to Guy. He couldn't be dead. He couldn't be. It wasn't possible.

This wasn't happening. Not again.

"Gail!" Jeremy raced up and pulled Guy's limp form off of me. I immediately scrambled to my knees.

The headache hit like a semi-truck.

One second, I'd been upright, and the next, I lay on

the ground, and it felt like somebody had slammed my face into the concrete. Sharp spikes dug through my eye sockets. I gasped. From far away, like I was underwater, I heard Jeremy's "Gail? Gail!"

I opened my eyes. The light only dug the spikes in harder, but Jeremy was *right* there next to me, crouched over Guy's prone form. He wasn't looking at Guy, though. He had his eyes on me and his lips were moving, but I could barely hear anything.

"Gail!" Suddenly his voice was crystal clear. "Gail, you're bleeding—what the *hell*—"

Dazed, I wiped at my nose. My hand came away red, but I didn't care. I reached for Guy's mask, to pull it off and check to see if he was breathing. He couldn't be dead. He *couldn't* be—

"Gail, no, don't."

"He's hurt." All of my strength had vanished. I tried to fight Jeremy anyway. "He's *hurt*, can't you see that, dammit—"

"You can't unmask him in public! Gail, we have to run, she's coming back—"

A scream cut through my determination. I looked up even though it felt like a hammer pounding directly into my skull. Chelsea hovered about twenty feet away, chin pointed down so she could look directly at me.

Every rational thought disappeared. I broke free of Jeremy, head throbbing, and ran at her. "*You!*"

She shot a blast of green and yellow at me. I batted it away as I sprinted. Chelsea had killed my friend and now she'd hurt Guy and it was *enough*. For an instant, I saw the whites of Chelsea's eyes. I tackled her.

"What did you *do*?" I didn't know what I was shouting, but words were coming out of my mouth. I punctuated them with my fists, hitting her over and over again as she writhed and tried to dodge on the ground underneath me. "What did you do to him? You sadistic *bitch*, he wasn't even the one you wanted—"

Chelsea tried to hit me in the face with another blast. I knocked her hand away and headbutted her—big mistake. Pain rang like a klaxon through my head. For a second, there were two Chelseas in front of me. The left one grabbed me by the throat as I reeled.

She launched us both off the ground and hovered, dangling me by my throat. My vision started to darken, so I grabbed onto her wrist. Her face pushed in close to mine, her free hand held up just over my forehead so I saw the swirling green and yellow in the vortex in her palm again. I couldn't speak, so I tried to struggle away. My feet kicked uselessly two feet above the pavement.

She moved her hand closer to my forehead.

"Kill me or drop me," I managed to wheeze. "But quit playing games already."

"You're not scared of me," Chelsea said.

The green-and-yellow sparks were starting to blind me a little, so I reached out irritably to bat her hand away. It tickled against my skin yet again. "Gee, what gave it away?"

"How is that not hurting you?" Chelsea asked, tilting her head. "How are you . . . you're like me, aren't you?"

"Wh—what are you talking about?" It was harder to breathe, but I kept kicking.

She only shook me. "Well?"

I wheezed something that wasn't very complimentary to her ancestors. Looking annoyed rather than furious now, she shook me a little. When I dug my nails in harder, she didn't even flinch—until a bolt of fire hit her in the face. It came so close to my face, I felt my skin go temporarily crispy.

Chelsea cursed and dropped me. I hit the pavement hard, skinning my elbow, and coughed. A second later, a black streak flew overhead, chasing after Chelsea's retreating figure. Vicki, it appeared, had recovered enough to rejoin the fight.

I was going to have to talk to her about her aim later on.

"Gail!" Jeremy was suddenly standing over me. He had Guy draped over his shoulder. "We need to get out of here, like, *right* now. Can you walk?"

I coughed.

"Taking that as a maybe," Jeremy said. He pulled me upright even though every little movement made me want to throw up. "Move."

"I've got a car," I managed to stay.

Jeremy grabbed my arm and started running. Every step jarred my entire system, and I felt something wet drip down my face. I put one foot in front of the other, focusing on that and not on the fact that Guy

SUPERVILLAINS ANONYMOUS 167

flopped limply over Jeremy's shoulder, or that he had
been on fire, or that Chelsea was getting away *again*.
Every part of me was wrapped in trying to fight off
the agony coating the inside of my skull with fire ants.
When Jeremy asked a question, I answered, but as to
what I said, I had no idea.

"Gail? What happened?" Naomi appeared as if by
magic. The car, I realized. We'd reached Sam's car.

Jeremy shoved me her way. "Hold this. Who are
you?"

"Naomi Gunn. I work for the Domino, and Gail
told me to wait here. Her friend took off and—" She
gawked. "Is that *War Hammer*?"

"Later," Jeremy said, opening the back door of the
car. He shoved Guy inside.

"Who did that to him? Was it Chelsea?"

"*Later.*"

I ignored them and scrambled into the backseat,
reaching for Guy's mask. His eyes were shut, deep lines
dug in around them under the mask, but he moaned. It
hurt my heart to hear that much pain, but it also meant
he was alive. I pulled off the helmet he wore over the
mask.

"Sure you want to do that?" Jeremy asked as he
climbed into the driver's seat. He jerked his head at
Naomi.

When it came to finding out if Guy was injured
versus one reporter knowing his identity, I didn't give
a damn. "She owes me," I said, and I peeled off Guy's
mask as Jeremy pulled into traffic.

What I found underneath made me gasp. I'd never seen Blaze bleed, ever, in all of the time we'd had together, but Guy's face was covered in burns, irritated and raw. A cut on his temple bled sluggishly so that blood dripped into his hair. He groaned and shifted away from me, but he never opened his eyes.

I sucked air through my teeth and held his mask against the wound. It wasn't the best solution, but it was the only thing I had. "He's bleeding!" I told Jeremy, risking a dizzy spell to look over at him. "We need a doctor or a hospital *right now*."

"I can take him back to Davenport, but I need to get you somewhere safe." Jeremy looked panicked as he twisted to glance at both of us. "And he's not the only one bleeding."

I hardly cared about some damn nosebleed, not when Guy was hurt so badly. He moaned again. "I don't care," I said. "He needs help."

"Holy shit," Naomi breathed.

"Davenport!" I said suddenly as an idea struck through the panic. "That's it. We don't need Davenport, we need *a* Davenport. Can you call Kiki?"

"Y-yeah, I have her number." He pulled his phone out of his pocket, his hand shaking. I shook Guy, trying to wake him up. His head lolled. I knew nothing about superhero physiology and even less about his, given that I didn't know *anything* about his past. He had accelerated healing, but how fast did it work? And would it be enough? I'd never even seen him really get injured.

"Kiki?" Jeremy asked into the phone. "Oh, thank god you picked up. We're in trouble. Are you hearing about Chicago? Chelsea's back. Gail?" Jeremy asked, and I looked up. But he hadn't been trying to get my attention, he'd been answering Kiki. He looked into the rearview mirror so that our eyes met, and evidently he came to a decision. "Yeah, she's here with me. She's almost as bad as he is."

"I'm fine," I said through gritted teeth, even though even I knew I wasn't.

Naomi gave me a wary look.

"N-no, it's a nosebleed," Jeremy said. "She's not bleeding out of her ears or any—what do you mean *yet*?"

"What?" I asked, looking away from Guy.

"You want me to go *where*?" Jeremy asked into the phone. "And no, I'm not getting rid of this, I just got it, and it's a bitch to transfer everything over and—okay, fine, don't yell at me. We'll be there soon."

And as I watched, one hand holding down the slowly reddening mask over Guy's forehead, Jeremy hung up, opened the window, and tossed his phone out.

"God, she's bossy. Everybody hold on." He made an illegal U-turn into oncoming traffic and stomped the gas, throwing me back against the door. We missed hitting a Hummer by a very thin coat of paint. "Kiki gave me an address. She said not to go inside but that you would know what to do from there."

"What are you talking about? What address?"

Jeremy listed it off.

"I have never been there in my life. What kind of game is she playing? We don't have time for this. Guy is hurt!"

"I know, and I told her that." He pressed harder on the gas. "I'm not seeing any other options, not unless we want to explain to all of Davenport why Guy's in his brother's outfit. Then you *both* end up in prison."

"I really have missed a lot," Naomi said to nobody in particular.

Guy's bleeding had slowed to a trickle, but he didn't open his eyes. Panic built up in my chest. Guy had never been injured. I was the one who'd always gotten hurt during our Blaze and Hostage Girl days. He'd always faced my injuries calmly.

I, on the other hand, wanted to jerk the steering wheel out of Jeremy's hands and drive to the nearest hospital, prison be damned. Why couldn't Kiki just tell us to show up somewhere so she could *fix it*? Why did we she have to be so cryptic?

"We're here," Jeremy said an eternity later. He'd pulled over to the curb in a fairly nice subdivision. Somewhere in the North Shore, I thought, but I couldn't have said more than that. He looked at the expensive-looking split-level he'd parked in front of. "Should I go up and knock?"

A chill crawled down my spine. "Wait," I said, looking around. Why did I feel strange? What was going on?

Jeremy twisted in the driver's seat. "What is it?"

"I don't know." I climbed over Guy and stepped out of the car, shoving the sick feeling at the back of my throat down. I'd never had any reason to come to this neighborhood before, but everything felt familiar. I stepped off the curb and into the road and the flashback hit me.

Headlights, coming right at me.

A minivan.

"Holy shit," I said. "I've been here before."

CHAPTER FOURTEEN

Naomi climbed out of the car as I looked around. Awareness prickled under my skin. I'd stood in this very spot once. I'd faced down headlights.

I'd woken up in an ambulance. Maybe. That part was unclear.

"What is going on?" Naomi said.

"Shh," I said, craning my neck to look around. How did Kiki know about this place? Was this some kind of game? Instinct told me to head west, so I started walking. "This way."

Jeremy and Naomi exchanged a look. "You stay with her. Make sure she doesn't pass out, I'll follow in the car," he said.

Naomi fell into step next to me. "Any idea where we're going?"

"Not sure yet."

"You realize this is crazy, right? War Hammer is

unconscious and bleeding in the back of the car, and we're going for a walk?"

"I *know*." Guy was hurt, and I was wasting time, but the farther I walked, the more sure I was that I was going in the right direction, that I'd walked this path before. Jeremy followed in the car as I pushed on, turning two corners and doubling back when a cul-de-sac confused me.

And finally, I knew it.

I'd found Mobius's hideout. Kiki had somehow led me there.

I stood on the perfectly manicured lawn under the sweltering August sun and looked up at a cheery little bungalow house. There were cranberry-colored shutters on the window. The front door was painted royal blue. My memories of the escape were patchy. I remembered bursting through the garage doors in his car and—this was new, I hadn't remembered this before—dark-clad figures with guns on the lawn. Shattering glass and Mobius's prissy, cultured voice telling me to run. One last look at his hideous Halloween mask of a face as he'd shoved me out of the car.

Jeremy pulled over to the curb and climbed out of the car. "What is this place?"

I had a hard time swallowing. "It's where I was kept. When Mobius turned me into whatever it is I am now."

Jeremy's brow crinkled. "It is? Why would Kiki send you *here*?"

"I don't know, but I'm going to find out." Something huge was going on. But right now, Kiki was going to fix Guy. And the minute that happened, I was getting some answers. I strode up the front steps of the house.

And I kicked the door to my old prison open.

Breathing hard, head splitting, I started to step inside, but a woman appeared around the side of the porch, her eyes wide and frantic. Kiki Davenport held both hands up to stop me. "Wait! Don't!"

"Give me one reason why I shouldn't," I said.

My old physician took a deep breath. The look on her face was the most terrified expression I had seen in a long time. "This place is a decoy. Trust me, you'll understand very soon, but right now we've only got three minutes, and if they find you here, it's all over."

"What are you talking about?" I asked.

Kiki shook her head tightly, darting around me to yank the door shut. She pulled her sleeve down over her hand—she was wearing a Cubs jersey, the first time I'd ever seen her in civilian clothing—and wiped frantically at the doorknob.

"We have to move," she said, words tumbling over each other. "They can't catch us. If they do, it's all over, and I have gone through *too much* to let him take this, too. Go, go, go!"

She shoved at my shoulder, and I had no choice but to jump off the porch. "Is that your car?" Kiki asked Jeremy.

He only nodded, a little dumbfounded.

"Get it into the garage next door. Do it now, or they'll think it's suspicious, and they'll run the plates." She pushed on his shoulder, too, shoving him away.

This time, she pointed the fob at the house next door, and the garage door began to trundle up.

I twisted, trying to follow Jeremy, but Kiki kept her grip on my arm. "Guy's in the backseat—he's hurt—"

"Gail!" Kiki yanked me around. For somebody who didn't have any superstrength, she sure had an iron grip. "As soon as we're safe, I promise, but we have to get inside."

"Guy—"

"Will be okay. They cannot get *you*, and if Guy knew what was going on, he would agree." Kiki tugged on my arm, and there was so much raw and naked terror on her face that I felt my stomach twist.

Jeremy ran for the car, leaving Naomi and me no choice but to go with Kiki as she grabbed my arm and hauled us both into the garage next door. When Jeremy pulled the car in, she hit the button to close the garage door. "This way," she said.

I wasn't going anywhere without Guy, and opened my mouth to say so.

"I'll bring him. You go with her," Jeremy said.

Kiki, worry lines etched into her face, sped into the house and hooked an immediate right, sprinting down a set of steps. Naomi glanced uncertainly at me, but we both followed her down into a basement. Instantly, cold spread over me, and I knew it had nothing to do with the temperature. Something about this place seemed horribly familiar. My stomach began to roil. My head began to pound even harder. The basement was dusty and filled with cobwebs, sectioned off by tall shelves so that I couldn't actually see much of anything.

Kiki hurried around me, grabbing my wrist and towing me along. Tall shelves full of old books formed a miniature hallway. She pulled me into a little space ringed by even more shelves and stacked boxes. Six dusty monitors had been embedded into the wall.

"What is this place?" I asked.

"It's a long story. Short version: next door's a decoy—" I opened my mouth to protest that, as I knew for a fact that the house next door had been the one Mobius and I had escaped from, but Kiki shot me a quelling look. "—and we have to be quiet because they're coming."

She fiddled with some knobs on the wall. The monitors flickered and sprang to life.

"*Who* is coming?" Naomi asked as I scrubbed my nails all over the back of my neck. Why did this place feel so familiar? Mobius and I had run from the house next door, I knew that much, so why did *this* place feel strange? Anxious and unable to say why, I craned my neck to look around. I didn't recognize any of the books or the old albums, or the old appliances gathering dust.

And then through a gap, I saw it. The shelves formed another little partitioned-off room right next to us. I could only see a sliver, but it was enough to give me a clear view of a scarred metal table in the center of the area, and the swaybacked shelves directly across.

My heart quit beating for a second. On the back of my neck, my fingers stilled, and I took one dizzy step forward, pushing the dusty popcorn maker aside. I had to be imagining things.

This couldn't be real. The laboratory was *next door*. The house I remembered breaking out of, that was next door. I remembered the lawn clearly—or at least I did now that those memories had been unlocked. So why was there a familiar, scarred metal table right there on the other side of the shelves? I could see the manacles dangling on chains, and I felt the phantom of unforgiving metal circling my wrists.

The lightbulb overhead was even still swaying, caught in perpetual motion.

"Shit! No, don't look at that." Kiki leapt to shove the popcorn maker back into place, but the damage had already been done.

My throat closed up. "That's—"

"I know. But you have to be quiet, they're going to be here any second—" Kiki looked over her shoulder at the monitors in a panic.

There wasn't enough air. Where had all of the oxygen gone? I clawed at my throat as I tried to gasp in a breath, but it did nothing. I was back in Mobius's lab. Any second now, I'd be back on that table again, where Dr. Mobius had kept me for weeks, two of which I couldn't remember. Why couldn't I breathe?

"Gail! Gail—shit, there is not enough time for this, they're going to be here any second!" Kiki's face filled my vision. I tried to shove her away. "Gail. You're okay. You're never going on that table again. Deep breaths. Breathe, Gail. It's okay. You're safe."

Naomi's voice cut in. "I don't think—what is that?"

Kiki looked over her shoulder and swore so viciously that it jolted me back. My eyes automatically cut to the monitors as she let go of me and leapt over to them. "Shh, they're here. Please, for the love of god, *please* stay quiet."

"I think she's serious," Naomi said. I felt her hand on my shoulder. I bent at the waist, still trying to suck in as much air as I could. It felt like an elephant had plopped right down on my chest, and I was fighting it for every precious breath. I felt my knees go weak. Naomi grabbed me before I could fall over. She helped me sit down.

"Damn it," Kiki said. The fear in her voice made me look at the monitors again. I recognized the house next door, the one Kiki had called a decoy. A van rolled up to the curb. As the three of us watched, the passenger and rear doors opened. Men in unassuming dark suits and shades climbed out.

"Who—" I tried to ask, but Kiki shushed me.

The men spread out over the lawn next door in a neat pattern. They never spoke or looked at each other. Even though the monitors weren't the greatest quality, I could see the little cables connected to their earpieces.

"What the *hell*?" Naomi whispered. Kiki shushed her by frantically waving a hand at her. Two of the suits climbed onto the porch. They vanished into that house while the others continued their sweep of the grounds. In the basement next door, we watched on the monitors as they searched the wrong house.

Eventually, the two suits that had gone inside reemerged. One shook his head, and the van door opened, bringing out one more person. Unlike the others, though, this man wasn't wearing a suit. He had on a bright white polo and navy shorts, and his sneakers practically gleamed in the late-afternoon sunlight. I didn't need to be close to know that his eyes would be a pure, steely blue.

What was Lemuel Cooper doing here? What was *going on*? Why was his own girlfriend hiding from him?

It took an eternity, but finally the agents climbed neatly into the van and left as unobtrusively as they'd arrived. The minute they were out of sight, Kiki seemed to sag like the string holding all of her body taut had been cut. She slid down the wall and sat on the floor, closing her eyes in relief and breathing hard. "That was close," she said. "That was the closest they've ever come to catching me. I didn't think I was going to get to you in time; and then it really would all be over."

I pushed myself to my feet. Or I tried to. Even climbing onto my hands and knees made the dizziness come swirling back in. My knuckles whitened against the cement floor.

I felt Naomi crouch next to me. "Gail? Are you okay?"

I shook my head, but before I could answer, Jeremy stepped in. He was sweating bullets and breathing hard, but he had Guy over his shoulder again. "Is he okay?" I asked.

"Put him on the stretcher," Kiki said, voice businesslike. Jeremy panted as he moved to comply. Naomi raced over to help.

I swallowed hard against the dizziness and climbed to my feet, staggering the two or three steps to the stretcher Kiki had pulled out. "Guy," I said. He'd stopped bleeding, and he looked pale, far too pale, deathlike and horrifying. I gripped the sides of the stretcher.

"Gail, sit down before you hurt yourself," Kiki said. The terror had apparently subsided, leaving her doctor mode in place. She picked up Guy's wrist, feeling for a pulse. "I can't take care of the both of you at the same time."

"I don't trust you. I don't know anything about you or why you know about this place, but I don't trust you. I'm staying right here," I said. The last time I'd seen Kiki bending over a stretcher, the patient hadn't made it.

"I am on your side," Kiki said, raising one of Guy's eyelids and shining a penlight from her keys into his eye. She repeated the process with the other eye as Naomi and Jeremy stood back.

"Your family threw me in prison!" The words came tumbling out before I knew they were there. "Your—I guess Eddie's your uncle, right? He said I was guilty without even giving me a fair trial, and they threw me in prison, and it *sucks*. Okay, this past week has *sucked*, and whenever I try to do anything, it only gets worse, and now Guy—"

I broke off on a hiccuping sob.

"Gail," Jeremy said, stepping forward warily.

But I shook my head, curling over the stretcher and holding on tight. Guy's chest was moving; he was breathing. He was alive. I had to focus on that.

"Sit down," Kiki said. "Please, before you hurt yourself worse. Gail, you're falling apart."

I stayed upright, never taking my eyes off of her. "I'm staying right here until I know he's okay."

Jeremy stepped up beside me. "Me too."

Kiki could have used her powers to make Jeremy do her bidding, as he didn't have the mental shield I did. But instead she told him, "Help me get his armor off."

With the breastplate and under armor removed, Guy's torso revealed a road map of old scars layered with small cuts and perfectly circular burns that had to have come from Chelsea's stinging powers. Several of them began to bleed when the uniform was peeled away.

"What did this to him?" Kiki asked. "I've never seen burns like these before."

"Chelsea," I said. "It was like she could actually hurt him, and she never has before. Not really."

"He wasn't on fire, by any chance, was he?" Naomi asked.

All three of us turned to face her as one. I narrowed my eyes. "You," I said, remembering exactly why Chelsea was after her. Naomi had known something about Guy and Sam she'd been trying to avoid sharing with my psycho nemesis. "This has something to do with you. What did you find out? Why is she able to hurt him now?"

Naomi hunched her shoulders and looked for an exit. I didn't plan on giving her one. "War Hammer and Blaze, they've got a weakness. Fire."

"That can't be right," I said. "I've seen him take a blast from a flamethrower when he was fighting L'onn Dartzz." He hadn't even flinched.

"No." Guy's voice was weak. "She's right."

"Guy!" My knees abruptly went watery as I whipped back around. His face was taut with pain, but his eyes were open. Dried blood streaked his face and in his hair. "You're awake, thank god. You're gonna be okay."

"Doesn't feel that way, but I suspect you're right." He started to lift his hand toward my cheek, but he grimaced, dropping the hand. I squeezed it instead. "And she's right. Fire did hurt me, but it wasn't—it's difficult to explain." He broke off into a rattling coughing fit that made my own torso hurt. "The fire was mine."

"But . . . but I've *never* seen you use fire on anybody."

He made a noise that was probably an attempt at a laugh, but it sounded more like a groan. His eyes were glassy and he was bone white underneath the angry red burns, which were already starting to blister over on his skin.

"All these years," he said, his voice hoarse. "All these years of those impossible saves together, and you never once wondered why a superhero named Blaze never used fire? I even have that little"—he groaned, squeezing his eyes shut—"flame logo and everything."

I'd always thought his name was symbolic. His uniform was so bright that when he flew fast enough and through a floodlight, for example, it looked like a blaze of green, streaking across the sky. It had never occurred to me to wonder.

"I have fire powers," he said, coughing again. "But when I use them, I'm vulnerable. In my flame-state, I guess. So I try not to use them. Only a few people know about it."

"How did *you*?" I asked Naomi, narrowing my eyes at her.

Kiki cleared her throat and leaned over so that she was in Guy's line of sight instead of me. "We can do this later. How are you feeling?"

"Like hell." He coughed, which racked through his entire body. I cringed in sympathy. My own dizziness was returning in force, making it hard to focus on his face, but I stayed right there. I clung hard to his hand. At this point, I was never letting go.

"Care to tell me your name or what day it is?" Kiki asked.

"I'm okay, Doc. It'll heal. It just takes time," Guy said, but his voice was still weak. He looked around in confusion. He looked around in confusion. When he looked at my face, he blanched even paler. "Why are you bleeding? Gail, are you hurt?"

"I don't know, I . . ." When something dripped down my chin, I touched my face and stared in bewilderment at the blood on my fingertips. I'd had a nosebleed earlier, and apparently it was back. "Don't feel good."

As if to prove my point, my brain tried to explode in my head, and everything faded to a dull gray static. I groaned and fell forward over Guy.

"Gail?" Guy's voice seemed to waver in and out. "Gail! Kiki, *something is wrong!*"

My knees gave out and I half sank, half toppled to the floor beside Guy's stretcher, my head pounding so hard that it felt like an earthquake. Through the gap in the shelf, I saw Mobius's metal table one last time before the light grew to excruciating levels. I squeezed my eyes shut with that table burned into my retinas, and clutched my temples. Pressure built inside my head, so complete that I curled up and sobbed.

"Please," I begged as blessed darkness finally came for me, "please don't put me back on the table. Please don't put me back on that table."

I was still sobbing that when the darkness descended fully.

CHAPTER FIFTEEN

I felt the metal at my wrists again, pinning me down. I couldn't struggle or even move. Every time I did, the cuffs turned to smoke, but my limbs turned to lead, and I could do nothing but lie there without a single spark of fight left in me, helpless all over again.

Alone and unrescued.

And then I woke up.

I drew in a deep lungful of oxygen, automatically groping in the darkness to make sure my arms and legs were free. Three of them were, but something tugged at my right hand. Not holding it down, but I was definitely connected to something. I grabbed plastic tubing of some type with my free hand, and yanked.

"Son of a *bitch*!"

Tape ripped off the back of my hand, sending sparks across my vision. To my right in the darkness, something jolted. "Gail? Are you okay?" Guy's voice asked.

"Ow," I said, and several details filtered in. I wasn't on the table. I wasn't tied down, though I could see the silver glint of an IV pole. And even more important than that, I saw Guy. He'd been leaning back in some kind of recliner, but he sat up now. He was shirtless, white bandages covering most of his torso and some of his head. It kind of made him look like a muscular, half-dressed mummy.

I rubbed my injured hand and looked around. I didn't recognize the room. Some kind of den, I realized, and I was currently on an ancient, battered couch wearing scrubs that felt weirdly stiff. "Where are we?" I asking, shaking my head groggily. Nothing hurt.

Why did that feel like a novelty?

"The living room." Guy rubbed his hand over his face. "Jeremy took off, and I think Naomi is passed out somewhere. Kiki suspected you wouldn't want to sleep in her old bedroom, so we put you in here."

"Kiki?" I asked, which apparently served as some sort of magic word. Memories came rushing back in one overwhelming lump. Going to the bar and finding Portia. Breaking into the facility. Fighting Chelsea. Guy's injuries. The men on the lawn, and Cooper. Mobius's lab.

I put my head in my hands and groaned.

A few seconds later, I felt a soft touch on the hand that had been hooked up to the IV, and a tug. Guy scooted the recliner closer. "Hey," he said, fingers slipping in between mine as I lowered my hand from my face. "How are you feeling?"

"Shouldn't I be asking you that?" I asked.

I *felt* his smile, the weary edges of it, so I raised my head. The bandage across his forehead made some of his hair stick up goofily, and he had a black eye I hadn't noticed earlier. "Kind of a rough day," he said.

"You're a master of the understatement." I reached up to try to fix his hair, and he ducked his head to give me better access. The number of bandages made me feel sick to my stomach. "Seriously, though, how bad are you hurt?"

"I'm sore, but I'll heal. It looks worse than it is."

"You scared me." I was going to see him plummeting toward the ground whenever I closed my eyes for a long time. I gave in and rested my forehead against his, careful to avoid any of the bandages. He smelled like whatever ointment Kiki had used on the burns. I really, really wanted a hug, and possibly to hold on and never let go until this unending nightmare went away. But I'd been hurt in too many hostage situations over the year. I knew comfort afterward could feel worse with his type of injuries.

Indeed, he sighed, his hand sliding up my arm and resting on the back of my neck. "It's part of the business," he said. "And I suspect we'll only have more scares in the future."

"We could get away," I said, leaning back a little so I could meet his eyes. "You're rich, you can fly, that's all you need to get us to some tropical island far away from all of this."

He laughed a little and leaned forward to kiss me.

"Redhead, remember?" he said.

I gave him a look. "Fine. You can buy me a ski chalet and support me in the manner to which I intend to become accustomed. But you should know, you're giving up me in a bikini and with these muscles, that's a sight to behold."

"There's always hot tubs. Mind if I switch to the couch?" he asked, grinning. I gestured for him to help himself, and he moved over, groaning a little. He settled back gingerly. "Nice try. The manner to which you intend to become accustomed, my ass. You're the most independent woman I know."

"At this point, I would be willing to give all of that up for some mai tais and sand. Or Irish coffee and skiing." I moved as close to him as I dared with his injuries. I had so many questions. As much as I wanted to pretend everything was okay and keep flirting, they were pressing against the back of my mind. I didn't know where to start, so I asked the first thing that came to mind. "Who's Brook, Guy?"

"Starting with her and not Mobius?" Guy asked.

"I am choosing one problem at a time. Mobius didn't do this." I ran my finger gently next to one of the bandages. Guy didn't shiver. Right, not ticklish. Which made sense, given that I'd once seen him break a knife on his own hand out of surprise. "Somebody named Brook did. She meant something to Sam, didn't she? The look on her face when you came in, in Sam's costume . . ."

"She's what I was scared would happen to you." Guy rested his elbows on his knees and faced forward.

You're like me, aren't you? Those had been the words Chelsea had used when she'd held me up by the throat. "What do you mean?"

Guy shifted, looking at the wall opposite rather than at me. He took a long time to answer. "I got my powers in high school. I was a sophomore. I was shy, I liked cooking more than I liked people most days, and Sam was—you know how it is. Every class has the king, right? Quarterback, could do anything, good-looking, all of that."

"In my year, it was a guy named Mike Roman. I hated that asshole."

"Asshole's a good way to describe Sam. He even had the, you know, the perfect girlfriend. Brooklyn Gianelli. They were together all of their junior and senior years, before the explosion. They stayed together a couple years after it, too."

"Wait, Chelsea's real name is *Brooklyn*? Did she— she just picked a different place in New York. That's . . . okay, I have to respect that a little. I still want to kill her, though." I shook my head when a ghost of a smile touched the corner of Guy's lips. Brooklyn. Wow. I would never have called that one. "Wait, when you say explosion, you mean . . ."

"The one that gave Sam, Pet, and me our powers," Guy said.

"Pet?"

"Petra. My sister." Guy's voice hitched. "That was what we called her. She hated it, and we were idiot boys, so of course we only used that more. She's in the Annals, you know. They never found out she had powers before she was killed, so she's in the family members section. It doesn't exactly . . . I don't . . . I don't like it. But maybe it's better."

"How did she die? If it's okay to ask, that is. If you don't want to talk about it, I understand."

"We don't know." Guy sighed and leaned back, wincing as he did so. Since it was growing uncomfortable to sit the way I was, I scooted over on the couch and pulled my legs up into a half lotus. I rested my elbows on my knees and propped my chin on my fists. "She disappeared. Sam's never stopped looking for her. He and Brook, they tried to stay together after the explosion, when we got our powers, and I think for a little while, it was working for them. But then Pet disappeared, and Sam became somebody else.

"Brook was devastated. It was really hard to watch it all go down, but what could I do? I was just the little brother. I could fly, and I could turn my entire body into fire, and it was *neat*, but Pet was gone, and my parents' marriage was falling apart because of it, and Sam was so busy trying to get to the bottom of it. And Brook, she wandered into the world of superheroes the same way you did."

I frowned. "By throwing a beer bottle at a psycho?"

"By getting kidnapped," Guy said, chest shaking with silent laughter. The smile disappeared from his face quickly, though. "Villains started kidnapping her about a year after we got our powers. Sam would usually show up to save the day. You know"—and his voice turned bitter—"if he wasn't out looking for Pet or her killer. It took him hours sometimes, and it was like he didn't care."

"That's why you always came to get me so fast," I said, as years of rescues began to make sense. There had always been a sense of panic to Guy's first entrance into saving the day, even after I'd long grown weary and sometimes completely unafraid of the villains altogether. History could only repeat itself so many times without growing dull.

"Yeah," Guy said, his voice flat. "That's why. She put up with it for a lot longer than she had to. But that's love, I guess."

"What happened to her, Guy?"

"She died. Or we thought she died. It was Deathjab. Sam had a strong lead on where Pet might be, and he didn't want to give it up. We didn't get there in time. In either case." Guy's throat worked. "Deathjab killed Brook, and Sam killed Deathjab. It was one of the hardest battles I've ever fought. Even without my blaze mode, he was still able to hurt me. I should have realized it—Brook, or Chelsea, or whoever she is now, she has the same powers. Felt like bees were trying to kill me. That's not something you should forget."

"How is Brook alive? How did she get Deathjab's powers and—wait, when was this?"

"She's been dead seven years. Or I thought she was. It was after our fight with Deathjab that Davenport found us. Raptor showed up, took one look at the— god, we were kids. I'd been out of high school maybe two years at that point. I didn't even really have a uniform yet, I was just wearing a T-shirt and some cargo pants, with a ski mask. But Raptor found us, brought us in."

He paused for a long time, and I stayed silent, letting him think. Grief and anger were both carved into his face now. "I don't know why," he said. "I don't know why I didn't think Chelsea was Brook right away, with those powers. I guess I tried not to think about her too much. Anyway, Davenport brought us in. Angélica was my trainer. Sam didn't want anything to do with Davenport at first, but I . . ." He rubbed his wrist, where a bandage had begun unraveling. "I liked finally having a community where I didn't feel like a freak. A couple years later, you started getting kidnapped all the time. It's horrible, but it established me as one of the bigger names in the heroing business."

"Wow," I said, leaning back as I tried to filter all of the information in ways that made sense. Guy's past had always been a big mystery to me. I knew he'd grown up in Chicago thanks to an offhand comment he'd made over dinner one time, but the origins of his powers had never been explained. "So you have no idea how Chelsea—how Brook can be alive?"

"Or where she's been. But I can understand why she would want to kill Sam, and me, I guess. We were supposed to save her, and we didn't."

"That doesn't make anything that she's doing right," I said. "There were people injured in that mall, and Naomi was unconscious for nearly a week. She killed Angélica. She might have been the victim, but she's the villain now."

"I wish it were that black-and-white."

"Yeah, nothing ever is," I said. "Even if she blames you, that doesn't give her the right to kill you."

Guy worried the edge of a bandage on his wrist. "I wouldn't blame her, though."

"I would."

Guy smiled and looked down. "Never change."

"Doing my best." I stretched my neck out since it still felt a little stiff, and the air felt heavy. I stretched my arms out, too, to free up some of the tension in my back muscles. My hand brushed against plastic tubing, and I turned to look. The IV that I'd ripped out of my still-aching hand. Right. I was so used to waking up in hospital rooms, attached to IVs, that I hadn't even given the matter any thought. I looked up at the bag and froze now, though. "Guy."

"What is it?" He sat up, already alert.

I pointed. "Why isn't that clear?"

The liquid in the bag was a murky sort of gray that almost looked like mercury. And it had been filtering directly into my hand and my bloodstream.

"Oh," Guy said. "It's okay. It's Mobium."

"*What?*"

"Kiki said you . . ." Guy paused and licked his lips. "Maybe I should go get her. It's a lot to explain. I don't think I can do it justice."

I stared at the IV bag. Mobium. So *that* was what it looked like in its liquid form. It had changed my life and my body, down to my cellular composition. I'd been told it was a mistake from a mad scientist with unexpectedly amazing side effects. Mobius had told me it was a drug that would cause debilitating addictions.

I'd never really known which explanation was right.

So why was Kiki administering it to me through an IV?

"Do you trust her?" I asked.

Guy shook his head. "I don't know. When she explained, it all made sense, but . . . I don't know, I've always steered clear of her and so have a lot of people at Davenport. Villain Syndrome's no laughing matter, and she's got two generations of it behind her. I'm surprised they even let her work at Davenport."

"It's because I'm family," said a voice in the darkness, and Guy and I jumped. A light in the hallway flicked on, and Kiki entered. She'd swapped the Cubs shirt for a band T-shirt, and her pajama pants had unicorns on them. Her hair was a mess. "They felt guilty. But they give me the same looks everybody else does. Everybody thinks it's only a matter of time before I become a villain."

"Pro tip," I said. "Lurking in hallways and eavesdropping on private conversations doesn't exactly reinforce the whole 'I'm not a villain' shtick."

"I heard my name as I was getting up to get a glass of water. I wasn't listening in." Kiki belatedly seemed to notice the IV needle on the floor. "Did you pull that out? You shouldn't have done that, you need it—"

"I'm not putting anything else in my body until I get some answers."

"That's fair," Guy said, giving Kiki a hard look.

"Okay. Okay, yes. You deserve answers. And I'm sorry I couldn't give them to you before. Hell, I'm sorry in general. I didn't know you were caught up in this until after you showed up at Davenport, and I didn't realize they had specific plans for you until—" Kiki abruptly stopped and took a deep breath. "I need a drink," she said. "Let's go into the kitchen. You'll start getting hungry soon."

With a start, I realized she was right. I wasn't hungry, which had been kind of a first until recently. I knew it had been a long time since I'd eaten. But I didn't feel particularly weak or in pain.

"I can cook something," Guy said. He groaned a little as he got up.

We moved into the same kitchen I recognized. I'd eaten in there before, during my captivity with Mobius, and it made my skin crawl. But I took a seat at the table while Guy searched through the refrigerator, and Kiki leaned against the wall, looking like she was trying to figure out how to continue.

"Well?" I said.

"I'm not sure where to start, except that—oh, wait, here." She crossed over to a drawer and rummaged through it. She handed over a small photograph. "This should explain some things."

I gave her a final suspicious look before I turned my attention to the photograph, which was one of those studio portraits. The old man in the photograph had aged quite a bit between this photo and his time kidnapping me, but I'd recognize that ghoulish Halloween mask of a face anywhere. I didn't recognize the pretty, auburn-haired woman standing behind him with a hand on his shoulder, but the third face, a girl that looked to be about four of five, I knew that face.

I looked up at Kiki again, mouth dropping open a little. She'd grown up, but she still had the same eyes and nose as the four-year-old in the picture.

"Yes," she said. "What you're thinking is right. That's me, and Dr. Christoph Mobius was my grandfather."

My first thought was that she should be grateful she'd gotten her looks from her grandmother. And then I stared. "You mean to tell me that Dr. Mobius and Rita Detmer did the nasty?"

"*What*?" Kiki asked, gawking at me.

"You said he's your grandfather. She's your grandmother, so—"

"I have two sets of grandparents!" Kiki planted her face in her hand. "Mobius is my maternal grandfather. Kurt Davenport is my paternal grandf—Nightmares. I'm going to have nightmares about my grandparents and 'doing the nasty' for a long time now."

"Believe me, it's not something I want to think about either." I shuddered. "Hold up. You've known who he is the whole time? How come you didn't say anything? You knew Davenport was looking for him."

Kiki took the picture back, looked at it for a second,

and moved to return it to the drawer. "It's complicated. Nobody trusts me at Davenport. No reason they should, I guess. Dad blew up half of the New York complex when I was three, Grandma Rita is Fearless herself, and hey, would you look at that, my other grandpa is a mad scientist—not that they know that part. And I'm not really that anxious for them to. Would you trust me?"

"Probably not," I said, "but I think that has more to do with the fact that you've been lying to my face since I first met you."

"I'm not the only one. My grandfather lied to you, and I'm pretty sure—well, no, Grandma Rita actually didn't lie to you, probably, but she likely twisted the truth. The Mobium you were given? Cooper's known all along what it was." Kiki took a deep breath.

"What?"

"My grandfather told you he was turning you into an addict. That was a lie. He knew you wouldn't—well, probably wouldn't—need more injections. And he picked you specifically."

"Why? He told me it was because he had a bone to pick with Guy," I said. Guy looked up from heating a pan on the stove, in alarm. "I thought he just hadn't received the memo that villains weren't kidnapping me anymore."

Kiki shook her head. "He chose you because you were Hostage Girl, not because of Guy. You're too famous to kill."

"Okay, that's a new one," I said. Villains liked to

take me because they had vendettas with Blaze, or they wanted their fifteen minutes of fame on the front page of the Domino. Or, as I'd most recently, to get an easy stretch of time in Detmer Day Spa. But because I was too famous to kill? Yeah, I hadn't come across that one before. "When you say too famous, you mean . . ."

"I mean, Guy would raise a stink if you were dead or vanished for too long, and that made you valuable to Mobius."

"Why? What was his plan?"

Kiki pushed both hands into her hair and left them there. "He picked you to receive the Mobium because he wanted to expose Cooper for the fraud he is. His goal was always to give you the Mobium and set you free so people would know the truth about his work. That's why he went through so much trouble to set this place up. He even set up two houses: the place Lodi thinks he kept as his lab is next door. He put fake notebooks and staged your escape from there, but everything's really in this house. It's all been hidden here, right under their noses, this whole time."

That explained some of my memory problems and the confusion between the two houses, but: "Why go through all this trouble? Why not just get straight to the point and tell them Cooper's a fraud?'"

"Because," and Kiki took a deep breath again, like she was about to reveal the biggest secret in her arsenal, "he was following orders. All of this has been my grandmother's plan all along. And Grandma Rita?

Does not believe in simple plans. Welcome to the hell I've been living for over a year."

"Okay, maybe you should start over," I said, since my head was starting to hurt. Mobius had picked me? Because of Rita? There were two secret labs? "And maybe draw, like, a diagram. I have a feeling it's going to be that kind of—"

Thumping upstairs cut me off. I looked at the ceiling. "What's that?"

Kiki looked puzzled for a second. "What's wh—oh my god, she can't do what I think she's about to do."

"What do you mean?" I asked, but Kiki was already racing for the door. Guy and I followed her. I had the impressions of a pleasant house, one with pictures on the wall and a lived-in feel, as I rushed after Kiki up the stairs.

Naomi stood on the landing, tugging so hard at a locked door that it thudded repeatedly against the door frame. "Get away from there!" Kiki's voice had risen to a screech.

"What's behind this door? Why is it locked?" Naomi tugged harder.

Kiki darted forward and hauled Naomi back. "Get away!"

I exchanged a look with Guy. "No," he said slowly, speaking for both of us. "I'm with Naomi on this. What's behind this door?"

"I promise, I will tell you, but you have to let me explain first."

"Nope." I was officially done with secrets. I stepped forward, kicked the door in, and, ignoring Kiki's whimper, stepped into what looked like an attic. Unlike the basement, though, there were no grimy boxes or appliances or cobwebs to be found. It was a room with sloped walls that rose to a peak in the ceilings, and everything smelled of antiseptic so strongly that I expected to see fluorescent lights overhead. But there was nothing but a skylight that dropped a square of sunshine right over a gigantic container in the middle of the room. It was about the same height as a deep freezer, but longer and wider. Medical equipment clustered around it.

I heard the beep . . . beep . . . beep of a heart monitor. There was something alive in there. Somebody with a beating heart.

My own heart in my throat, I crossed the room and looked through the glass lid.

My entire body went numb. "What the *fuck*?"

"What is it?" Guy asked, hurrying up. A second later, he gasped.

In the box, eyes closed and face pale, lay my trainer, Angélica Rocha.

And she was very much alive.

CHAPTER SIXTEEN

All I could do was stare. Angélica was right there. Angélica was alive. Her chest was moving. She lay on her back, eyes closed, floating in the middle of the chamber. I couldn't see anything holding her up, but she seemed to drift a little up and down in suspended animation, arms and legs limp and loose.

It was such a far cry from the vital, always-moving woman I remembered.

I blinked, and Guy was no longer beside me. He had Kiki by the upper arms. "What have you done?"

"Guy!" The last time I'd heard him that angry, it had been after Shock Value had nearly killed me. "Guy, don't."

They both ignored me. Kiki gave him a level look. "Hands off."

Guy only stepped in, so they were eye to eye. I could see him actively vibrating with rage, but Kiki didn't even flinch. "You've known all along she wasn't dead. Gail went to *prison*, and this entire time, you could have said something!"

"Both Angélica *and* Gail would be dead if I had. Let me just explain—"

"You can explain in prison," Guy said. "I think I'm done with you screwing my girlfriend over."

Kiki narrowed her eyes, and I felt the hair on the back of my neck rise. A second later, Guy gritted his teeth. He dropped Kiki's arms and grabbed his skull.

"Hey!" I started for Kiki, but Naomi stepped into my path.

"Here's an idea," she said. "Why don't the three of you *calm the fuck down* and tell me why there's a dead woman pulling a Snow White in this creepy casket thing of yours? Why don't we do that? Because if you keep trying to fight each other, this building's gonna get destroyed real quick, and I'm pretty sure that'll be a dead giveaway to those scary dudes who think the real base of operations is next door."

Guy, breathing hard, turned his glare on Naomi.

"I'm just saying," she said, folding her arms over her chest.

I took a deep breath. "Her name's Angélica," I said. "She's not dead, which is a surprise since I was sent to prison for killing her."

"What?" Naomi said.

"I *can* explain," Kiki said.

"You'd better," I said. I looked at the medical equipment around Angélica's container, trying to make heads or tails of it. The machine monitoring her vitals, that was easy to pick out, but there were other screens and readouts I didn't understand. How did I get her out of there? I went still, though, when I saw the IV bag.

"Why don't you start with that?" I asked, pointing at it.

"What *is* that?" Naomi asked. Her fingers twitched, like she was itching for her notepad.

Guy made a strangled noise. "Mobium," he said. "It's Mobium."

Horror grew. I had to swallow hard several times just to keep calm. The ringing in my ears that had nothing to do with one of Raptor's flashbangs. "What have you done?" I asked Kiki.

"I saved her life. That's the transition chamber—you were in there before, when my grandfather gave you the Mobium. He only put you on the table downstairs after you already had the Mobium, for show. I didn't want to do this to her, but I didn't have a choice. It was the only way to save her life after Chelsea killed her."

I sank to my knees, next to the Mobium coffin. "Explain. Start from the beginning."

Kiki's story wasn't easy to unpack. First, there was the problem that Guy, Naomi, and I all had varying levels of knowledge about Davenport. We kept having to stop and explain basic things to Naomi ("No, when you're introduced to Davenport and until your powers settle in, they keep you underground. It's nice, except for the lack of sunlight. There's a lot of food."). I stayed where I was, one hand braced against the chamber, as Kiki told her tale.

She started not with Dr. Mobius but with Lemuel Cooper.

"He came to Davenport about three years ago," she said. "He's the most invulnerable man I've ever seen, pretty much impossible to kill."

"Nobody's impossible to kill," Naomi said. "All of you have some Achilles heel."

Since she'd been hired to discover Guy's weakness, I gave her an unimpressed look.

Kiki wrapped her arms around her knees. "I never found his weak spot. And I never even suspected that he might be involved with anything nefarious. Not until after I started sleeping with him. Little things didn't match up about him. Probably because he's a spy."

"A spy for what?"

"The Lodi Corporation. They're another company trying to shoehorn their way into the hero game. My grandfather—Kurt, this time—he didn't intend for Davenport Industries to be the be-all and end-all for superheroes. He really did just start it with the idea in mind of helping, which is why we never charge the powered people that want protection. And why we're supposed to protect them. Lodi's not like that." Kiki rested her forehead on her knee. "They want to *create* superheroes. Which is why Mobium exists at all. My grandfather invented it years ago. Lodi must have discovered it because they kidnapped him. I thought he was dead, I really did."

People really did have a habit of coming back from the dead today, I thought.

"And I didn't know they had him until Cooper"—Kiki shook her head—"he had a dream about Mobius. Sometimes when people aren't as on guard, I can see their dreams when I sleep."

"How do you know it was his dream and not yours?" Naomi asked. Her fingers were really moving now, still itching for her notepad. This entire day would be like a jackpot to a reporter covering the superpowered beat. "How can you tell the difference?"

"When I see other people's dreams, they're clear. Like a movie. And Cooper dreamed about my grandfather so clearly when I knew they'd never met."

"Okay, obvious question," I said, "but if Cooper is as dangerous as you say he is, why not *tell somebody?*"

"I tried to. I tried to tell Uncle Eddie." Kiki closed her eyes. "He told me that I was just having weird psychic fits again, like I used to have when I was a kid."

"You know, for a guy who's in charge of the company that oversees pretty much everything having to do with superpowers, Eddie Davenport sure is a dick to people with them," I said, and Guy nodded. "So you went to Eddie, and he didn't believe you? What does this have to do with Angélica being in there?" I jerked my thumb behind me.

"I'm getting to that. Eddie didn't believe me. If Cooper figures out that I know what he's doing, he'll kill me. I'll disappear without a trace, and even worse, everybody will say, oh, that was bound to happen, she's Rita's grandkid." Kiki shuddered. "Ironically, Rita was the only one who ever believed me."

"Oh," I said.

"He's the golden boy," Kiki said, her voice turning bitter. "He's brought so many advances to Davenport, in how we work with new heroes. But I—I *know* him. I've seen his dreams. He's a remorseless killer and stronger than any of us."

I scratched the back of my head. The man she was describing sounded nothing like the friendly doctor who had greeted me on my first day at Davenport. But then, Shock Value looked like an accountant. So it fit.

"When you came to Davenport, Gail," Kiki said, "he covered up the truth about what the Mobium really does. He couldn't risk Davenport finding out what it was, what it *really* is. That's why he told you some bullshit story about leukemia."

I jerked back so hard I nearly hit my head on Angélica's chamber. "I don't have leukemia?"

Kiki wordlessly shook her head.

I looked up at the skylight. I had to. I'd thought I was out of tears to cry, but the edges of my eyelids felt wet again. I didn't have cancer. It was all a nightmare, and I didn't have leukemia.

"It was a story to distract you and keep you from questioning things too deeply. A scare tactic. He's a bastard. But . . . do you understand what it really is?" Kiki asked.

I was too busy reeling with the news that I *hadn't* been walking around with cancer for the past month. "Huh?" I asked, shaking my head to clear it. "What? Oh, the Mobium. Yeah, it enhances things. It makes me able to heal, keeps me in top shape mentally, or whatever."

"Gail, it's adaptive."

"Well, yeah, sure, it made me stronger."

"And it's giving you more powers as it picks them up along the way."

"What?" Guy and I asked as one.

"It's—I hesitate to call it the next step in evolution, but it's not just some sort of metabolism enhancer. Look, it's like this. You need to run somewhere? The Mobium figures out to maximize your performance. If you're exposed to a gas, the Mobium learns how to counteract it. I could poison you, and you would probably be fine ten minutes later. Have you done anything weird lately?"

I automatically opened my mouth to say that I hadn't. But that wasn't right, was it? "Chelsea's powers," I said, looking at Guy. "She opened up, full force, right on my face, and it was like it tickled."

"The Mobium had time to learn how to counteract the effects." Kiki nodded, like she'd expected that. "I wondered when that would happen."

I, on the other hand, reeled. "This whole time, Chelsea couldn't hurt me at all? I could have fought her instead of Guy and Vicki? I could have saved Guy from—well, that?" I gestured toward him, and all the bandages on his torso and head.

"I think Brook was pretty determined to do this to me either way," Guy said. "Also, she can fly, and you can't. Yet. Or can you?"

I shook my head, bewildered. "If I can, it's news to me."

But Kiki was also shaking her head. "It takes time for the Mobium to really integrate. If you try using too many new abilities too fast, it deteriorates because it's not exactly . . . stable. Yet. It's getting there, but yes, that's why you've been feeling sick."

"Because I'm using new abilities?"

"I'm guessing you've had migraines, fainting spells, dizziness. I gave you an infusion so you'd have some fresh Mobium. It should help balance you out." Kiki banged the back of her head against the wall a few times. "You don't really know when you're using the new abilities, you just kind of do it. Which Angélica picked up on."

I looked over my shoulder though I couldn't see Angélica from where I was sitting. She was on the other side, inside the Mobium chamber. "She did? She didn't say anything."

"You were altering your velocity the way she does when you were fighting her," Kiki said. "She brought up her concerns to Cooper."

I gawked. I had no memory of doing any of that. I'd sparred with Angélica quite a few times. It had taken me forever to figure out what she was doing, she'd been using her powers so subtly. And in the end,

I'd been doing the same thing? It made my stomach twist.

"Why didn't she tell me about this? Don't you think I deserved to know?" I asked.

"It's pretty common practice to for trainers to talk these things over with Medical before bringing it up with the trainee," Kiki said. "She was following protocol, but Cooper couldn't risk anybody's finding out the truth about what you really could do. He couldn't outright kill or disappear you yet is my guess, He would've had to be careful about it because you have some powerful people on your side. That's why I pulled some strings, got you mentored with Vicki even though she wasn't due for a mentee for a long time. Vicki's not exactly role-model material."

"Hey," Guy and I said at the same time.

Kiki hunched her shoulders. "I protected you as best I could, but I couldn't save Angélica. He poisoned her."

"*What?* No, Chelsea—"

"Angélica could survive her powers a hundred times over. Or she could, if she hadn't been poisoned by something that interacted horribly with the stinging ray. I think he must have dosed her food," Kiki said. She looked troubled.

"How did he know anything about Brook's powers?" Guy said. "Nobody knew who she was, or that she was going to be at that mall unless . . ."

"Unless he tipped her off himself?" Kiki shook her head. "She's connected to all of this."

"*How?*" I asked. My voice was starting to rise in pitch. When were the hits going to stop coming?

"Lodi. Where do you think she's been all these years?"

Guy, Naomi, and I all stayed quiet as that conversational bomb hit and exploded between all of us.

"Kiki," I said slowly. "Chelsea has Mobium, too?" Was *that* what she was talking about, when she said I was like her?

"They've had her for a long time. When Rita orchestrated my grandfather's escape from Lodi, he broke Chelsea out, too. I didn't know about that until I visited Rita at Detmer, and she told me everything that's really going on."

"Brook," Guy said. He sat across from me, but he didn't look up. Instead, he was staring very intently at the floor between his feet. "Her name is Brook."

"Sorry," Kiki said.

"Guy, this isn't your fault," I said.

"Isn't it?" He never looked up. "They must have had her for *years*. Doing, what, experiments on her? And we had no idea, this entire time. How is that not my fault?"

"I prefer to blame the bad guys," I said, swinging my head to look at Kiki.

Guy's jaw flexed.

The rest of my brain caught up with me. "*Rita* orchestrated Mobius's escape from Lodi?"

"This is my problem, you see," Kiki said. She banged her head against the wall. As much as I worried about that, I figured somebody with psychic abilities would want to protect her brainpan above all else. So she knew her limits. "If they had just let me handle it, I could have come up with something a lot simpler. But *no*. My grandmother has to be Fearless. My grandmother has to have the worst case of Villain Syndrome ever. And to save me, my grandmother has to ruin the lives of at least ten people, all of them innocent. Welcome to my hell, and on behalf of the Detmers, Davenports, and Mobius brigade, I am so sorry for everything."

Warily, I pushed myself to my feet and turned so that I was looking down at Angélica's floating form again. So Cooper had used poison and Brook to kill her and keep the Mobium secret. The poison made sense, as I'd seen Angélica heal from a bloody nose in less than a second. Brook's powers should never have been able to touch her.

I rested my hand atop the glass covering her as my brain tried to put it together.

Rita had orchestrated Mobius's escape from Lodi. Mobius had tracked me down because I was too well protected to kill. He'd infected me with the same thing that Brook, also on the loose from Lodi, had been dosed with. I'd arrived at Davenport with no idea what was happening to me. They'd assigned Cooper as my doctor, but if Kiki was telling the truth, Cooper knew the most about Mobium except for the doctor himself. To keep Davenport from realizing the truth, he'd had Angélica killed and framed me?

"There's something I don't get," I said.

"What?"

"Why I went to prison. Was it Cooper who sent those texts to Brook?" After all, it was the only evidence they'd needed to throw me behind bars.

"Rita planned that, too," Kiki said, her voice hollow. "It was only a matter of time before Cooper would get bolder and try to take you out, so she framed you. She was sitting on the evidence the whole time. And when Angélica was killed, she deployed that particular missile because hey, you were safe in prison. Cooper couldn't get to you. Davenport and Detmer doctors, they're not supposed to cross over, ever. It protects all of us in case a villain escapes."

Cooper had tried multiple times to get in and see me at Detmer. I thought he'd been on my side, but now my stomach dropped. Rita had broken me out of prison the night before I was supposed to receive a visit from him.

"Plus," Kiki said, "I think Rita wanted a chance to work on you herself."

I thought of the pepper spray. The constant attacks. The insults. "Work on me. Right. So . . . all of this is her twisted, Machiavellian plan?"

"Pretty much." Kiki sagged. "My grandmother redefines meddlesome in a deadly way."

"So what's her endgame?"

"She wants me safe from Cooper. That's always been her goal. Look, she's a villain, but she loves me. I'm family. And Rita Detmer will do anything for family."

Another thought occurred to me. "Rita doesn't care about anything that's not her family, right? But I'm not family. Why all of the trouble to keep Cooper away from me?"

"Because she's not done with you," Guy said, looking up. "She's got more plans for Gail, doesn't she?"

"I'm afraid so." Kiki looked miserable as she curled in on herself.

My heart lodged in my throat. "What does she even want from me?"

"Isn't it obvious?" Naomi said, making the three of us look over at her. She'd been so quiet that I'd forgotten she was there. "She thinks you can take Cooper out."

"Of course she does," I said. I was starting to get another headache, but this time it didn't feel like it came from deteriorating Mobium. I pinched the bridge of my nose. "She didn't perhaps give any hints about why she would think this, did she?"

"That's the thing about Villain Syndrome." Kiki gave all of us a long look in turn. "They're not really the kind of people who share with the class."

"Perfect." I kept my gaze on Angélica's slack face. "That's just . . . great. I'm—yeah, I need a minute."

"Take as much time as you need." Kiki pushed herself to her feet. "I'll go make us all something to eat."

I stayed where I was as Kiki left. Naomi, apparently deciding Kiki was the juiciest source of information at the moment, took off after her. I listened to Guy breathe, deep breaths that were so even, I knew that he had to be deliberately controlling them.

I wasn't the only one Angélica had taught that trick to, it seemed.

"I thought," he said after a couple of long minutes had passed. "I thought that Brook would be the worst news I received today. I mean, I got you back, and out of prison, and for a while you were safe, and I thought Brook would be the worst, but it's not even *close*."

"It's not every day you end up in the middle of a conspiracy perpetrated by the world's first supervillain," I said, my voice distant to my ears.

He kept breathing like that, in and out, slow and even.

When he punched the wall, the entire building shook. I watched him, feeling curiously empty. Being told everything I thought I knew was wrong was not a feeling I particularly cherished. But then, the last month of my life had been full of so many twists or turns that now all I felt was exhausted and somehow cut off from everything.

The phrase *Why me?* did come to mind.

Guy punched the wall again, this time only shaking the attic. He dropped to his knees and seemed to sag. "Seven years," he said. "And that's not even touching what these bastards did to you, too."

"That beach is looking better and better, isn't it?" I asked. "We could go now. Nobody would blame us."

"If Kiki's telling the truth, Lodi will pay for everything they've done." Guy's jaw clenched. "And so will Cooper."

"*Is* she telling the truth?"

"I don't know." He looked worn-out.

"How powerful is Cooper, though? If he's as scary as she says he is, why doesn't anybody suspect him?"

"You never suspect the truly evil ones," Guy said. "But Kiki's one of the smartest people I know, and she's clearly terrified that he's stronger than anything Davenport can throw at him. So maybe she has a point."

And Rita Detmer somehow expected me—tiny Gail Godwin, the person who hadn't even realized she *had* powers not once but several times—to somehow take out this monster. *And* his organization, I realized. Rita didn't believe in small goals *or* simple plans.

I dropped to the floor next to Guy and hugged him because I couldn't think of anything else I could possibly do. He hugged me back, and I turned my face toward Angélica's chamber. "You have to admire the insanity of it, I guess."

"Always finding the silver lining." Guy shook his head.

"I'm on the run from one company, another company is trying to kill me, and a crazy old woman expects me to kill a guy who's invulnerable. Silver linings—and you—are all I have right now."

"Yeah," Guy said, and he sighed.

We stayed like that, both staring at the chamber holding Angélica, for a long time.

CHAPTER SEVENTEEN

I stayed by Angélica's side after that. Part of it was worry that if I left her alone, she would vanish, and the nightmare would return, and she would be dead again. I needed some kind of link, a reassurance that I wasn't going crazy, that I hadn't actually helped kill her. I didn't realize how much that fear had been pushing into my mind, how much it had permeated the cracks and seeded my doubts over the past week, until it was out there in the open for me to pick it apart. After all, I *didn't* remember those two weeks I'd been unconscious. There was a blank space in my life, and while I wasn't *really* worried that I'd been somehow programmed to work with Brook, it had apparently been on my mind.

But no. That, like everything else about me, was a lie. Just like what had really happened to me with

SUPERVILLAINS ANONYMOUS 217

Mobius, just like the leukemia they'd told me I had. Just like everything I'd learned since waking up at Davenport.

Guy disappeared half an hour into my vigil and returned carrying the couch from downstairs, which he set in front of Angélica's chamber. He kissed me on the top of the head and left. I suspected he needed his own alone time, so I didn't say anything.

Naomi silently brought up a plate of food and left it without saying a word.

"Everything I thought I knew was a lie," I said to Angélica as I dug into the grilled chicken. It was remarkably similar to the meal Dr. Mobius had given me ages ago in this very house, but I tried not to think about that. "And they lied to you, too, about me."

Unlike me, she'd noticed, and she'd paid the price for it.

"First they told me it was an accidental thing, the Mobium. And then maybe it was intentional. I can do *things* now, and I don't even know I'm doing them, and that's a little scary. I wish you were here to show me how to do everything and not stuck in a weird Snow White glass coffin. I'm sorry I didn't know you were alive. I feel like I should have. Or I should have tried harder to avenge your death like one of those old kung fu movies. I'm sorry. I'm a bad student."

I chewed without tasting the food and talked. At first it was venting, the way I'd done whenever I didn't like what she was teaching me. Of *course*, I said. Of course I would somehow end up in the crosshairs of some kind of gigantic conspiracy. Never mind that my life had already sucked enough.

But at least I didn't have cancer. I wished Kiki could have found some way to tell me that earlier. If nothing else, she would have saved me a lot of time in the quiet moments, when my brain wasn't occupied and drifted back to the constant, underlying fear that the Mobium was killing and healing me at the same time. But I really didn't want to think about that, so I employed an old tactic from my days of constantly being kidnapped: I focused on other things. Like the source of my current troubles.

"I don't think you'd like Rita," I said aloud. I folded my legs under me, rested my hands on my knees, and propped my chin on the tops of my fists. "Though I also worry you two would get along like a house on fire, you twisted sadist. But I guess you mostly told me the truth, and I don't think she's ever told the truth in her life. Like grandmother, like granddaughter."

After that, I talked about Detmer. There was so much that I'd been through that I didn't feel comfortable telling Guy or Vicki about, not without upsetting them. But Angélica probably wouldn't remember anything about being in that chamber, so I told her about the food and how I could now say I'd tried snails—not my thing—and how much she would love the gym.

"It's even better than Davenport's, and you know Davenport's. It's nothing to shake a stick at. But wow, this place—if it weren't for the involuntary imprisonment and the fact that I was basically one badly timed sneeze away from being killed by any of about fifty enemies? It probably would have been perfect. I mean, sure, I never saw myself becoming an IRS agent or a villain, but I don't know. After the week I've had, burning a few buildings to the ground in rage seems more and more like a reasonable response." I thought about it. "I won't, I promise. But I can understand the urge. I wish you were awake."

She'd tell me it would be okay, after all. I wouldn't believe her, like I didn't believe any of the others, but it would be nice to hear.

I drifted off, throat sore from all the talking. Curled up on the couch, facing my friend, I fell asleep.

An explosion woke me up.

Or at least, that was what it felt like. The entire house shook, and the walls shuddered, and it knocked me clean off the couch. In an instant, I'd rolled over, crouching on all fours and looking around me. Was it Raptor? Had she found me again?

The irate hero that stormed in wasn't Jessica Davenport.

"Where is she?" Vicki ripped off her mask. "I want to see her now, you had *no right* to lie to us like this—"

"Vicki, calm down," Kiki said as she hurried into the attic after Vicki.

Vicki was having none of it. "Where is she, Gail?" she asked.

I rose to my feet and pointed. Vicki vaulted over the couch and crossed the three feet of space to the chamber. When she looked inside, she gasped. The look she shot Kiki was full of poisonous anger. Without warning, she turned and punched the glass, shattering it and sending shards everywhere. And as Kiki and I gaped, she reached in, scooped Angélica up one-armed, and set her on the couch where I'd been sleeping.

"You don't get to play life or death with us," Vicki said, rounding on Kiki. "That's not your call to make. This stops now."

Kiki gave her a distressed look and climbed over the couch as well. She ignored the glass all over the place and began to probe Angélica's face and neck with her face. "Now you've done it," she said. "It looks like she was in there long enough, so she's okay. No thanks to you. You might have killed her."

Vicki made a scoffing noise and stood back, arms crossed over her chest. She gave me a little nod, a jut of the chin. "Hey, Gail. Feeling better?"

I nodded. "Didn't know you cared so much," I said. "Are you and Angélica even friends?"

"We're coffee buddies sometimes. I'm more pissed off on principle." Vicki looked down at the destroyed chamber that she was leaning against. "What'd I just break, anyway?"

"You fighters are all the same," Kiki said under her breath as she carefully turned the still-unconscious Angélica onto her side. "Punch first, ask questions later. If you'd let me *explain*—"

"Guy called and filled me in. Needless to say, I'm not

impressed." Vicki swung about to look at me. "How's it feel to be in the middle of things?"

"Not great," I said, completely honest.

"I'm here for you, Gail." Vicki rested a hand on my shoulder and gave me a tiny shake. "And for your trainer. See? Looking out for you, like a good mentor."

I decided not to say anything about the fact that Kiki had gamed the system to make her mentor not because of compatibility but because Vicki was too powerful to cross. I had a feeling that, out of everything, would break her heart the hardest.

Pounding on the stairs made all three of the conscious people in the room look over as Guy, Naomi on his heels, burst inside. He skidded to a halt, took one look around, and relaxed. "Hurricane Vicki strikes again, I see."

"Hi," Vicki said.

Guy wandered over to the couch, concern etched on his face as he looked at Angélica. "Is she okay?"

"No thanks to the masked menace over here." Kiki glared.

Vicki dusted a piece of lint off the shoulder of her uniform. "You don't exactly have the moral high ground here. Look what you've done to my friends."

"Kept them alive against my grandmother's best attempts to use them like tissue paper?" Kiki's chin firmed up.

"Because of *you*," Vicki said. "You could have come to me at any time for help. God knows I've wanted to punch Cooper in the face for a long time."

"You have?" I asked, as the first time I'd met Vicki, she'd been flirting with Cooper pretty hard-core.

The others ignored me. "Right," Kiki said, glaring at Vicki, "you would have believed me. Sure. Because you don't give me the same suspicious looks everybody else does—"

"Were we wrong?" Vicki asked.

"And even if you *did* believe that I was telling the truth, I'm pretty sure you would have screwed it up!"

"When have I ever done that?" Vicki asked.

Kiki made a strangled noise and gestured at the glass all over the floor, and I realized maybe she had a point. "You're lucky you didn't kill her!"

"I could say the same for you!"

"I was saving her life."

"*After* you put her in danger by not telling any of us anything!"

"Gail," Guy said quietly, sidling up to me. "You might want to get out of the blast radius."

"Not without Angélica," I said, as if I was in danger, so was she.

Guy sighed like I had a point. He grabbed Vicki by the scruff of her uniform, Kiki by the back of her Cubs tee, and picked them both up, setting them on the other side of the couch. "You want to argue," he said, "you do so away from the patients. Take it downstairs."

Vicki swiped at Guy's arm, breaking his grip. "You're such a hall monitor sometimes," she said, stalking toward the door and towing Kiki behind her. I stood where I'd been rooted, feeling like I'd just brushed the edge of a deadly storm.

"I'll get a broom," Guy said, sighing again at the shards all over the floor. It was probably a good thing I hadn't moved, as I'd kicked off my shoes before going to sleep. I didn't particular relish the idea of getting the bottoms of my feet cut to ribbons. "Stay put."

"Actually." It was awkward as hell, but I leaned over as far as I could, planted my hands on the edge of the couch cushion. I kicked off, did a small handspring off the edge of the couch, and folded my legs over the back. It left me sitting on the back of the couch, facing the door. "I'll stay here, in case she wakes up."

"Resourceful as ever." He headed back into the rest of the house, brushing past Naomi, who was just standing in the doorway gawking. She had Vicki's discarded mask in her hands.

I gave her an odd look. "What's up with you?"

Her jaw clicked shut. I could see the whites of her eyes clearly in the darkness. "What the fuck was that?" she asked, her voice a hoarse whisper.

"Vicki being Vicki," I said. "You get kind of used to it—"

"Victoria fucking Burroughs is *Plain fucking Jane?* You talked about a Vicki earlier, but—Victoria Burroughs. Oh my god, everything makes *so much sense.*"

"Oh, right. I forgot you didn't know," I said. That was just my world now, I realized, where I regularly forgot that a world-famous supermodel was also a well-known superhero. How far had I come, that it just made sense? "Yeah, that's . . . a thing. Are you okay?"

"I kind of feel like I'm about to have an aneurysm. Do you realize I now know more about the world of superheroes than any other journalist out there, and the minute I say anything, some psycho bitch will hunt me down and kill me?" Naomi moaned and rested her forehead on the back of the couch, next to me. Vicki's mask dropped to the cushions, bounced, and clattered to the floor. It lay there, looking up and judging us.

I fought the urge to kick it away. "I won't lie," I said. "They're not going to let you out of this house until you sign the biggest nondisclosure agreement known to mankind."

Naomi moaned again. "I won't be able to write a single thing without lawyers all over me. I'm going to have to quit my job. Do you know how much my parents are going to gloat when I do that? They think I should get a real job."

"I'd say you're less likely to wind up in the cross-hairs of a supervillain if you have a 'real job,'" I said, making the finger quotes in the air, "but I am living, breathing proof that that really is not the case."

"Your life is messed up, you know that?"

"So is yours."

Naomi took a deep breath and straightened up. She seemed to pull herself together, pushing her shoulders back, lifting her chin. "We got off on the wrong foot," she said, sticking her hand out. "I'm sorry. Naomi

Gunn, reporter, and not as much of a pain in the ass as you all think I am, I promise."

I shook her hand. "Gail Godwin. I *am* as much a pain in the ass as everybody thinks I am, though the fault is mostly not mine."

Naomi grinned, briefly. Her smile flickered and died. "I didn't tell Chelsea—Brook, whoever the hell she is—I didn't tell her about Guy's weakness. When I figured out what it was, and why she wanted it, I ran. I never wanted him to get hurt."

I took a deep breath. "So how did she know?"

"My guess? She found my notes and traced them to the same old article I did. It mentions War Hammer and a purple fireball. You can kind of draw your own conclusions from there." Naomi pulled her arms in around her midsection, hunching over.

"Oh," I said. "I'm sorry you went through all of that. With her, I mean."

"Thanks. I have to ask: what's going to happen to us? You realize that if Chelsea—Brook—whoever she is, if she has the same thing you do, she's only going to get stronger. Yeah, it's selfish, but I'm a little person-ally invested in making sure that *doesn't* happen as she probably would have killed me if you hadn't busted me out of the hospital today."

"I don't know. I guess I understand her a little better now, though." After all, how would I have reacted if instead of Davenport, I'd ended up in a cage? "Though I have to wonder at her priorities. I'd rather take out the bad guys than the ex. Of course, maybe she shares

Kiki's school of thought, where Cooper and Lodi are too powerful to even consider, so hit what you can."

"Or she snapped, and now she's crazy," Naomi said. "I mean, that's an option."

"A depressing one."

When Guy came in to deliver the broom, he was shaking his head. "We're one wrong word away from Vicki burning the house down," he said as he started to sweep. "Just so you all know."

"I still can't believe Victoria Burroughs is Plain Jane." Naomi shook her head like she was trying to get water out of her ears. "That's . . . I still don't know what that is."

"She's a character, all right." Guy's gaze lingered on Angélica for a second before he turned a determinedly cheerful expression toward us. "How are you two holding up? We're not going to have a repeat of the Kiki vs. Vicki situation, are we?"

"We're friends now," I said.

"We are?" Naomi immediately perked up. "So I can ask what the deal with you two is?" She looked hopefully between Guy and me.

"No. We're not that good of friends," I said, and Naomi snapped her fingers.

Guy swept the little pile of dirt and glass into the dustpan. "Got a minute?" he asked me.

Since Naomi offered to sit with Angélica, I followed Guy downstairs. I was still having a hard time wrapping my brain around the fact that I'd been held captive in this house for over two weeks. It felt so suburban. And really kind of cozy, when you looked at it. I wondered if the house next door, the decoy house that the Lodi Corporation thought was Mobius's real laboratory, had the same decorations.

Shouting from the kitchen made Guy pull up short. "Why don't we talk in here, instead?" he said, and ducked through the doorway to his left. I followed and immediately had to stomp down hard on the desire to run away. The dark pink carpet and pink wallpaper were as familiar to me as my own bedroom in my abandoned apartment though in reality I'd spent less than twelve hours in this room when Dr. Mobius had held me there.

I looked automatically at the window. The last time I'd been in here, I'd been zapped trying to escape through the window. It had been boarded up then, but now the curtains were just drawn closed.

"Kiki says she disabled everything," Guy said, understanding right away. "She shocked herself pretty good doing it. This is her old bedroom, apparently." Guy took a seat in the desk chair. "She said you were kept in here?"

"Not for long, but long enough." The book I'd been reading during my captivity was still on the nightstand, which did unpleasant things to my stomach. I sat on the edge of the bed. "What did you want to talk about?"

Guy sighed. "I need to get out of here, and I don't want to leave you behind. But this is the safest place for you right now."

"I want to stay wherever Angélica is," I said. "If she's like me now . . ."

"I understand. She's going to be pissed about that, you realize."

"At the moment, I'm not happy about it myself. Where do you need to go?"

"Sam."

"Ah," I said. I could see the lines on Guy's face. The knowledge that Brook was alive and had been through hell for years would probably eat at him for a long time. And Sam definitely needed to know that his ex-girlfriend was both alive and at large.

"It's not exactly news you deliver over the phone. But he needs to know, and we need to figure out what to do about her."

"I understand," I said. "I'd do the same thing if I were in your shoes."

"It shouldn't take me long," Guy said. "I'm just going to talk to him, then I'll come right back. We'll come up with a plan to deal with Cooper and the Lodi Corporation."

Something crashed loudly from the direction of the kitchen, and raised voices let us know that Vicki was now in the dish-throwing portion of tonight's entertainment.

"Right. A plan. On a scale of one to ten, just how terrifying is Cooper? Theoretically," I said.

Guy's troubled look returned. He took a long time to answer, which I knew was him considering his words before speaking. Unlike me, he actually took the time to debate his options, whereas I tended to blurt out the first thing that could get me in trouble.

"When you came to Davenport," he said, "you had Cooper and Kiki doing all of your physical testing, right?"

"Yes," I said, and tried not to think about how much that made me want to shudder now. "Why do you ask?"

"They had me with another physician to do the physical when I first arrived at Davenport. Cooper came in to do the punch test. They do that to you?"

I nodded. One of the first things Davenport had asked me to do was to punch Cooper as hard as I could. He'd been wearing monitoring equipment, and I'd worried about breaking him with my newfound strength. I could only imagine how that must have gone for Guy, who was a lot stronger than me and likely had an even harder time hitting an opponent who hadn't hit first.

"It didn't even hurt him," Guy said. "I mean, I knocked him off his feet, but he didn't even flinch."

I gawked. Guy had once punched through reinforced steel doors since I'd been trapped on the other side of them.

"So, theoretically? It's not good," Guy said.

"How do you beat somebody like that?" I asked, feeling even smaller than usual.

"We'll find a way. We've faced longer odds, believe it or not."

"I don't believe it, but if you do, that's fine with me."

Five minutes later, dressed in the War Hammer costume again, Guy carefully checked the street and flew off through Kiki's window, while I watched from deep inside the room, out of view in case there were any random passersby at three in the morning. After he left, I hurried out of the room as fast as I could. I didn't want to spend a minute longer in there than I had to. Since Kiki and Vicki still both sounded aggravated when I passed the kitchen, I went back to the attic.

"Any change?" I asked Naomi.

"She mumbled something a couple minutes ago, but other than that? No. It's a little weird hanging out with a coma patient when you know she's got superpowers, I won't lie." Naomi flattened her hair a little bit, but it sprang right back up. "Can I ask you a question?"

"Sure." I sat on the floor, resting back against the empty chamber again.

"So somehow you're the key to get us out of this."

"Yeah." I snorted. "Because I've totally got the resources to take out what's probably a multimillion-dollar company and its spy, who can incidentally withstand a punch from my incredibly strong boyfriend without flinching. Yeah, that's me in a nutshell."

Naomi raised her eyebrows. "So *do* you have a plan?"

"I never have a plan."

"Want me to come up with one?" Naomi asked. When I squinted at her, she shrugged. "Just trying to help. I've never been on this side of the superhero line."

"It's not that great, honestly," I said, closing my eyes.

"Gotta be better than getting kidnapped all the time, though."

I thought about it, about all of the terror and anger and frustration I'd lived through since that fight with Brook and her cronies in the mall. "It's not really that different," I said. "Just more work expected of me, in the end."

Naomi laughed. "Anybody ever tell you you're a bit of a downer?"

Guy had told me I always found the silver lining. I wasn't sure which perception of me unnerved me more, so I smiled at Naomi and shook my head. "Welcome to my world."

"I was serious about coming up with a plan," Naomi said. "I might not have powers, but I graduated top of my class."

"From where? The School of Hard Knocks?"

"Harvard, you idiot."

"You went to Harvard, and you run a superhero gossip blog?"

"A *well-respected* superhero gossip blog. But you can see why my parents are harping at me to get a real job." Naomi brushed the knees of her jeans off. "I'm going to talk to Kiki. Hopefully, Superhero's Next Top Model down there has stopped throwing things."

"Doubt it," said a rusty voice from the couch.

I sat bolt upright. "Angélica!"

Her eyes were open though they were mere slits as she took in the room and me, and Naomi. Her skin had gone even waxier, but she apparently had the energy to lift her head an inch. "That's me," she said. "Somebody mind telling me where I am?"

CHAPTER EIGHTEEN

Everything descended into brief, loud chaos. I nearly burst into tears, Vicki and Kiki pounded up the stairs together, and Naomi scrambled to get out of the way before she could get stepped on. For a second, I couldn't hear a thing, as we were all trying to talk at once.

"Hey," said a voice from the couch, and Angélica gave us a malevolent look. "Anybody ever teach you idiots how to act around sick people? Vicki, go away."

"But—"

"Go make tea or something. Gail looks like death. Who let my trainee almost die?"

"If you want to get technical? Cooper." But Vicki listened to her and stomped off, which was almost as amazing as Angélica's waking up at all. After a second, Naomi glanced at me and decided to follow after her.

I crouched by Angélica. "I don't feel as bad as I suspect I look."

"Liar." She coughed weakly. "Where am I?"

"Long story. You're safe."

"From *what*?"

"Never mind that." Kiki nudged me to the side and began checking her pulse. "How do you feel?"

"You don't want me to answer that." She coughed again. "Why aren't we at Davenport?"

"Because the world thinks you're dead," I said.

Angélica's eyes cut to me. "What?"

"Gail, don't get her excited at this stage, she's likely to—and there she goes." Kiki sighed and rested back on her haunches as Angélica's eyes rolled back into her head. Kiki bit off a curse. "In this state, when the Mobium is first dealing with full consciousness, any excitement will take the patient back under. My grandfather's journals were clear about that when that happened with you."

"Excitement? You mean him letting me believe I was a robot? Yeah, no wonder I passed out." Warily, I brushed a little of Angélica's hair back. "How long will she be out?"

"Probably an hour or two. I take it you want to stay with her?"

"Yeah."

Kiki moved over to the Mobium chamber and picked up her clipboard from where it hung on a little peg. As she scribbled something onto the chart, she made a noise in the back of her throat. "Did Guy take off?"

"He wanted to talk to his brother. He should be back soon."

"Hopefully, he comes back before daybreak. I don't want to draw too much attention to this place."

"He'll be discreet."

When she left me alone, I reclaimed the seat I'd taken before Angélica's brief spell of consciousness, my heart hammering with the leftover adrenaline. Angélica was okay. Seeing her alive had been one thing, but she'd woken up, and she'd been so *her* that it made my chest constrict a little.

"You shouldn't die ever again," I said as I put my head back and felt my eyes drift closed. "It's really exhausting, okay? So after this, *if* we get through this, no more dying."

Angélica made a noise in her sleep that I took for assent. I let myself doze. Not full sleep, as I was too keyed up for that, but a twilight doze where I could keep an eye on her.

Angélica was going to be like me when she woke up. How would she feel about the ability to gain new powers? How did *I* feel about it, come to think of it? I'd processed the news when Kiki had dropped that particular bomb because I needed to. But I hadn't really thought about what it meant. How did the Mobium really work? Was the substance making up a large part of my body simply observant enough to look at the powers around me, say "I want that," and begin to use that power? Or did I need to be exposed to it through bodily fluids somehow?

Wow, that was kind of gross. Had I absorbed Angélica's powers because we'd sweated on each other during our sparring matches? I gagged a little at the thought.

And I'd kissed Guy several times. Did that mean I was going to get his ability to fly? Or his strength or imperviousness to pain? His ability to turn into a green fireball? God, there was so much about me that I didn't know. I needed get my hands on Mobius's notebooks, I realized. Those could be very valuable reading material.

I opened my eyes when Vicki came in with two cups of tea. "I can take a shift if you want to go shower or something," she said.

"Is that your way of telling me I smell?" I asked as I took the tea from her.

"Yeah, actually." She dropped down next to me. Given that she was over a foot taller than me, it was a much longer drop, and she had to fold herself over to fit between the couch and the chamber. "Hygiene is important, my mentee."

"I'm kind of nose-blind to it," I said.

"Trust me, the rest of us aren't."

"So mean." I nudged her with my shoulder.

"I nag because I care." She sipped from the tea, wrinkled her nose, and set it off to the side. Her sigh was gusty and seemed to go on for nearly a minute. "She's alive. Isn't that a kick in the ass? Makes more sense than her being taken out by one of those piddly little sting rays of Chelsea's."

"Brook," I said. Vicki's chin had a red mark in the spot Brook had hit during the battle earlier, but I wasn't going to point that out. "Apparently her name is Brook."

"I'm still wrapping my head around that. My arch-nemesis is the ex of the man I'm sleeping with. I don't like that."

"That she slept with Sam? They were together for a long time," I said.

But Vicki shook her head. "Oh, that, I don't care about that. I just don't like the cattiness of it all. You know?"

"If it makes you feel better, your rivalry was there before we knew her identity."

"That does make me feel better, actually." Vicki tried her tea again, wrinkled her nose even harder, and set it aside once more. "Never was a tea drinker. I don't understand you people that are. What's wrong with coffee?"

"I find it relaxing, myself." I picked up her tea and poured it into my cup. No use letting it go to waste. "I'm surprised you didn't bring Jeremy with you."

"He's back at headquarters still, looking into the Lodi Corporation."

I felt a spurt of alarm. Jeremy didn't have any powers to defend himself if Cooper found out the truth. "Is that safe?"

"I mean, Cooper doesn't know we know, so if Jer can pretend everything is normal, it should all be okay. Though Kiki can't stay here much longer without blowing her own cover." Vicki reached forward and brushed Angélica's hair away from her face the same way I had earlier. "I can't stay here either. Jer needs some backup, and if we *all* drop off the grid, it looks suspicious. They already think I'm helping you."

"But you *are* helping me."

"Yeah, but they don't need to know that." Vicki scooped up her mask and pulled it on. "I'll go out the same way Guy did, I think. Stay here, and stay safe."

"I'll do my best."

Vicki made it almost all the way to the door before she turned around. "Hey, is there something wrong with your reporter friend? She keeps giving me the weirdest looks. It's a little freaky."

"I think she's working on reconciling Victoria Burroughs and Vicki the Plain Jane," I said, laughing.

"Oh, right. Sometimes I forget." With a cheery little wave, she headed off.

Angélica woke up three more times, a little longer each time. Naomi and I rotated shifts, so Kiki could get some sleep. I took a shower—this time not in the chemical shower closet in the basement—and changed into some of Kiki's spare clothes, as Vicki had a point about my starting to smell.

And then there was nothing to do but wait.

"Look at us," Naomi said as I pulled a card from the deck. Kiki had taken off an hour before since the sun would be up soon. "Couple of fugitives, doing very important things. Got any twos?"

"Go fish," I said.

Naomi picked up a card. "Damn it," she said. "The good news is that I talked to Kiki about a plan."

"And the bad news? Any fours?"

She handed over a card. "Bad news is that you guys weren't kidding. This guy is built like a fortress. Taking him down is nigh impossible. No wonder he's gotten away with so much for so long."

"How about sixes?" I asked.

"Go fish. How do you deal with it? I mean, you're collecting powers like baseball cards, but you're not that strong yet. How do you deal with knowing that everybody around you is stronger?"

"You be better." Angélica's voice was once again rusty as she spoke. She stirred and stretched, yawning widely. "If they're stronger, you're faster. If they're faster, you're smarter. It's just how it goes. Good morning. Why . . . am I so damn hungry right now?"

"Long story," I said far too brightly. "But I have something to fix that!"

She squinted at me like a woman with a hangover. "There's a catch here somewhere," she said.

"No, it's food. Theoretically." I held up a bag Kiki had left behind, full of little silver wrappers. "Aren't you excited?"

She groaned and sat up with some difficulty, arms shaky as she pushed herself up. "This is revenge, isn't it?"

"It's a dish best served cold." I unwrapped a crap-cake and held it out. Naomi, who'd nibbled on one, immediately wrinkled her nose, and I didn't blame her. There was no proper way to describe the taste of crap-cakes, which would keep a person with an average metabolism full for an entire day. I preferred to think of them as utterly disgusting and leave it at that. After all, the only thing worse than the taste of a crap-cake was the aftertaste.

Angélica sighed and ate the whole thing. She frowned. "I'm still hungry."

I handed her a second, unwrapped crap-cake. "It'll be like that for a while. You're still getting used to the Mobium Kiki gave you to save your life. Or possibly bring you back from the dead. That part of the story's not clear."

My trainer blinked both eyes open and gave me a look. "Mobium," she said, flatly.

"It's the miracle drug."

Naomi, on the other hand, leaned her head back all the way, looking up at the ceiling in exasperation. "Houston," she said, "we are go for explanation round three."

Angélica ate three more crap-cakes in the time it took Naomi and I to explain why we were playing card games in the attic of a house in the suburbs. She took the news that she'd died remarkably well. Just some quiet, vociferous cursing in Portuguese, followed by some louder swearing in English. By the end, she shook so badly that Naomi and I shared a silent fearful look. She didn't pass out. She took deep breaths and finally nodded.

"Cooper," she said when we finished relating *that* part of the tale. "Cooper poisoned me?"

"You didn't take anything from him, did you? Right before we went to the mall?"

"He gave me a stick of chewing gum when I stopped by to talk to him." Angélica groaned and pushed the side of her fist into her forehead. "It all makes sense. He told me I was seeing things, but I *saw* you phase, I know I did. And you were strange afterward. Weaker. I got in an easy hit, bruised your cheek up pretty bad. Do you remember that?"

That had been the day I'd gone to the Annals, I realized. I'd had a nasty bruise that had unfortunately hit every color of the ugly rainbow as it had healed.

"Yeah," I said. "Yeah, I remember that. Would've been nice to know about that before I started—" Wait. Weaker. I didn't remember being fatigued after that hit from Angélica, but I remembered a sudden dizzying migraine while fighting the Raptor.

She'd said I'd 'ported. I'd assumed she just hadn't seen me climb the stairs or had underestimated how fast I could be. But I remembered the rooftop, her fist coming right at my nose, too fast for me to dodge, and then I'd just been somewhere else.

"Holy shit," I said.

Both of my companions looked panicked. "What?"

"I can 'port! I did it once when I was—no, I've done it twice." That was how I'd reached Guy in time when he had fallen, after Brook had nearly killed him. "I can 'port. Oh, god."

Angélica closed her eyes and lay back down. "Of

course you can," she said. "Of course that would be the power you pick up almost right away."

She had a point. 'Porting, they'd told me when we had visited the way station in New York to travel to Chicago, took years and years to master, which was why so few people could do it. It was difficult to control and probably fatal if you screwed it up. I had no idea what the principles were behind it, but each time I'd 'ported, it had been short distances, and I'd felt like death afterward.

Great. I'd gained the coolest power, with apparently no way to control, and no time to learn *how* to control it.

That was just helpful, that was.

"Gail, and I mean this with love, but you are shaping up to be the most problematic trainee I've ever had," Angélica said.

"You mean, they haven't killed you over your *other* trainees? Gee, I'm shocked."

Angélica managed a smile. She reached out and squeezed my shoulder, but it lacked her regular strength. "I think I need to sleep some more," she said, her voice growing slurred. "Once I'm up, I'm reporting in to headquarters, and I'm going to kick Cooper's ass myself."

"Get in line," I said, thinking of Vicki.

Since she was actually sleeping this time rather than passed out, Naomi and I gathered up the cards and carried them to the kitchen. I didn't feel like cooking, so I bit the bullet and swallowed a crap-cake whole. I stuck a second one in my pocket, just in case. As much as I complained about them, the little bars were actually incredibly handy to have around.

"I still can't believe you can eat those," Naomi said, wrinkling her nose as she poured herself a glass of water.

"Just part of my life now. Do you want—"

The house shook. This time, it had nothing to do with Vicki.

Something *boomed* from outside, rattling the whole house. I tackled Naomi to the floor. From the direction of the front door, my ears picked up the sound of glass breaking. And then a hissing noise that filled me with dread.

"Gas!" I shoved Naomi to her feet. "Go out the back!"

She started coughing, so I yanked off the flannel overshirt I wore over my tank top and shoved that at her. Then I pushed her until she complied, racing for the back door. I turned and sprinted instead for the stairs. Angélica was too weak to get herself out of there. She had to be my priority.

How had Cooper found us? What had given us away?

There was a second *thunk*, followed by a hiss. I cursed under my breath. At least it was the same stuff Rita had ensured wouldn't bother me. It irritated my eyes and throat as I ran, but I didn't care.

A third window shattered right as I reached the

stairs. Instinctively, I ducked forward. Something whipped over my head. When I looked up, I was eye-ball to eyeball with a bird logo on a throwing disc sticking out of the wall. It was nice that she believed in putting her logo on *everything*, but—"Oh, hell."

Not again. How had *Raptor* even found us?

I tried to keep running for the stairs, but a second disc sliced into the wall, blocking my route. She'd effectively cut me out. I spun and ran the other way. I'd have to scale the outside of the place.

The net *whooshed* as it flew behind me. I dropped into a roll, flinched when a piece of glass bit into the bottom of my bare foot, and leapt straight through one of the windows in the living room. It exploded outward in a shower of glass. I hit the flowerbed and landed on all fours, immediately springing to a crouch as I looked around. She had to be near, if she was throwing all of those toys at me.

I didn't see anything in the front yard. Not even the Raptorcycle.

This had to be a trap.

Trap or not, I needed to get to Angélica. I raced for the drainpipe on the corner of the house and started to climb. It was out in the open, leaving me vulnerable, but I didn't have a choice. At least it was still dark, and the windows in the neighboring houses hadn't lit up.

How had she found us? Was our cover blown? Were the others okay?

I climbed, pushed up with my feet, and grabbed the overhanging eave on the second floor with both hands.

When I moved to pull myself over, a *thwipp* noise filled the air, and I felt a rope snap my ankles together. I cried out, nearly losing my grip, and tried to pull myself up anyway. It was all for naught: something sticky hit the center of my back. One sharp tug, and I fell backward. Oh, god, this was going to hurt—

I hit some kind of cushiony surface with an "Oof!" A gel, I realized as my body began to sink. A bright *pink* gel, which only made it worse. In less than a second, I was completely trapped in the gel from my shoulders down. My body was immobilized; I tried to call up as much of my strength as possible, but all it did was nudge the rapidly hardening gel a tiny centimeter.

"Don't waste your energy." Raptor's modified voice emerged from the shadows. She followed a second later. The light from a nearby streetlamp cast her face in deep shadow.

"What do you even want with me?" I asked, panting.

She crouched next to the giant glob of Gail-filled tactical jello. "You have the worst survival instincts of anybody I've ever met," she said with a frown. "You keep going up. You could have gotten away just now, and you went up."

"My friend—she's in the attic—"

"The gas won't kill anybody. I don't use lethal tools." She shrugged to herself. "You've got a prison to go back to, young lady."

"Young Lady" only felt mildly less insulting from a woman my mother's age than it did from a man, I discovered in that moment.

"No, you don't understand," I started to say, but Raptor touched a button on her wrist cuff. The gel around me turned a blindingly bright pink for a second.

It tasted inexplicably like cotton candy when it knocked me out.

When I woke up, I was upside down, gagged, and blindfolded.

Sadly, this was not the first time that had happened.

Everything ached. The blood had long ago rushed to my head, so I had a headache on top of everything, but I sorted out as many details as I could. New-car smell and a sensation of movement in my stomach, so I was clearly in somebody's car. I wasn't entirely upside down, I realized after a second, since I lay on my stomach. Only my head and shoulders were hanging downward. I could lift my head, which I did.

"Sorry about that," a voice came from somewhere in front of me. "You fell out of the restraints, and I didn't have time to get you set to rights. How's your head?"

I turned my face in the direction of Jessica Davenport's voice and made a noise through the gag.

"You're not the first person to tell me that," she said, understanding my insult perfectly. "Points for creativity, though. Why a goat?"

I made another noise.

"Yeah, I hate all Davenports, too. But you belong in prison. Your ride should be here any second to take you back."

Wait, my ride?

I realized abruptly where I must be: the Raptor Tank. Jessica Davenport's tricked-out utility vehicle that they said contained over five hundred weapons *and* could fly. Of course it would always smell like a new car, since the Davenports were richer than Midas. I'd wanted to see inside it for a long time, and so it just figured I'd be blindfolded now.

I felt the car decelerating, which slid me forward a little so that my neck and shoulders were again over the edge of whatever I was atop. Raptor climbed out of the tank, and I heard her greet somebody else. I tried to wiggle my wrists and see if there was any give in my handcuffs, but no joy there.

From behind me, I heard the creak of a door. Apparently, the Raptor Tank had a back hatch.

"I know it's unorthodox," said a new voice. I froze in horror. "I appreciate you letting me transport her back. I've been worried about how they've been treating her in Detmer. Her cancer isn't something to be taken lightly."

"She's pretty spry for somebody with leukemia," Raptor said.

I couldn't move. I'd gone absolutely stiff with fear and cold, and the way Lemuel Cooper laughed now, lighthearted and cheery, only made things worse. "Isn't she, though," he said. "Where'd you find her, anyway?"

"Few miles from here." I felt myself being pulled backward and immediately started struggling. Raptor grunted.

"Here, let me help."

When I felt a second pair of hands hauling me back, I struggled harder.

"Gail, it's only me," Cooper said.

That was the problem.

No matter how much I struggled, though, they were stronger than me. I was pulled out of the Raptor Tank and carried into what I guessed was a second car, buckled in while blindfolded and gagged.

I felt a gloved hand on my shoulder. Raptor. "Straight back to the prison," she said to Cooper. "This one's already gotten away from me once. My reputation will be in shreds if she does it again."

I heard her footsteps walking away and tried to scream through the gag.

"Don't worry," Cooper called after her. "I'll take care of her."

I was afraid of that.

CHAPTER NINETEEN

I was alone in the car with the man who had in the most indirect way possible caused me to fall victim to the machinations of the world's first supervillain. A man who was stronger and more indestructible than Guy, could punch harder than Vicki, and essentially had no reason to fear *anything*. A man who, if Kiki was to be believed, had the morals of a rabid weasel and was involved in the testing of a compound designed to turn ordinary people into superpowered freaks of nature. A man who had allegedly been looking for an opportunity to kill me since the first day I had set foot in Davenport Industries.

Not only was I alone in the car with him: I was alone, blindfolded, gagged, *and* handcuffed.

So that was great.

I flinched in terror when I felt him touch the blindfold. A second later, it was pulled off. I blinked rapidly several times.

"Better?" Cooper asked. He held the blindfold loosely in one hand. I tried to scramble away from him. "Gail! Gail, relax. I'm here to drive you back to Detmer. I wanted to make sure you hadn't hurt yourself. Your condition is delicate."

I screamed through the gag and tried harder to get away. The seat belt creaked against my weight.

"Whoa! Whoa, Gail, it's okay. You're safe." He held his hands up. "What's the matter? You do recognize me, don't you? It's Cooper. I'm your doctor, remember? Did you get hit with a memory gas?"

A cold, striking fact broke through the terror.

He had no idea.

He had no idea I knew who he really was. He was operating under the assumption I was just out of my mind with fear rather than specific terror at the sight of him. Which meant that Raptor must not have told him anything about where she'd found me. Otherwise, he would know everything.

"Doing better?" Cooper asked.

I took a deep breath through my nose. If he didn't know, then I could—what? What, Gail? I was still cuffed and gagged, and he was tremendously strong. What could I *possibly* do?

First rule of hostage situations: never let your captor know how much you know.

And if Cooper didn't know I knew about him,

there was always a chance I could bide my time and get away.

My last meal fought to make a reappearance, but I battled it down. Could he see that I was shaking? I felt like it was obvious. "Sorry," I tried to say through the gag.

"Why don't I take that off?" he asked.

I stayed as still as he peeled the gag away from my face. Raptor might have entrapped me using high-tech gel, but it was kind of nice to see that she sometimes used duct tape like the rest of us plebeians. When it was finally off, I gasped.

"Better?" he asked.

I nodded past the sick feeling in my throat. "M-much."

"Remember me yet?"

I nodded again. "Been a rough couple of d-days. I haven't slept much, and Raptor—she came out of nowhere, and I panicked and—"

"It's okay." Cooper patted my knee, and I did my best not to flinch away. "I've got you now."

Yeah, that was definitely not as reassuring as he meant it to sound.

"I want to do a physical, to make sure you haven't sustained any lasting injury from your time on the run," he said.

"Aren't the prison doctors going to do that?"

"Humor me." His smile was probably meant to be reassuring and helpful, but it only made me tremble harder. Cold sweat coated the back of my neck. He tapped his thumb on the roof of the car in time to the song playing faintly on the radio. "I'm just going to take you to a nearby Davenport facility. I'll run some tests, let you have a nice meal, and I'll take you back. I hope you at least had *some* fun on the run."

"Oh, yeah, it was a blast," I said, the sarcasm appearing without prompting.

He shook his head, shut the door, and moved over to the driver's seat. In that moment, he certainly didn't *look* like the evil mastermind who could and would kill me at the drop of a hat. But if there was one thing my multiple kidnappings had taught me, it was that evil came in all shapes and faces.

"I didn't know Davenport had a facility around here," I said. I had no idea where we were. The sun was just beginning to rise on my third—or maybe fourth— day of being a fugitive.

Cooper winked at me. "Davenport, home of many secrets."

He made small talk as he drove, asking me about my adventures over the past few days. I made up a few lies—sleeping behind a dumpster on the Navy Pier might have been overselling it—and tried to pay attention to road signs we passed without seeming obvious.

Less than ten minutes, Cooper pulled into a parking lot. He badged in past the front gate, crossed around the car, and unbuckled me. "Our humble offices," he said with a grand sweep of his hand. "Not much to look at, I know, but Davenport prefers to put all its goodies inside."

The building was a flat and square, unobtrusive. It could have passed for a dentist's office or accounting firm. There wasn't a single sign anywhere to be found as we walked into the building together. He didn't grab my elbow as expected, but I didn't run. There was nowhere I could go.

The security guard at the front desk looked up to smile at both of us. "Hey, Coop. One guest?"

I gave him a smile back that hopefully hid the ill feeling behind my sternum. Where were the signs? They'd been all over the place at Dartmoor Incorporated, to the point of obnoxiousness.

This was definitely not a Davenport facility.

Cooper scribbled something on the clipboard the guard held out. "Name of Doe, Jane, for an examination."

I tensed without meaning to. Jane Doe? There was no way *that* could lead to anything good.

"Davenport policy," Cooper said easily as he handed the clipboard back. "We don't log real names here, right, John?"

"Right, Mr. Smith." The guard winked at him as Cooper ushered me out of the foyer and into a hall that could have been in any office building anywhere on the planet.

None of the doors were marked, and everything felt quiet and still. My gut said this building belonged to the Lodi Corporation, I saw no clues for that, either. All I knew was that none of my friends knew where I was, I knew where none of my friends were, and I'd just officially had my name stripped away from me. Singularly, these were all terrible signs. Together, they spelled my doom. The skin on the back of my neck prickled as we walked farther and farther into the facility.

"Ah, here we are," Cooper said, stopping at an unmarked door. "After you."

I stepped into an examination room and lifted my chin, mostly so I could swallow the panic. The eye chart on the wall, the blood pressure cuff, the little cabinet that held swabs and needles, all of it felt like any hospital room. Cooper closed the door behind us. With one of his long arms, he reached out and patted the crinkly tissue-paper-covered examination table. "Have a seat."

I did so though I stayed tense. What if I took off right now, while his back was turned, and he was sitting down to log data into the computer? He was stronger than me, but was he faster? Could I get out of the facility before any of the guards caught me?

All signs pointed to no. Especially with my hands still in the cuffs.

"So how have you felt lately?" he asked as he picked up a clipboard. "Any issues with the Mobium or the cancer?"

"I—I got dizzy a little," I said, as the best lies were wrapped in truth. "A couple nights ago. It was probably because I didn't eat. Do you really have to send me back to prison? I didn't do it, you know. I'd never work with Chelsea."

Oh god, I'd almost used her real name.

"I don't make the rules. I just follow them." Cooper scribbled a note and looked up with a genial smile. He asked the expected follow-up questions about the dizzy spell. I'd been through the checklist so many times that I answered almost on autopilot. My brain scrambled to come up with some kind of escape plan.

"I'm going to take your blood pressure and check your pulse," he said. I coughed to hide my instinctive flinch when he stood up. He frowned anyway when he laid his fingers on the pulse point at my wrist. "Your heart is racing. You doing okay?"

"Just—*really* don't want to go back to prison," I said weakly. "Do you know how many enemies I've made in there?"

"Oh, come on. We both know you never did anything of note to them. That was all your boyfriend."

"Yeah, I don't think they're all that wrapped up in the technicalities, thanks," I said, thinking of my enemies in Detmer.

"Well, if you're innocent, I'm sure they'll get you out of there as soon as they clear matters up. Shame we lost Angélica. She was one of the best."

Yeah, I bet you think it's a damn shame since you're the one who actually killed Angélica, I thought. The rage that rose up was so sharp and potent it nearly made me dizzy, and I struggled to keep it inside. Hopefully, none of the sudden malevolence showed up on my face. I didn't need that kind of trouble until I found a way to escape. *If* I found a way.

"I miss her," I said. "I didn't know her long, but she was the best."

"Mm. Hold still." He held a device like a hole punch over my arm. I tensed. Should I fight him off? I could kick him pretty easily, though standing over me like that, he had me at a crazy disadvantage. The device bit into my arm, eliciting a yelp.

I looked at the bleeding puncture in my forearm. "A little warning might have been nice."

"It hurts more if you know it's coming." He turned away to shove an actual piece of my skin into a test tube. I eyed it uneasily. He was collecting samples. I had officially become a specimen to study, like Brooke.

Just one more way we were alike.

"If you're taking pieces of me," I said, wiping the blood on my pants, "I'm entitled to a warning. And shouldn't you have used a local or something?"

"You heal fast." He rifled through a drawer. When he pulled out a syringe with a giant needle attached, I had to swallow hard several times. "Ten minutes from now, it won't even hurt. That Mobium of yours is pretty great."

"I don't know," I said. "Right now it just feels like more trouble than it's worth."

"Mm. Well, now that we're done with the formalities . . . ." Cooper waved a distracted hand at the wall, and the door burst open.

I didn't have time to shout when the men rushed in, crowding the space and reaching for me. Every survival instinct kicked in at once. I fell back on my elbows and kicked out, catching the first man in the chin with the blade of my foot. As he careened to the side, a second man tried to grab me. I twisted left and ducked under his arm, smashing the back of my fist into his ear. I blocked a strike from the third man. He lunged for me. I tried to scramble away, but there was nowhere for me to go. They pinned me to the wall, all three of them holding me down. Even with my enhanced strength, there were too many of them for me to wrestle off. That didn't stop me from trying or from turning the air blue once I failed.

"Told you she's a fighter," Cooper said.

I panted hard. The men holding me down were all giants, but they grunted at the effort. I wasn't going to make any of this easy for them. "What the hell is going on? I thought you said this was a checkup!"

Cooper ignored me and palmed a button on the wall. It slid away with a whisper of noise, revealing a doorway. Beyond it, I saw a surgical operating room that made all of the blood in my body turn to ice. No amount of struggling seemed to help; the men picked me up and carried me inside.

"Just running some tests," Cooper said, as I was strapped onto the operating table on my side, my wrists and ankles locked into place. In a flash, I was back on Dr. Mobius's table with his ugly mug leaning over me. I'd been on my back then, stretched out and staring up at a lightbulb in a dirty basement. Now I was in a polished operating room, and I was on my side with my knees locked into place against my chest. Other than that, it was essentially the same.

I squeezed my eyes shut and strained against the cuffs as a tear broke free.

Cooper wiped it up with a piece of gauze. I flinched away.

"Don't worry," he said, flicking the gauze toward a trash can. "With your pain tolerance, this will hardly register at all. Some quick tests, and we'll have you right on your way back to prison."

"You're lying," I said, since the clueless act was starting to get a little thin. "This isn't a Davenport facility at all, is it?"

"Oh, Gail." He nodded at the men, who all pushed down on my side to keep me still. I felt their breath on my skin and tried to fight harder, but they were rapidly draining my strength, and I was getting nowhere. When Cooper pushed the needle into my arm, I screamed.

It echoed off the walls of the operating theater around me. A feeling of weightlessness began to flood through me.

Cooper tucked his tongue in his cheek as he bent over so that our faces were level. "I won't lie to you. If that hurt, you're in real trouble. We haven't even started on the *real* pain."

"Get fucked," I said.

He tsked. "Language."

"You sound like a bad Saturday morning cartoon

villain." The room began to shift around me. Everything stopped feeling permanent or solid, and my eyes had a hard time focusing on anything in the liquid aftermath. All sense of up and down became incomprehensible. Instead, I drifted vaguely sideways.

"She'll shake off the drugs quickly, so I'd better get to work," Cooper told the men as he stood.

Telling him off again didn't seem like a worthy expenditure of my remaining strength, so I rested my forehead against the cold metal and let another tear leak across the bridge of my nose. At least we had confirmation that Kiki had been telling the truth, my brain pointed out, though I hadn't really doubted her.

It was just depressing to note that I'd finally faced a true bastion of evil, and I'd gone down with barely a fight.

Story of my life, really.

Something cold slithered up my back. Cooper cut off my tank top, leaving me in my jeans and bra. "Really?" I asked, my voice slurred. "Must we?"

When he swabbed on some kind of liquid up my spine, I closed my eyes against the familiar yellow smell of iodine.

"Little pinch," Cooper said, and stabbed me in the back.

I screamed as the needle went into my spine, punching through my skin. The pain hit in waves. It radiated from my back and raced all the way to my toes. Even high as a kite, I felt my mouth drop open. Cooper chuckled and did *something* that made my vision go white. When I screamed again, it echoed.

An eternity later, he pulled the needle out. "That's that," he said.

"So we're done?" My voice was barely a whisper. I was sweating and overheated, and my back throbbed so hard I could feel it in my teeth. I tried to raise my head, but I couldn't even do that. Everything hurt too much. "This was fun. Let's never do it again."

"Such a little optimist. Let's move her onto her back, gentlemen."

I don't know how long it took to do all the tests. All I knew was that by the time Cooper had finished, he didn't even need the drugs to subdue me anymore. I was so out of it from the agony that they were able to unchain me from the table, wrap my wrists in a length of rope that chafed at my skin, and drag me down the hall while I was too weak to protest. My feet dragged behind me on the linoleum as they pulled me through the facility.

I was covered in sweat and shaky. They hadn't replaced my shirt or given me shoes. My lower back actively throbbed in time with my midsection (which he'd also punctured). It made me ill to know that there were bits of me sitting in little specimen jars in his minifridge, but I was too weak to fight for my life, let alone mete out punishment for that.

"Is she going in one of the cages, boss?" one of the men asked as they hauled me along.

"I'd love to keep her. A perfect specimen, and I've never seen such a stable reaction to the Mobium before. The good doctor must have altered his formula. But unfortunately," Cooper went on, sounding more and more like far too many mad scientists I'd had the displeasure of meeting, "I've learned a thing or two watching this girl."

"Yeah?"

"She has an unbroken streak of getting rescued, usually by that idiot savant in green."

I still couldn't raise my head, but my fists clenched a little. He would pay for the torture he'd just inflicted on me, sure, but insulting Guy? I'd happily strangle him for that alone.

"So this one, I can't keep," Cooper said. "I've probably pushed my luck as it is. Time to dispose of the body."

This really was not my day. I jerked my head when we passed through a door, and I felt sunlight on the back of my neck.

"Ah, here we go. This way, gents."

When they stopped walking, I gritted my teeth and picked my head up. They'd dragged me to some sort of loading area behind the complex. It was empty, save for a beat-up old clunker and a black van, both of them horribly ominous. The clunker had its trunk open. A man leaned against the open driver's door, wearing a ball cap and sunglasses.

I really did not want to be shoved into that trunk. It was an irrational dislike, but if I was going to die in a car trunk, the car should not be older than me.

"Hold her arm out," Cooper said as he pulled on a fresh pair of latex gloves. He'd avoided touching me, I realized. He didn't want the Mobium absorbing his abilities. When the men raised my cuffed arms, he pulled out his pocket knife and flicked the blade open. "Sorry to damage the goods, but we need the decoy to be convincing."

I stared at the edge of the blade, the way it glinted evilly in the light. "That's a lie. You're not sorry at all."

When he dug the knife into my forearm, squeezing so that blood dripped into the trunk of the car, I didn't give him the satisfaction of screaming. I clenched my jaw and sucked air through my teeth, shallow breaths that didn't hold off the sparks at the edges of my sight. My knees buckled.

I didn't scream, though I did spit at him when he yanked out a hank of my hair. "Asshole. I'll kill you for that."

"I sincerely doubt you could, Gail." He sprinkled the hair over the trunk and jerked his head at the men holding me. "Put her in the van."

My arm, stomach, and back all bled as they dragged me off, but I kept my head up. I looked back over my shoulder in time to see Cooper pass over a wad of cash to the man in the ball cap. The gun the man handed back was unmistakable. He climbed into the clunker and started the engine, driving off right away.

So that was how Cooper was going to kill me.

How utterly and boringly pedestrian.

They threw me in the van, which had one of those partitions between the driver's seat and the cargo area. Dust geysered as I landed on a rolled-up carpet, making me cough and hack as I lay there. I fell sideways off the carpet and lay on my side, curled up as though that could stop everything from hurting so badly. When they slammed the doors closed behind me, it left me alone in the semidarkness, looking up at the metal shelves that lined the van.

Bleeding, tied up, and in the back of an unmarked van. I'd faced greater odds, but not that often.

When the engine started up, I moaned. The vibrations sang through my injuries so that everything throbbed in great detail, from my teeth to my toenails. When I lifted my head, I could see several airtight containers near the back of the van, held down with bungee cords. The skull and crossbones on the jars made me do a double take. Was that acid? Great. So not only was he going to shoot me in the head, he was going to dissolve my body, and none of my friends or Guy would ever know what had happened to me. They'd find the car with my hair and blood in it in some junkyard somewhere, but I'd always be a mystery.

I rested my head back against the carpet and closed my eyes. Everything smelled like dust, making my nose itch. To make matters worse, the universe seemed to be laughing at me because something was poking into my side. Frustrated, I wiggled around until I could pull it free. I nearly tossed it away before I realized what I had in my hand.

A gas mask.

With a Raptor logo on the front.

A post-it note was taped to the back: BRACE YOURSELF.

I fumbled to put it on, pulling the straps as snug as I could around my head. It wasn't easy with my hands tied. Then I wiggled until I was under one of the shelves, pulled the rolled-up carpet in to serve as a cushion, and waited, not even daring to hope.

Ten seconds later, all hell broke loose.

CHAPTER TWENTY

By now, the shattering glass and the *pop-hiss* of a smoke grenade going off was old hat to me, but I still shrieked when the canister bounced into the back of the van. It hit the floor and ricocheted onto the shelf opposite, spewing clouds of bright blue gas into the air. Cooper's ripe curse followed a split second later, and the van began to swerve. I gritted my teeth and held on to one of the posts holding the shelving up with what remained of my strength. Agony sang through my battered body as I bounced from the carpet to the outer wall of the van. Through it all, I could hear something sloshing around near my feet.

I held on as hard as I could, squeezing my eyes shut behind the mask. Cooper began to cough, deep, hacking noises that led to gagging. From around the van, I heard *pops*, like firecrackers going off.

An explosion shook the ground under the van,

briefly tilting my entire world to the side. Somehow, though, Cooper must have regained control, for the van slammed back onto the ground, juddering hard enough that I hit the front of my mask against the bottom of the shelf and saw stars. My brain helpfully chose that moment to inform me what the sloshing noise was: the acid. A second later, it reminded me that when the skull and crossbones was red, that meant Lazarus acid.

"Oh, *shit*," I said, my vision going briefly white with sheer terror. It was enough to inspire at least a *little* strength, enough to pull me out from under the shelf, at least. Cooper must have really wanted me gone. Lazarus acid could eat through a battleship hull in under a minute. A disgruntled chemistry-professor-turned-supervillain who'd kidnapped me two years before had been all too happy to provide multiple demonstrations.

And now I was stuck in the back of a van with three large containers of it. A van driven by the most evil man I knew and under siege by the Raptor. Just great.

I fought my way out into the open, grunted when a particularly nasty bit of swerving threw my back into the shelf, and pounced on the sliding door. I needed to get out of the van before Raptor did something like hit it with a missile, as I didn't particularly fancy having my life saved, then being subsequently melted.

I looked around frantically until I spotted a jagged bit of metal on the underside of one of the shelves. I sawed away at the rope as fast as I could, which wasn't easy with Cooper's driving like we were on an obstacle course. My terror amplified every swish of the acid against the sides of the containers. When the rope snapped, I pushed myself to my feet. Unfortunately, Cooper chose that moment to slam hard on the brakes.

I hit the partition between the driver's seat and the rest of the van and saw stars. When I reached out to steady myself, my hand landed on something rubbery: a HAZMAT suit. Cooper really had come prepared. That sort of foresight might have been admirable—provided I might have admired his foresight if he weren't currently using it to kill me. He jumped out of the van and slammed the door behind him.

Gunshots outside made me drop to the floor. The sliding door was locked when I tested it. When I tried to yank on the handle as hard as I could, it broke off in my hand.

"This is really not my day," I said, throwing the handle at the wall. A new spate of gunfire made me drop to a crouch again.

From outside the van, I heard Cooper's voice, but it was muffled. I couldn't make out anything he was saying, but if he was like any of the other villains who had kidnapped me and stuffed me in the back of a van, it was probably something mocking.

"Release the hostage and surrender." Raptor's altered voice boomed through the walls of the van; she must have had speakers on the Raptor Tank. "Put the weapon down."

Fat chance of that. I tried kicking the door; it didn't

budge. And then my gaze fell on the HAZMAT gear, and I had a horrible idea.

A brilliant, horrible idea.

The gear was meant for somebody Cooper's size, but at least the pants came with suspenders. I shimmied into the pants and scrambled into the jacket, fingers fumbling in my haste. I yanked the hood up so that it covered my skin around the gas mask. It was difficult to get the cap off the first container of acid with the stiff gloves. I prayed to the patron saint of hostages, cursing when that didn't immediately solve my problems.

The cap came off with a snap.

"Here goes nothing," I said under my breath as Raptor demanded Cooper drop the gun once more. Standing as far back as I could, I splashed the acid right at the back doors. A stream of highly corrosive acid hit the doors dead center. The air filled with the acrid stench of burning. The doors began to *sizzle* and *pop*.

The shooting stopped as the acid, smoking hard enough to make me glad for the gas mask, ate a fist-sized hole in the door. Sunlight filtered in through the smoke. I stepped closer, until I could kind of make out the Raptor Tank in the distance. The hole grew bigger and bigger. Cooper stepped into view, gawking at the rapidly melting doors.

I threw the rest of the acid in the bottle. It hit him in the chest, splashing everywhere. If he'd been any less indestructible, it would have killed him instantly. Since it was Cooper, he merely dropped to his knees and clutched at his face, letting out an unearthly scream.

Two seconds later, the doors lost their structural integrity and fell right off the van. I took a deep breath, stepped back, and ran as hard as I could. Even in my weakened state, I was able to launch myself. I flew over the screaming Cooper and tumbled to a stop on a clean patch of asphalt. I started for the Tank even as I ripped the HAZMAT suit off.

Raptor appeared around the side, stocky and formidable in her armor. I opened my mouth to scream when I saw the gun in her hands, but she immediately pointed it beyond me, at Cooper.

Gunshots erupted again. Something clipped the pavement a foot to my left and ricocheted. I cut right, automatically falling into a zigzag pattern. Safety. That was my only goal. If I could get to the dark bronze tank, I would be safe. I just had to get there.

Raptor covered me, gun muzzle flashing every time she fired it toward Cooper. Bullets ricocheted off the ground and the tank in front of me, but I ran on. By some miracle, I was suddenly there, throwing myself around the back and to safety. When the hatch opened, I scurried inside. It slammed shut behind me as I ran my hands over any part of my body I could reach in a panic. Had I gotten any acid on me? I knew what it could do, I didn't want to die like that—

Raptor dropped in through the top hatch. "You didn't get any on you. You're safe."

Even an hour ago, those words would have caused terror. Now I just wanted to break down and sob. I fell forward, mouth open as I tried to pull air into my lungs and *breathe* again. Safe. Raptor had come to my rescue. Cooper wasn't going to shoot me in the head and dissolve my body in acid. I was safe.

And then I heard the Raptor swear, and looked up. The interior of the Raptor Tank wasn't actually that large: it held a bay area, where I was currently staving off a panic attack, and two padded seats in front of a console loaded with switches and gauges. Raptor had immediately taken the seat on the left. Ahead of her, through the window, I could see Cooper's van peeling out. The second door crumpled and fell off. It lay in a smoking heap on the pavement.

"Aren't you going after him?" I asked between gasps. I didn't know what I wanted the answer to be.

Cooper was dangerous, and I needed to stay as far away from him as I could get.

To my shame and relief, Raptor shook her head tightly. She pushed back her cowl so that she was Jessica Davenport again. "Can't. I've got more pressing problems to deal with. You're not the only one who's bleeding."

"What the—oh, hell." There was something wet on her glove when she lifted it, and now that I wasn't so focused, I could smell the coppery tang of blood in the air. A lot of blood. He'd clipped her in the thigh, it looked like. "It didn't hit the femoral artery, did it? Crap, that's a lot of blood. Um, okay, I know how to handle this, this happened to me once. I can—"

"Get in the seat." She reached overhead, and pulled down a kit.

"O-okay." Apparently we were working together now. I climbed into the passenger seat, though every move jarred my stomach and back. "Should you be driving with that?"

"No, which is why you're going to." She flipped a switch. A panel opened in front of me and what looked like controls for a 747 silently slid out. I gawked at them. "What are you waiting for? Drive."

"I've never—okay." I could roll with this, if it put me far away from Cooper. I pressed on what I hoped was the gas pedal, and the Raptor Tank shot forward, making me feel like a teenager with her first stick-shift car all over again.

"Who the hell taught you how to drive?" Jessica asked as she calmly sorted through the first-aid kit. Blood continued to leak onto the floor, but she was probably used to that.

"You know," I said, pushing more slowly on the gas (the Tank jumped again, but not as badly), "you *really* remind me of your mother. Where are we going?"

Jessica flipped another switch, and the windshield seemed to light up. A blue line appeared in the middle. "Follow the blue line." She grunted and peeled back a panel on her pants to expose a patch of skin marred by blood. "Missed the artery. Looks like you're not driving me to the morgue after all."

"Uh, yay?" I was still weak and dizzy, and the fact that the vehicle I was driving had a console full of more controls than a plane cockpit really wasn't helping either matter. I just had to hope that I wasn't going to accidentally flip a switch with my elbow and level a city block with a missile or something. I'd heard a lot of rumors about the Raptor Tank, and right now I really had no desire to discover if any of them were true. "But seriously, where are we going?"

"Unfinished business. You'll see in a minute." Jessica ripped open the packaging of a small, flat item. I shook my head, took a deep breath, and decided that for now I would just follow the blue line superimposed over the windshield. It made me take a U-turn. I only put the Tank up on two wheels for a second. Jessica sighed at me as she placed some kind of bandage over the gunshot wound on her leg. "How bad are you hurt? And where?"

"He cut me up some," I said. I still didn't have a shirt, so the trail of blood from the incisions on my midsection and along my spine were pretty easy to see, even in the dark. And my arm had already started to scab over. "I'm safe to drive, if that's what you're worried about."

"Whether you're actually a good driver remains to be seen."

"You could give me just a *little* leeway, considering this is my first time driving a *tank*."

"There," Jessica said, pointing up ahead. I leaned forward to squint through the windshield, and cold washed over me.

"You can't take me back there," I said, sick fear coating the back of my throat. The facility Cooper and I had just left behind was just ahead. I could see people in the parking lot now, but they were clustered far away from the building. "They *do* things there—they did this to me—"

When I tried to stomp the brakes, Jessica grabbed my elbow, her gloved fingers digging in. "Don't do that. Flip that switch by your left hand."

"Why?" I tried to pull my arm free; her grip only tightened.

"Are you going to question everything I do, or are you going to do what I say?"

"Ask your mother," I said, but when Jessica gave me a hard look, I reached over and flipped the switch.

The building exploded into a spectacularly large orange fireball. The percussive wave threw the people closest back. It barely even nudged the Raptor Tank.

"Holy *shit*!" I gawked at the plumes of black, oily smoke. "What the hell did I just do?"

"Isn't it obvious?" Jess gave me a cranky look.

I turned on her, which hurt my stomach and back. "How many people did I just kill?"

"I pulled the fire alarm. It should have been empty. Drive." Not at all bothered by the massive destruction of property we'd inflicted on the mysterious building, Jessica leaned forward and began turning dials. Belatedly, I put my foot on the gas, hard enough to leave rubber marks on the street behind us. People were too busy gawking at the burning building to really pay much attention to the armored utility vehicle that had just leapfrogged into action. "I'm putting us in stealth mode so nobody should notice us unless you keep driving like you are."

"Are you this mean to everybody you save?" I asked. Outside the tank, the air seemed to shimmer like massive amounts of heat radiating off its surface. But when I passed the mirrored windows of a storefront, I saw nothing but an overlarge SUV going by. So *that* was how the Raptor sneaked her overly conspicuous transportation around town. I'd always wondered. "Uh, thanks for that, by the way. I didn't really want to end up in a shallow grave today."

Instead of answering, Jessica sorted through the first-aid kit again. The bandage on her leg had actively begun to sizzle, which was a little worrisome, but she wasn't dripping blood on the floor anymore. "You know who told me where you were hiding out?" she asked.

"Huh?"

"My mother called me from prison in the middle of the night and gave me the address of where you were staying."

"*Rita* gave me up?" I asked. "That . . . that *bitch*."

"Don't take it personally. One thing I have learned over a lifetime with my mother is that she doesn't do things without a purpose. So when Cooper put his request in, I figured something was up." She pushed on my shoulder, luckily one of the few nonsore parts on my back, until I leaned forward. It wasn't easy to drive like that, and it put my nose perilously close to some of the switches. At least she didn't have to rustle around under my shirt since I wasn't wearing one. "Turns out I was right. Sorry to make you the bait. I needed to know how deep the corruption went. How bad did he hurt you?"

"These are probably the worst of it." I hissed through my teeth when she poured something on my back, over the place Cooper had operated on. It stung, but in the grand scheme of things, it was a tolerable pain. "So wait, were you in the building with me the whole time?"

"Explosives don't plant themselves." With a briskness that told me she was well practiced at this, she smoothed a bandage over my wound.

"You were never going to let him kill me, were you?"

"I don't believe in killing. On either side." She sealed the bandage down with her thumb and sagged back against her chair, one hand creeping toward her leg. Her breathing was beginning to grow labored, I realized. The gunshot wound hurt more than she was willing to let on.

"Are you okay?" I asked, glancing at her quickly before I focused on the road again. In the past three days, I'd driven more than I had since moving to Chicago five years before. "You don't look so hot."

"The injuries hurt worse the older you get." She finger-combed her hair back impatiently and sagged against her seat. "There's a strong chance I am about to pass out."

"What the—no, don't do that! I have no idea what the hell I'm doing."

"Something tells me you'll be all right. The GPS

will take you to a local base, and Audra will know what to do."

"Who is Audra?"

Jessica's head lolled forward suddenly.

"Raptor? Raptor! Jess!" Reaching over and jiggling her shoulder did absolutely nothing. "Damn it, don't do this, I don't know who Audra is, and I've *heard things* about your bases. I don't particularly want to get blown up today."

But it looked like I didn't have a choice. Nothing I could do would rouse Jessica Davenport. Given that she'd passed out from the bullet wound in her leg—shock, I had to figure—she needed a hospital. But I also couldn't take the *Raptor* to a hospital in her full gear, as nobody even knew she was a woman, let alone who the Raptor really was. And Jessica was a Davenport, which meant people would notice if she randomly showed up at the hospital with a gunshot wound. Surely, the Raptor had been shot and injured before. She didn't look like she was healing rapidly, so this couldn't the first time she needed medical assistance.

And she hadn't said go to the hospital. She'd said Audra would know what to do.

I really hoped she was right about that. Shaky, still weak from surviving whatever the hell Cooper had done to me, and terrified even though I was in what was probably the safest vehicle on the planet, I followed the blue line of the Raptor Tank's GPS system. It took me to a neighborhood I only knew because my old boss had lived close by and had hosted the holiday party for work a few times. When it bade me to turn into a parking garage, I took a deep breath and obeyed though I had no idea why Jessica would pick some place so public as a parking garage to house the Raptor Tank.

The attendant didn't even look up from his phone as he let us in, which was a good thing. I didn't really know how this hologram system of hers worked. Sweating and glancing nervously at the unconscious Jessica every couple of seconds, I drove in and parked in the spot it directed me to. What was I supposed to do now? There wasn't exactly a key in the ignition I could twist and remove. I had no idea what any of the switches did, and Jessica didn't look like she was going to be contributing anything to society anytime within the next ten seconds.

The Raptor Tank began to sink. I gasped in surprise before I realized this was supposed to be happening and we weren't, irrationally, melting. I stayed stiff as a board as the tank was lowered, the pavement around us rising and rising until it was level with my chin, over my head, and finally I could see some sort of underground room. It was spacious and lit moodily by the same dim yellow light that was inside the Raptor Tank. To the left, I could see an array of other vehicles: the Raptorcycle, a few fancy sports cars, what looked like some ATVs, and a—was that a *jet*? All of them bore the raised-falcon emblem associated with the Raptor. To the right, monitors covered an entire wall, with several computers spread out below. I could see a boxing ring shoved into the corner, as well as weight-training equipment and a treadmill. A little kitchenette area stood in another corner.

Standing in the middle of it all was a woman. She wore a crisp blouse and a skirt, with her hair twisted into an elegant chignon, and she honestly should have clashed with the moody cave all around her. But she watched our platform lower itself all the way to the ground, her expression politely disinterested. When we touched down with a tiny gust of air, she stepped forward and clicked a button on a little pad in her hand.

The top and back hatches of the tank opened as one.

Time to face the firing squad, I thought. I climbed out of the seat and crawled through the back hatch. Immediately, I put my hands in the air. "I can explain, I swear—"

"No need for that." The woman sized me up quickly and coolly. "Gail Godwin," she said. "She mentioned she might have you with her. I am Audra Yi, Miss Davenport's personal assistant. How much medical assistance do you require?"

"At this point, probably just some Neosporin, but Raptor—Jessica—she's hurt bad."

"They are already taking care of it."

"Who . . ." I turned and stopped midsentence. Somehow, so silently that even my enhanced hearing hadn't picked up on it, two wheeled robots had appeared with a stretcher. A robot arm had descended from the ceiling and was lifting the still-unconscious Jessica onto the stretcher. It was the most futuristic technology I'd ever seen, so it wasn't surprising that I gawked like a schoolgirl. They wheeled the unconscious superhero off to another part of the room that I couldn't see. "Oh."

"Davenport money," Audra said, her voice dry. "It buys the best. If you'll follow me? I'm sure you would like a change of clothes."

"*Please.*" It was cold in the cave, and my shirt was little but a memory now. The concrete flooring was also freezing against my bare feet. I shivered hard as I followed the personal assistant. "What is this place?"

"The Raptor keeps several bases around the planet, as I'm sure you've no doubt figured out by now. This is her secondary Chicago residence." Audra's heels clicked on the floor as she led me through the base. "I've been pushing for her to make things a bit homier, but, unfortunately, she prefers the spartan approach in most everything she does. Would you like anything to eat or drink? It might be some time before Miss Davenport wakes up."

"Is there a way I can get a message to somebody?" I asked, ignoring the edge of hunger gnawing at my middle. If Cooper knew his cover was blown, Kiki and the others needed to be warned.

"If your message involves Dr. Cooper," Audra said, "there is no need to worry. Miss Davenport uploaded the data she gathered at the Lodi Corporation base straight to the heads of Davenport Industries. Dr. Cooper is now at large, but all of your friends have been warned."

"And do they know I'm safe?" I asked, a tight feeling my chest. "I need to get to them right now. If they think Cooper has me, they might try to take him on, and I just saw that man blink off a faceful of Lazarus acid. They need to stay far away."

"Your friends have been notified that you are safe with the Raptor. As for now, Miss Davenport left instructions that we should maintain radio silence," Audra said, opening a small door off to the side. The lights came on automatically, and I followed her into what looked like some kind of armory. Shelves and cabinets filled the place, all neatly labeled with each type of weapon. I saw throwing darts, several types of guns, and even a small cannon. An RPG rested carefully on a custom-built shelf. Audra ignored all of these and instead strolled on as I followed her. She stopped in front of an alcove that held several Raptor suits, neatly, on hangers. Ignoring those, she collected a shirt and a set of pants with cargo pockets. "What is your shoe size?"

Dazed, gazing at the Raptor suits, I told her.

"You're in luck. Miss Davenport's youngest wears that size."

Great, I had the same size foot as a ten-year-old. The realization that Raptor kept gear in her secret base for her kids was a little disconcerting, as well, but I accepted the boots that Audra passed me with a grateful nod.

Twenty minutes later, I was clean, my midsection had been bandaged, and even better, I had a shirt on again. It was long-sleeved and dark gray, which would be miserable if I had to go outside into the August weather. But in Raptor's superchilled underground base, it was perfect. Audra had handed me a dark green package, one of those meals that they gave people in the military when they were deployed places. The food tasted a little bit like cardboard, and it took me three tries to figure out the food warmer, but it was sustenance. I ate it all as I sat on the corner of the boxing ring.

In truth, it was nice to be left alone. I'd come so close to a shallow grave that I would probably shake for days. A chance to sit and digest my near-death experience was almost a luxury at this point. I stayed where I was, resting one side of my back against the post at the corner of the boxing ring so as not to jar the injuries from the surgeries.

When I heard the approaching *click* of an altered gait, accompanied by the tap of a cane, I turned and raised an eyebrow at Jessica Davenport. "So you *do* heal faster than average."

She snorted. "Keep telling yourself that. You okay?"

"I've been better, but that's not saying much." My hands had finally stopped shaking, at least. "Why did you use me as bait? You couldn't have known he wasn't going to kill me on the spot."

"I had a listening device on you." Grimacing and keeping her injured leg straight, she lowered herself to sit on the edge of the ring, outside the ropes. She held her hand up and only because I looked closely did I see the thin piece of hair dangling from between her fingers. "I attached it to you before I handed you over. I will say this for you: you don't flinch in the face of danger. If he'd made any move to kill you, I had a backup plan in place." She coughed a little. Her skin was so waxy pale that it made her blonde hair look dark by comparison. "Always have redundancies. First rule of this game."

"That must be nice. Plan A never works, and I never have a Plan B."

"You'll need to change that if you want to survive. Though you seem to be doing a pretty good job of it so far."

"No thanks to your mother," I said, since everything that had happened in the last two months was definitely Rita Detmer's fault.

"How did you get mixed up in her plans?" Jessica looked me up and down. Unlike Audra's clinical interest earlier, it felt more like a threat assessment. "Did you cross one of the few people she calls a friend?"

"As far as I can tell, it's because I'm too famous to kill." Though it hurt my sore midsection and stretched the bandage across my back, I hugged my knees to my chest. "So yay for my infamous celebrity status, I guess. So you know the truth, then? I didn't kill Angélica. She's alive. And your family didn't even give me a trial."

"I know."

"That's not right," I said.

"I know."

"You're not going to apologize?"

"There are reasons we do what we do. They're not perfect, but there's past precedent." There wasn't an ounce of apology in Jessica's face when I glared at her. She looked as though she'd made her peace with the way the superhero world worked a long time before. I could sense an undercurrent of pity that I hated.

"It's wrong," I said.

"Then fix it." Jessica said it like it was that easy, like the entire world hadn't been built to keep people in the dark and away from the knowledge they needed.

Fury tried to bubble up in my midsection. I swallowed until I could control it. "I don't want to fix it. I want . . ."

"You want what?"

"I want this to be *over*," I said, my voice breaking. I could feel the imminent threat of tears, but I closed my eyes and willed them away. I'd cried enough. "I want to be in the know again, not to have to question everything and be lied to all the time. I want to know where I stand with people and with whatever it is I am now. I want Lemuel Cooper gone and away from where he can hurt anybody ever again. And I want to see Guy."

"That last one, I can help with," Jessica said, and I looked over at her in surprise. The contrition I longed for had never appeared, but she looked a bit sardonic now. She tapped her leg under the injury. "I'm out of the fight against Cooper. So I can't help you with that. But I can help you with other things."

"Why would you?"

"Honor system. Your friends are all holed up in a place where they hope you'll return next."

"Where's that?"

Jessica smiled without showing her teeth. "Audra will take you."

CHAPTER TWENTY-ONE

When Audra pulled the perfectly plain and serviceable SUV up in front of the building, I gaped. "Really? They're here?"

"According to Miss Davenport. I've very rarely known her to be wrong." Before I could climb out of the car, she held out a business card. "Just in case."

"In case of what?" I asked, but Audra only gave me a tight-lipped smile. I sighed at her and climbed out of the car. "Thank you for the ride. I think I'll be able to find my way from here."

"I figured," she said, and pulled away from the curb in front of my building.

I stayed on the sidewalk for a minute, pushing my shirtsleeves up against the heat. I hadn't seen my apartment since the morning I'd left it to go find Naomi and been attacked by Chelsea, née Brooklyn, nearly two months ago. Vicki had told me that Davenport would keep up the payments for me, but I'd kind of figured being sent to prison meant that had lapsed. Evidently, it hadn't.

I took the outside steps up to my place two at a time, the way I always had. Everything felt familiar and foreign at the same time, like my skin didn't quite fit. On my doorstep, I paused. It felt absurd to knock on my own door, but I did it anyway.

It was wrenched open less than three seconds later. "Gail!"

"No, don't—" I said, but not in time, since Guy scooped me up and squeezed me. It made my vision go temporarily hazy since I hadn't completely healed from the surgeries. "Oof."

"Sorry!" Guy, apparently realizing his mistake, all but dropped me back on my feet, his eyes wide in horror. "Are you okay? You're hurt!"

"I'm getting better." I breathed through my teeth until the sharpest pain had subsided. "Been kind of a crazy morning. How are you? Are you okay?"

"Of course. Nothing's happened to me. All I did was get back to the house to find you gone." He shook his head in confusion as he stepped back to let me into my own apartment. I could tell right away that the air-conditioning had only been kicked on less than an hour before. I wanted to sink to the ground there inside the doorway and just look around. I hadn't really had an attachment to any of my stuff—my apartment had been wrecked too many times for me to have nice things—but I didn't realize until that moment just how much

I missed what little I did have. "I've been worried sick. Are you okay?"

"That's . . . a difficult question to answer at the moment," I said as honestly as I could. "Raptor handed me over to Cooper and used me as bait. So far today, I've been treated like a lab rat, nearly ended up in a shallow grave, I've burned Cooper with acid, and I have discovered more than I ever really thought I would know about the Raptor."

"So a regular day for you?" Angélica called from my living room.

"Or thereabouts." I squeezed Guy's arm and headed into my living room. Naomi was on the floor with my old laptop, frowning intently at something on the screen, and Angélica lay on the couch, looking a little less like death than the last time I'd seen her. I let out a breath. They were both okay. They hadn't been hurt during Raptor's siege on the house. "Hi," I said. "I'd say welcome to my apartment, but it looks like you guys have already made yourselves at home. Sorry about the mess."

"We weren't sure where else to go," Guy said, sounding apologetic. "We really need to set up some fail-safes for this sort of situation in the future."

"If Cooper doesn't kill us all," I said. I dropped into the battered old recliner I'd picked up at a yard sale and made Jeremy muscle into my apartment a long time ago. "Sorry. It's just been that kind of a day."

"I'll go make some tea," Guy said.

Angélica pushed herself so that she was standing. She lifted her foot.

Naomi looked up. "No, not again!"

But it was already too late. Angélica took a step, and an instant later, there was a crashing sound from behind my chair. I leapt to my feet, fists up, but it was only Angélica, shaking her head in a daze. There was now a dent in the drywall.

"What?" I asked, looking back at the couch like I fully expected to see another Angélica standing there.

"We think it's the Mobium," Naomi said, setting the laptop aside.

Angélica muttered something in Portuguese.

"Is she okay?" Guy called from the kitchen.

I dragged Angélica back to the couch. "For a fixed value of okay," I called back. When Angélica was safely back to where she wouldn't slingshot herself around the room and cause any more property damage, I raised my eyebrows. "That looked fun."

She groaned. "Shut up," she said. "I'm supposed to be helping *you*, not the other way around."

"I think you get a pass when you die and come back to life thanks to a miracle isotope." I looked over at Naomi, asking a wordless question.

"It's been happening all day," she said, understanding me perfectly. "And no, we can't get her to stop getting up and down. We've tried."

"Angélica," I said.

She muttered something else that I heard perfectly but chose to ignore.

"So what happened?" Naomi asked, looking up from the laptop. "You look like death warmed over, and you have new clothes, so I'm assuming there's a story there."

"And it's a doozy." When Guy came back with the tea, I filled all of them in on my morning.

"So Davenport knows I'm alive after all, huh," Angélica said. "It's nice that you won't be going back to prison for that."

If Cooper found us again, wrongful imprisonment was going to be the least my worries. He'd been planning to dissolve me in acid, after all.

"Yeah," I said, meeting Guy's gaze across the room. I could see that he was clearly furious, but his color looked so much better. The burns from Chelsea's powers were just faint red marks on his arms and neck. "That's one thing we don't have to worry about."

"Just a thousand others we have to deal with," Naomi said, still typing away at my laptop. "So Raptor's injured?"

I gave her a look.

"What? I'm still a journalist at heart. These things are important to know."

Angélica shook her head. "I'm going to have a long talk with Jessie."

Jessie. Guy and Angélica both called the most famous superhero "Jessie."

"Her ethics do seem to leave a bit to be desired," Naomi said, "leaving you to undergo that kind of torture, Gail."

"Tell me about it." I was pretty much done with all Davenports, Kiki included. It wasn't her fault, and she'd done the best she could under the circumstances. I could begrudgingly admit that, but from where I was sitting, I was a little tired of all of them. Speaking of which . . . "Where's Kiki? Somewhere safe?"

"She's been checking in regularly." Guy held up his phone. "And Vicki and Sam have, too. They're out looking for Cooper."

"Like we should be." Angélica closed her eyes and rose unsteadily to her feet again. When all three of us moved to stop her, she glowered us into silence. "It's not going to get better if I don't learn to control it. Stop hovering, you nags."

"Stop damaging my apartment, then," I said. "Obviously, I'll never get my security deposit back, but the dents don't exactly go with the decor."

"Bite me," she said, laughing, as she carefully put her foot down. "And stop watching me, you freaks. I just have to go to the bathroom."

She took another step and blurred back into existence down the hallway, right in front of the bathroom door.

"Was that on purpose?" I called.

"We'll go with yes."

I immediately turned to Naomi. "What do you have?"

"Pretty much *nada*. There's really nothing on this Cooper guy online. There was a news report about a gas leak and a fire about a building a few miles over—"

"Raptor," I said.

"And it looks like there's some roadwork nearby that due to a chemical leak—"

"Me," I said.

"And the typical minor villains are up to their usual antics. The official press office for superheroes—which I'm guessing is secretly run by Davenport—put out a release that there's a villain at large and local law enforcement should not approach him." She turned my laptop screen so I could see a company shot of Cooper. The Davenport Industries logo on his polo shirt had been cropped out. "Doesn't exactly look like the mad-scientist type. But—oh shit."

"What?" Guy and I both asked.

"I'm sorry—you've still got your e-mail program open on this, and it came up, and, well, look." She turned the laptop around to show us, and my abdominal muscles clenched so hard it made the incision ache all over again. The sight on the screen was a very familiar one to me: nondescript room with no identifying features, bad lighting, and an unconscious hostage. A smug, superior hostage taker.

I was used to being the hostage. And so was Brooklyn Gianelli. By all appearances, she was unconscious at the moment, head lolling forward. Cooper had one hand wrapped around her neck. The other held the camera over his head, maximizing the angle for his completely macabre selfie. A patch of disfigured and red skin ran up the side of his neck and covered most of his face, but his eyes were clear and malevolent.

"Hi, Gail," he said to the camera. "I figured this would be familiar to you, so we don't need to go through all of the bells and whistles. Not with you. We both know I'm done, as far as Davenport is concerned. No use pretending I was ever going to keep that job. But it's not over yet, and I know Mobius had notebooks he kept from us." His smile turned surprisingly brittle. "So here's how it's going to be: you've got two hours. Get Mobius's notebooks and bring them to me, or I kill this woman. Come alone if you don't want her or anybody else to die."

I half expected him to say something ridiculous like "Peace!" Instead, the screen just cut to black.

"Is he *serious*? Like I'm going to drop everything to save the woman who almost killed Guy?" I said. A second later, I ran my hand over my face. It did nothing to stop the sudden tension headache. I might hate Brook and everything she'd done to people I loved, but she was a hostage. "Of course I'm going to, and he knows that. Ugh."

"Gail," Guy said, a warning note in his voice. "You're not thinking about—"

"I hate her," I said, glaring at the black screen. Fear and panic wanted to well up and overpower me, but, honestly, I was so done with being scared at this point. I hadn't lied when I'd told Jessica I just wanted it over. I wanted Cooper gone, blasted into orbit preferably. Maybe he could survive up there, maybe he couldn't. I didn't care. "But she's been through enough, and if there's anybody on the planet that gets that, it's me. Where are the notebooks?"

"Kiki has them," Naomi said.

Angélica stepped out of the bathroom, tripped over

her own feet, and grunted as she phased herself to the couch. "Guy's face tells me I missed something," she said.

"Cooper's holding Chelsea hostage. He wants the Mobium notebooks, and he wants Gail to bring them. Alone," Naomi said.

Angélica's look told me all I needed to know about where she stood on that issue: no way in hell was any of that happening.

"I know, I know," I said. "I'm not just going to go waltzing up and hand everything over. But how do you take down a man like that?" I wanted to shudder. Everything he'd done to me was so fresh in my mind, and it would take weeks—weeks I probably didn't have, with Cooper after me—to unpack all of it. He'd been so merciless. It hadn't bothered him in the slightest to torture me. I pulled my knees up to my chest and wrapped my arms around my legs. I wanted to be as small as possible, which was pretty easy to do for somebody my size. "He's the next best thing to indestructible. You saw his face in that video. That's all the Lazarus acid did to him."

"Maybe we could throw him in Detmer with all of the other supervillains?" Naomi said. "Though, given how easy it is to escape from there, and how bad he has it out for you . . ."

"We aren't justice. We just save the day," Guy said though he looked like he wanted to agree with Naomi.

"All right." Angélica climbed back to her feet. "Let's go beat his ass, then. He can't take all of us."

"Excuse me?" Guy said. "You're not going any-where."

Angélica made a noise like an incorrect buzzer at a game show. "Try again."

"You can barely take two steps without running into a wall. In this state, you're more of a liability than a help. You need to stay home and rest. Trust me," Guy said. "We'll have *plenty* of people to take out Cooper."

"That asshole killed me. I am *not* staying home like some—"

"As helpful as this superhero posturing isn't," Naomi said, cutting off my former trainer, "it's not ex-actly coming up with a plan, is it?"

A plan.

I unfolded myself abruptly, sitting up and tilting my head.

"Oh-ho," Naomi said, pointing at me. "Gail's got idea-face. This is going to be good."

It really wasn't, I thought, as my brain whirled. Unformed bits and pieces that had been sitting at the edges of my mind began to take shape into something that vaguely resembled a plan—if you squinted or were very drunk. "Raptor told me," I started to say. I paused and licked my lips. My throat was dry. "Raptor told me that I need a plan, and redundancies. And she's right. I saw Cooper earlier. The acid didn't kill him, but it *hurt* him. And when Raptor gassed him, I heard him coughing. It affected him, and I didn't even realize until now that that's weird."

"He overcame it, though," Angélica said, a frown line appearing between her eyebrows.

"He did," I said. "Maybe there's a brief window in time where something *will* affect him, or maybe he evolves like I do, but either way, I've got an idea. Somebody call Kiki. We're going to need a doctor."

CHAPTER TWENTY-TWO

It didn't take much research to figure out where Cooper was holding Brook hostage. After all, he'd already made such outrageous demands, it figured that he likely didn't want to throw any more roadblocks up against my meeting them. In the end, it wasn't me we should have worried about.

It was Guy.

"I haven't been back here," he said, not looking up from the steering wheel of the van I'd borrowed from Jessica Davenport (who had not been surprised to receive my "just in case" phone call almost right away). His jaw was clenched so tightly that I was suffering from a sympathetic tension headache. I couldn't be sure if it was because he *really* didn't like the plan or if the area was affecting him. Either way, I stayed quiet. "Not since the explosion—and I didn't even want to be here that night in the first place. It just figures he *would* pick this place. Why is he such a bastard?"

"I'm gonna guess 'dropped on his head as a baby,' since any other answer makes me feel depressed about humanity in general," I said.

It surprised a small smile out of Guy. He looked through the windshield and down the road. We couldn't actually see the abandoned cement factory, since it was over half a mile away. But that didn't matter. Not only had Cooper kidnapped Brook, the woman he'd been experimenting on for years, but he was now holding her hostage at the same factory where the Bookmans had received their superpowers. The genesis of it all, as it were. It was such a grandiosely cruel thing to do that I had to wonder why I hadn't immediately pegged him as a supervillain upon our first meeting. You'd think his cologne would have given him away or something.

"You going to be able to handle it?" I asked Guy.

He nodded. "I've been through worse. Hell, I've been through worse just today. Coming back to Mobius's house and finding you gone, that wasn't fun."

It hadn't been fun for me, either, but I didn't say that. I only reached out and grabbed his hand. The texture of his glove was familiar against my palm. He was back in his Blaze gear again, and I could openly admit that I felt a sense of relief to see him in the green and black once more.

"It's not too late to escape to that beach resort and get away from all of this," I said, mustering up a smile I didn't feel.

"And let all our friends have all of the fun without us?" he asked.

"Good point. They would be lost without us."

"You realize we can hear you two jerks," Naomi said in our ears.

Guy and I winced as one. Apparently I wasn't the only one who had forgotten we were both wearing earbuds.

"Your flirting is also completely sad," Naomi went on.

"I don't know." Vicki was whispering, which made sense as she was already in place. She, Jeremy, and Kiki were already in the building. "They're kind of adorable, don't you think? In a G-rated sort of way. Hey, are you two going to get it on now that that Gail's no longer a jailbird? Curious third parties want to know."

"Vicki," Guy said.

"Quit talking, Burroughs," Naomi said. She had set up camp over two miles away, in another one of Raptor's vehicles. It looked like a bakery delivery van, but it was lined with monitors. I could just picture her inside, typing away at one of the twelve keyboards. "You'll give your position away."

"Fine." I heard Vicki let out a huff of breath before she clicked off.

Guy tapped his ear to turn his microphone off. "Whoops," he said. "That could have gotten embarrassing rather quickly. Gail—"

"I'm not going to change my mind," I said, stopping him before he made the same protest he'd made three times on the way over. The clock was running out.

There simply wasn't *time* to come up with a new plan. "I'm doing this whether you like it or not. It's easier for all of us if you just get on board."

"And if he shoots you on sight?"

"I'll duck," I said with a confidence I didn't feel. "You and Vicki will be there to look out for me. I'm not worried about it."

"That makes one of us."

"Don't let him shoot me, then," I said. "Otherwise, we're never making it to that island."

He squeezed my hand. "You're very into this island idea."

"I just really want a vacation." We didn't have much time left, and I didn't want to spend it rehashing a point that neither of us was going to back down over. I slid closer to him and kissed him. He didn't even tense up in surprise this time, which was a step forward, though he did pull back more quickly than I would have liked. I gave him a questioning look. "What?"

"I'm not taking you to a tropical island for our first date," he said.

I started laughing. "What? Why not?"

"Because at some point, I will need to top that date, and like I said, you're very set on this island idea. So let's work up to it. Maybe start with dinner and a movie?"

"Deal. And—oh, she's back." I jerked my head at him to pull down his mask.

With a sigh, he obeyed. "Time to go."

Portia appeared right next to the passenger-side door with an annoyed look on her face. The first time she'd done that, after transporting Vicki into the abandoned factory, it had made all of us jump. By now, I was completely used to it. "Last trip," she said, looking considerably harassed. "*This* is why I never told you about what I can do, by the way. For precisely this reason. This is so gross."

"Saving the day is gross?" I asked Portia, as Guy climbed out of the van and gave me one last look. Even with the mask on, I knew his expression. He wouldn't talk in front of Portia, though. Jeremy had worn a ski mask before we'd met up with Portia beforehand, just to keep Blaze's identity safe. She hadn't even appeared to notice when we skipped him in the introductions.

Portia rolled her eyes. "You know what I mean," she said. When Guy scooped her up the same way he'd carried me away during countless rescues, they both vanished, and I was left alone with the van.

I clicked my mic back on and tried to ignore the fact that my hands were shaking. "Last package on its way," I said. "Putting five minutes on the clock to let Portia get out of there safely."

They were the longest five minutes of my life, as only Naomi was able to talk. Everybody else was already hidden away in various parts of the factory. A single noise from any of them could bring the entire plan crashing down. We'd used Portia to sneak them inside without being seen. She hadn't promised to stick around for the actual fighting, which was understandable, but it looked like I was going to be doing a *lot* of work in PowerPoint when this was all over.

The clock finally hit zero. I took a deep breath and started the engine. "Here goes nothing," I said. "Good luck, everybody. And if I don't see any of you again—"

"Oh, don't even start with the bravado talk," Naomi said. "Just shut up and drive."

I grumbled wordlessly at her. It took every bit of courage I had to stop the van in front of the factory. The building was tall and squarish, several stories in height. It looked like it was built out of concrete cylinders and sheet metal, weirdly enough. Everything was dusty and dirty in a neglected way, though some teenagers had halfheartedly scrawled graffiti over one of the walls. Several smokestacks stretched high.

I stepped over the uneven gravel, grimacing as it gave way under my feet. Some of the rocks underfoot were the size of softballs. Just walking on them dislodged them. Great. Cooper had picked a place where I'd never have my footing. At least I had the body armor Jessica had insisted I use. The material was some kind of next-gen fabric that hugged my figure but would apparently deflect bullets. I really, really had no desire to test it.

"Hello?" I called, clutching the brown paper package Kiki had given me. "Anybody in here?"

"This way," Cooper called. It was barely noon, but when I stepped inside, gloom immediately descended. The building was little more than concrete framework and open levels. I looked around, memorizing as much detail as I could, before I turned in the direction of his voice.

I didn't have to fake the way my teeth chattered. This was where Guy had gotten his powers. This was where it had all started for him. I could see the damage from the explosion, the way the back half of the building was blown out, the scorch marks covering what few concrete posts remained. Through cracks in the wall, I could see the sky. It didn't cut through the dimness at all.

When I stepped around a half-decimated wall, I saw them: Cooper, standing behind Brook, who was definitely no longer unconscious. She *was* tied up, though, her hands shoved together so that her palms faced each other. Smart. The only person she could zap that way was herself. She was also bolted to the floor with one of the thickest chains I had ever seen. "Nice place. Cozy. You're just trying to hit *all* of the supervillain clichés, aren't you?"

Cooper lazily raised his gun. "I thought you'd appreciate the ambiance. Surprised you actually listened to me and came alone. That was foolish."

I raised my hands over my head. "I brought the journals, just like you asked. Now it's your turn. Let Brook go."

Brook's eyes widened at her real name. So did Cooper's.

"Yes, I know who she is," I said. "And I think you've done enough to her. Take the notebooks and go. It's not going to take Davenport long to catch you. Might as well enjoy what time you do have."

"I should have just killed you, perfect subject or

not," Cooper said, shaking his head. Brook narrowed her eyes at me, like she was trying to figure me out. "That's the last time I let my curiosity get in the way of my common sense."

He thumbed the safety off. In slow motion, I saw him move his aim from my Kevlar-protected chest to my head.

There was a *crack* of a gunshot in the air, but something hit me and knocked me to the side. I landed and automatically rolled.

When I looked up, Sam Bookman stood between Cooper and me, out of costume and furious.

The Bookman brothers shared some features: the same patrician nose, the shape of their faces. But Sam was solid and broad where Guy was slim. And his hair was the color of straw rather than fire. Either way, though, I'd seen the same fury on Guy's face that I saw on Sam's now. Or at least, I saw the fury for a split second, before Sam launched himself into flight and straight for Cooper.

The floors rattled as Cooper was thrown back into the wall behind him.

"What was *that*?" somebody asked over the earpieces.

"Plan A going straight to hell," I said. "Sam's here!"

"Gail, get out of there!" Guy said over the comms.

Cooper launched himself away from the wall and tackled Sam into a pillar, hard enough that it cracked. Brook and I, both frozen in our respective spots, flinched. "But Brook—"

"I'll get her! Go!" I heard a crashing noise behind me that must have been him emerging from his hiding place. Right as I turned to get the hell out of there, a flash of green and yellow at the edge of my vision made me stop. I turned back around. Brook's face was screwed up in concentration and hatred. A halo of green-yellow light so bright that it hurt my eyes glowed around her hands. I could see red-hot stress points forming in the metal chains around her wrists.

"Oh, that's *not* good," I said, and Brook's handcuffs exploded. "Guys, she's loose."

And pissed, judging by the way she immediately turned and flew right into the melee. It wasn't Cooper she aimed for, but Sam, a primal scream of rage bursting out of her.

"Guy, Vicki, *now* would be a good time to intervene," I said. What the hell was taking so long?

I scrambled to my feet and took off right as two streaks blurred right by me, one black, the other green: Guy and Vicki arriving to save the day. Or maybe just Sam. My own part of the plan was to provide backup for Jeremy and Kiki. I tucked the notebooks under my arm and scrambled over the uneven ground.

"Cut a left," Naomi said, nearly making me miss my step.

I bit down on the yelp and obeyed. As I ran, I had to battle down annoyance. Our plan was admittedly so flimsy, one solid breath could knock it over, but Sam's showing up out of some misguided sense of responsibility for an ex-girlfriend who wanted to kill him just really blew everything to hell. I understood a great deal more about Kiki's aggravation with superheroes who punched first and asked questions never.

"How's everything going?" I asked, wincing as the ground shook under my feet. This place didn't look like it could stand much more structural damage. "Is everything in place?"

"Getting there," Naomi said. "Make a right and go up the stairs."

"This place is a lot twistier than I expected," I said as I made the right turn. "Are we sure they're going to be able to lure him all this way?"

"Why do you think the others took so long to get to you?"

I reached the top of the steps and finally spotted my friends. Angélica, arms crossed over her chest and tension evident in every line, glared down into the open pit of rocks and garbage below. Jeremy was plugging something into a generator, and Kiki had scaled the tiny control room overlooking what had probably been the main production floor of the factory. Now it was just a little room that gave a bird's-eye view of the place—and even better, was a small, enclosed space. As I waved to Angélica and raced across the catwalk to the control room, Kiki looked up. She'd been threading a hose into the control room through a hole cut in the wall.

"He doesn't know we're here, does he?" she asked right away.

Out of all of us, she had the most reason to fear Cooper. She'd been the one closest to him.

And she was the bait.

"Not yet," I said. "How's everybody do—"

"Uh," Naomi said over the comms.

Jeremy stopped, still crouched over the generator. "Uh?" he asked for all of us.

"I just checked the camera Vicki put up outside. There are men in SWAT gear out there, and they're heading for you, not for Cooper and the others."

"Oh, good." Angélica tilted her head, popped her neck, and pushed her shoulders back. "I was worried this was all a little too easy. Cooper must've called on backup from Lodi."

I looked at Kiki and Jeremy. "You two keep working. Angélica—"

"Hey, you don't give the orders here," she said, laughing. She gave me an imperious look and gestured. Though I was taking my life in my hands, I climbed up onto her back, clinging tightly as she scaled the railing. She launched both of us into the air and, in the blink of an eye, we were on the ground.

Which was a good thing: less than twenty seconds later, the enemy began to swarm in.

CHAPTER TWENTY-THREE

If they wanted to catch anybody off guard, they shouldn't have picked the woman who'd survived two encounters with the Raptor in a very short amount of time. I charged for the first soldier through the door, clotheslining him with a sweep of my arm. It knocked him back into the man behind him. He didn't have time to react before I yanked the pull tab on the flashbang on the front of his vest, midspin. I completed the spin by kicking him in the chest and sprinted away as he landed on two of his buddies.

The flashbang took out the three of them.

To my left, Angélica ran at another one of the men. She disappeared, reappeared behind him, and took her opponent down without missing a beat.

A commando stormed in through a broken-out window behind me. I knocked away the muzzle of his rifle, grinding my teeth at the volume as he fired several times. I grabbed the gun, kicked the man in the knee, and yanked the gun free as he fell. When his buddy jumped in behind him, I swung the weapon like a baseball bat.

He hit the ground with a *thud*.

The cacophony of gunshots filled the air, echoing off the concrete walls and barking back to my already-hurting ears. I whipped around as five more commandos rushed in, already firing. One turned toward me and in the next instant, Angélica appeared, grabbed the back of my shirt, and phased us out of there. We hit a small mound of rocks together as she miscalculated. Winded and a little dazed, I crawled for the nearest pillar. She followed.

"Are you ever going to get that under control?" I shouted over the sound of gunfire.

"It's been less than a *day*! Get to the next pillar. I'll cover you." She rolled her eyes at me. When she moved, there was a flicker of color, then a soldier to the back of the group lay on the ground, wheezing. I sprinted for cover as his friends all turned to look.

Angélica was suddenly right beside me again. "How many do you count?"

"At least twelve, not counting the ones we took down already. This will be fun." I was a little startled and afraid to find out that I wasn't being completely sarcastic. Angélica's brief grin told me she knew exactly how I felt. "I'll follow your lead, boss."

"Thought you might." She mouthed a countdown, and we split up. Gunshots pinged against the walls and the concrete, ricocheting dangerously as we sprinted. I could hear the shouts of the troops as they set in to follow us. Their footsteps sounded just as unsteady as ours over the uneven ground.

The perfect way to fight the men from the Lodi Corporation would be to lure them into the maze and pick them off one at a time. Out in the open, we were both vulnerable. I might have the armor, and Angélica might be able to throw herself around in a fight, but ultimately, neither of us was bulletproof. But we also couldn't leave Jeremy and Kiki, who'd ducked into the control room out of sight, in the open for long.

Still, with no other choice, we raced for the hallway that led to the rest of the factory. Inside, we banked a sharp left. When the first group of soldiers pounded in after us, we set in on them. Angélica had taught me everything I knew about how to fight until Rita had come along, so it wasn't surprising that we worked together like a well-oiled machine. When she hit high, I dropped low to sweep a man's feet out from under him so I could choke him out. The brief, furious scuffle left three soldiers on the ground.

Angélica raced off in a direction that kept us parallel to the chamber where both Jeremy and Kiki were hiding. I jumped to my feet to follow, and the entire factory shook.

Distracted, I swung in the direction of where Cooper and Brook were taking on Vicki, Guy, and Sam. That hadn't been one of my friends, had it?

"Gail!" Angélica pivoted at the same time as the

soldiers rounded the corner between us. Three turned toward me. I saw the gun muzzles swing in my directly slowly, like time had slowed to a crawl. There wasn't anything for me to hide behind, so I did the opposite. I leapt up, grabbing the wire for the hanging bulb overhead. It snapped, but I was already flying feet-first toward the enemy.

I caught the first with the blade of my foot, landing on him when he toppled. The two soldiers on either side tackled me from both sides, dogpiling on top of me. I shoved one with my shoulder, just enough to throw him off-balance, and headbutted the woman behind me in the chin. When she stumbled back without letting go, I fell back on her. I kicked her partner in the chest with both feet and flipped over the woman behind me. She had no choice but to go with me. She plummeted like a rock and hit the pavement hard. I landed with my feet on either side of her and punched her partner.

The ground shook again.

Please don't be Guy, I thought, and turned to check on my fighting partner. Three of the enemy had gone after me, but five had chased Angélica down the hallway. I could see them ahead, two on the ground, three more still trying to capture and shoot her. She phased in and out, bouncing off of the walls, little sneak attacks.

Which would have worked better if her powers were working right.

I only saw the inaccuracies, the way she was a few

feet or inches off of her mark, because we'd sparred so many times. Three Class D fighters, combat-trained or not, should have been nothing for my old trainer. And for the most part, they were. She took the first out with an uppercut, the next with a combination that echoed brutally in the hallway. The third, though, was proving difficult as I sprinted for the pair of them. He blocked enough of her hits to tell me there was serious training there.

I could see the sheen of sweat on Angélica's forehead, the frustration on her face.

And from behind her, I saw the man with the rifle step into the hallway.

Angélica couldn't have seen him as he raised his rifle and aimed. I put on a desperate burst of speed, kicked off the wall to get around the two combatants, and threw myself through the air right as the man opened fire. The explosion of gunfire drowned out all noise, but I felt three bright points of pain blossom across my torso. It felt like I'd been sucker punched by a ball-peen hammer.

I hit the ground, out of breath, my vision flickering in and out. In a blink, Angélica snatched up the knife from her opponent's vest and flung it.

It hit the gunner in the face. Angélica cursed vociferously. A second heavy thud followed as the man she'd been fighting hit the ground at the same time as the gunner.

Angélica knelt by my side. "You *idiot*," she said. "What the hell kind of stunt was that?"

I grunted and rolled onto my back. Contrary to everything my brain screamed at me, there were no bullet holes in my torso. Instead, the armor Jessica Davenport had given me was scuffed in three places, but unbroken. "Bulletproof, remember?"

She smacked me upside the head. "I take hits for *you*, not the other way around."

"Yeah, because that worked out so well for me last time," I said, groaning. We both flinched when the floor shook again. "Help me up?"

"When we get back to Davenport, I am putting your ass through a wall for this," she said, but I could hear the shakiness in her voice that she wasn't quite able to mask. Whether it was from overextending herself so soon after waking up, or from actual fear that I'd been dead, I didn't know. She pulled me to my feet, and I sucked my breath through my teeth. "Gonna live?"

"Regrettably, yes."

"Good." She didn't smack me on the head again, but I could see the desire to do so written plainly on her face. "Can you fight?"

"Yes."

"Then follow me."

We had to get through two separate skirmishes to make our way back to the open foyer and the control room. Amazingly, though, there were no more troops waiting for us. Instead, there was only Kiki and Jeremy, both of whom looked pale. "How's it looking?" Angélica asked, running her arm over her forehead. "Are we ready?"

"My part is," Kiki said, casting an uncertain look at Jeremy, "but . . ."

"But what?" I asked.

"They messed everything up," he said. He was kneeling next to the generator, and he ran his hand through his hair several times in agitation.

"Is it broken? We need it for—"

"It works, but I won't be able to trigger it remotely and there's no time to rig anything up." Jeremy leaned back like he might actually be ill. "One of us is going to need to be up here to trigger, it and nobody else knows anything about how to work this. It needs to be me."

"No way," I said right away. "You don't have *any* healing ability, he'll kill you without blinking."

"Not if the rest of you do your jobs." I could see the obvious fear, but Jeremy raised himself to his full height. "It'll be fine. You know I've been wanting to play hero for a while. Be nice not to have the rest of you hog the spotlight."

"Jeremy," I said.

Angélica stepped between us, though. "If we can protect you from Cooper, is it safe for you?" she asked, looking up at my ex very seriously.

Jeremy outright squirmed under her gaze. "Mostly. This plan is incredibly dangerous to begin with."

"No," I said. "This isn't going to fly. Teach one of us what to do, and you get to safety."

But Angélica shook her head. "If the man says he can do it, we need to let him. Kiki, is everything—"

"Guys," Naomi said in all of our ears, making all

four of us flinch as one. "There's a problem. It's Brook, she—"

This time when the walls shook, more than concrete dust was knocked loose. I saw pillars actively shiver.

"What was *that*?" I asked, looking nervously in the direction of the other fight.

"Sam," Naomi said, her voice subdued. "That was Sam."

Angélica swallowed hard. "Is he . . ."

"No time!" This time it was Guy's voice in our ears. "We're coming your way! Get ready!"

Jeremy swore. "The water! Don't get any near the generator, and I'll be okay."

All four of us dove for the giant bottles of saltwater that Vicki and Guy had flown in. This was the last step of the plan for a reason: if it dried before Cooper arrived, we were up the creek without a paddle and not even Sharkbait in his really stupid costume could save us then. We scrambled to drench every part of the control room that we could reach.

"Ten seconds!" Guy said over the comms. I could hear the fight getting closer.

And then all I heard was gunshots, and Jeremy's vociferous curse. He was out in the open, exposed up on the catwalk, as one of the soldiers we'd taken out earlier raced in, spraying bullets everywhere. He dropped the bottle of saltwater as he staggered back.

Angélica hit the soldier with both feet, kicking him back into the wall.

"Five seconds!"

"Get out of here!" Kiki threw her water bottle down and grabbed my arm, shoving me out of the control room, toward Jeremy. She slammed the door after me and ran out the other way, out of sight on the other catwalk.

"Are you okay?" I asked Jeremy, who had managed to grow even paler. We raced for the stairwell where we would need to hide. I hit the stairs first and crouched, Jeremy sliding for home behind me. "You didn't get hit, did you?"

"N-no, he missed me, I'm okay."

I didn't get a chance to ask anything else, though, for in that second, Guy burst into the room in a blur of green and black. I could tell from how he was flying that he'd been severely hurt, but there wasn't any time to focus on that. Vicki followed a half second behind; and then, shouting in rage, Cooper charged in. He didn't pause before he leapt through the air, latching onto Guy and doing his best to rip one of Guy's arms off. They grappled in midair, Guy struggling against Cooper's superior strength. I stopped breathing.

Guy broke free. Cooper dropped sixty feet through the air, landed heavily on the ground, and leapt again. This time, it was Vicki he aimed for.

She flicked her hand and blasted him in the face with one of her firebolts. Cooper just shook his head like he was clearing water out of his ears. He landed and jumped again.

"Now!" Naomi said in our ears, and Kiki stepped into view.

"Lemuel!" she shouted.

All three of the Class A fighters swung about. Even though Guy and Vicki both wore masks, I could read the feigned shock in their body language as they took in the sight of Kiki up on that catwalk.

"What are you doing?" Vicki shouted a little melodramatically. She made a show of waving frantically. "Kiki, get out of here!"

A look of confusion spread over Cooper's face, followed rapidly by disappointment, and anger. He took three running steps and jumped yet again. "*You*," he said, lurching toward Kiki as he landed on the catwalk. Covered in sweat, his eyes crazy, he stalked forward. Kiki backed up toward the control room. "You did this. *Why?*"

"For my grandfather," Kiki said, and Cooper drew up short.

"Now!" Naomi said in our ears, and four things happened at once:

Cooper lunged for Kiki.

Jeremy and I sprinted for the generator.

Brook burst in and flew straight for Guy.

And Kiki threw herself off the catwalk.

As expected, Cooper overshot, slipped on the water, and tripped right into the control room. Vicki snatched Kiki out of the air three feet before she hit the ground.

Cooper leapt to his feet, but Angélica phased back

onto the catwalk and slammed the door on the opposite side shut, tripping the valve release. Cooper took two steps to the door—and began to claw at his throat. The gas that flooded the room wasn't combustible, but Kiki had sworn that even Cooper wouldn't be able to breathe. At least for a little while. Which was why we had the second part of the plan.

"Now, Jeremy!" Angélica called.

Inside the control room, Cooper turned red and began to lurch about. Out in the open, Brook kicked Guy in the center of the chest and sent him tumbling back. Vicki, who'd apparently deposited Kiki somewhere safely out of the way, joined in the scrum.

"*Now*, Jeremy!" Angélica said again, louder this time. She'd braced herself on the other side of the control room, but none of us was going to be able to keep Cooper in there if he shook off the gas.

I realized that Jeremy had gone bone white and was staring at the generator. Or more precisely, at the giant plastic bottle of saltwater that he'd dropped. It had pooled everywhere around the generator and under the door of the control room.

There wasn't a safe place to stand.

"Oh, shit," I said. There was no way that Jeremy could trigger the generator without being electrocuted.

"What is it?" Angélica said.

I looked at Jeremy. "Don't even think about doing what I think you're about to. We'll come up with a way—maybe I can—"

His eyes never left the puddle. "You can 'port, right? That's a thing you can do now?"

Desperation flooded me. What good was having a power if it couldn't save the day? In the control room, Cooper had dropped to one knee, but he'd stopped clawing for his throat, and that couldn't be good. "Yes, but I can't control it, so it would never work—"

"Good, then you'll survive this," he said, and he shoved my chest, pushing me right off the catwalk.

I fell, mouth open in a scream that never came out. Shock coursed through me. I saw in that weird time-lessness before gravity took hold, Jeremy run forward in slow motion forward. He stepped into the puddle, flipped on the generator—

And suddenly I was on the catwalk again, running toward him. It was like racing toward a weird mirror: Cooper on one side of the glass, body taut as the current raced through his body, and closer to me, in the open, Jeremy stuck in exactly the same position. Both of their faces were contorted with agony.

I leapt over the water and tackled Jeremy right off the catwalk, heart in my throat again. Everything sped up again so that all I could see was the ground rushing at both of us. I twisted in midair so I would take the brunt of the landing. It would hurt, I knew, but that seemed inevitable at this point. I squeezed my eyes shut.

A split second later, something hit me from the side, and Jeremy was torn away. My trajectory went from a steep plummet to a sideways flight. Either way, I hit the ground hard enough that it pushed all of the air out of my lungs and pounded hard into the earlier injuries from the fight. I lay where I landed, looking up in a daze. Every part of my body hurt, but all of that had nothing on my head.

I was never 'porting ever again. It just wasn't worth it.

"*You*," said a voice from over me, and I opened my eyes just the merest slits. I wasn't surprised at all to see Brook standing over me, vibrating with fury. Blood gushed from a cut on her forehead, but I could see her eyes clearly. They were even more crazed than usual. I was a little more concerned about the gun in her hand. Where was everybody? Where was Guy? And Jeremy?

"Leave me alone," I said, my voice hoarse. "At this point, you're just a pain in my ass. Your powers can't do a thing to me."

"No," Brook said. "But this can."

She raised the gun. Abstractly, I recognized it as Cooper's, the same one that had been meant to kill me. She thumbed off the safety. I didn't bother to watch my life flash before my eyes, as I knew it always had been and always would be depressingly full of encounters with supervillains. Instead, I lay there, unable to move after my fall, and glared up at her. It was almost peaceful, in its way.

Clang.

Brook's eyes rolled back in her head. Almost predictably, she dropped like a rock.

Angélica lowered the shovel she'd used to clobber my nemesis and spit on the ground for good measure.

"Been waiting to do that all *day*," she said, lowering a hand to help me up. "What a bitch."

"No kidding." Sitting up only doubled the amount of pain trying to cram its way into my skull, so I groaned. "Guy? Is Guy okay?"

"I'm fine." And like a miracle, he was suddenly there, kneeling right beside me. When he pulled his mask off, his hair was a mess, and he had a couple of cuts on his face, but he was there, and *alive*. He looked back at me in the same shell-shocked way that told me he was giving me the same once-over. "Angélica just beat me to the punch. Are you okay?"

"Sort of. Jeremy—where is he?" Panic flooded in. Had I gotten to him in time? Had he landed safely? I looked around, frantic now. I didn't see him anywhere nearby. "Where is he? Where did he go?"

"Vicki caught him and flew off." Kiki ran up, panting heavily. "I think he's dead."

"What?" I said, the word coming out as a screech. My heart stopped beating.

"Cooper! I think Cooper is dead, not Jeremy. God, I'm sorry. I mean—it worked." Kiki shook her head, looking as dazed as I felt. "He's not moving, and when I just looked in, he wasn't breathing. I think it worked." She took a deep breath and looked at each of us in turn. "I think we really did it."

CHAPTER TWENTY-FOUR

They had two doctors declare Lemuel Cooper dead.

I was still in the factory when Zaptastic arrived to undo the work Jeremy had electrocuted himself for. From where I sat, back resting against a column and head throbbing in time with the "William Tell Overture," I watched the electric superhero disable the generator so that medics in gas masks could break open the windows to the control room.

They carried Cooper's body away on a stretcher with a sheet over it. My entire throat felt coated with sickness. I'd helped kill a man. Even though I knew he had been trying to kill me, he was still a man. He and the Lodi Corporation had destroyed lives in their pursuit of creating superheroes from scratch, but I couldn't quite call myself a good guy in that moment, not while I watched them cart a dead man away.

They carried Brook off, unconscious and cuffed.

Taking her down didn't make me feel like a hero, either. She was a victim, too. A twisted one, but a victim nonetheless.

When the paramedics came for me, I was bundled off into an ambulance. Guy had flown back to Davenport with Sam to get him medical attention, so I only had Angélica with me. She nagged the paramedics about me while I lay on the stretcher with my eyes closed. My torso hurt from the bullets my armor had stopped, but none of that had anything on my headache.

Kiki stayed behind to handle the scene, I figured. At some point, I also suspected Naomi would emerge from the ether and start questioning everybody. Once a journalist, as she liked to say.

I started laughing when they took us to Dartmoor Incorporated, right there in the Willis Tower. The paramedics gave me weird looks as they carried us past the still-destroyed lobby, but I didn't bother to explain. They gave me my own room, prescribed me painkillers for the headache and rest for the exhaustion. Angélica was also given a full checkup, though they had to drag her away from me. She returned even grouchier than she'd been before.

"Long day, huh?" she asked as she dropped into the chair by my hospital bed.

I squeezed one eye open, even though light still felt like a personal affront to my corneas. I'd spent years in and out of the hospital, but it was a little disquieting how soothing I found the beep and hum of the monitors all around me. Like an old, forgotten lullaby.

"How is everybody?" I asked, closing my eye again.

"Sam will need some time to recover." I felt the bed move as she propped her feet up on the edge.

"And Jeremy?" I asked, my voice cracking a little.

"He's—he's not responding to anything. It was a miracle he survived at all. That much electricity should have killed him right away."

"I know." I was too hollow and tired to cry. I understood Jeremy and how impotent he must have felt for months, trapped in an underground superhero complex and surrounded by people more powerful than him. His life had been taken away by Guy's decision to let people think Blaze was Jeremy Collins rather than giving up his identity. And he'd been a general pain in the ass over it, but I was still fond of Jeremy. We'd been through too much together for me to hate him. "He's not going to make it, is he?"

"It's too soon to be sure. I've seen people come back from worse."

I could only nod.

"But you should sleep while you can." Angélica shifted in her chair. A second later, I heard a curse from all the way across the room.

I didn't bother to open my eyes. "You're really never going to get that under control, are you?"

"It has been less than a day, *idiota*." I heard her annoyed huff of breath as she dropped back into her chair.

When I opened eyes again, the headache was gone, the room was dark, and Angélica was nowhere to be found. Instead, Guy had taken up residence in her seat.

From the angle of his neck and shoulders, he was going to wake up with a cramp. I sat up and stretched, slowly.

The bed creaked, which made Guy jolt.

"Just me," I said when he went tense.

"Good morning," he said. His hair was sticking up in the back. He yawned and peered at me. "Doing okay? You were sleeping like the dead."

I didn't tell him that the beep of the monitors felt more like home than my apartment really ever had. "I'm feeling better. You can go back to sleep, if you want."

He pushed at his hair, yawning again. "No, I'm up, I'm up. I'm—I'm sorry I wasn't here earlier. I had to stick with Sam, and then somebody had to hold Vicki back when Jeremy flatlined—"

"What?" I asked, rolling immediately to my feet.

"They brought him back," Guy said. "But Vicki didn't handle it well. He's in a coma, Gail. I'm sorry. You saved his life, but the doctors don't think . . ."

"He wanted to be a damn hero, just like everybody else," I said, my voice rough.

"It's a problem in our line of work," Guy said.

And Jeremy *had* been a hero. Without his bravery, Cooper would have probably taken us all out. But I was tired of my having my friends make the sacrifice play. The last time that had happened, it had been Angélica, and I'd spent over a week thinking she was dead. Now it was Jeremy. "Are we sure Kiki's not faking it, and he's secretly fine thanks to some giant conspiracy?" I asked, weakly.

Guy's smile was tinged with sadness. "We only get that lucky once. Do you want to see him?"

"Please."

It was worse than even I feared. I'd been in some bad spots before, but Jeremy looked like a pale, faded facsimile of himself. He was strapped to a breather, and there were so many different diagnostic machines poking out of his arms and his chest that he looked like some kind of cyborg. I stopped in his doorway and stared, my breath hitching.

It didn't look like Jeremy at all. Not the man who had spent hours in the gym or was not-so-secretly vain about his looks.

"Hey," Guy said from behind me. He put his hands on my shoulders. "He's still alive. There's still hope."

I tried to reply, but my words stuck in my throat. Dread mounting, I stepped forward and around to the side of Jeremy's bed, which wasn't easy to do with all of the machines clustered around him. I looked hard at his face, like I could bring his sarcasm and life back by sheer willpower. There was absolutely no change.

"Gail," Guy said.

"I could have survived it, you asshole," I said, glaring at Jeremy's face. I felt my hands clench into fists. "I could have—" My breath hitched. "I could have made it, you didn't *have* to do that, you utter, insufferable bastard—"

"Gail." Guy grabbed my arm. He looked at the door and at the nurses beyond, but I didn't care. I wanted to reach past all of the tubes and wires and shake Jeremy so that he came back so I could yell at him properly. "Gail, I can't believe I'm about to say this, but please don't punch the coma patient."

"He didn't have to do it," I said. My cheeks were wet. When had that happened? "He pushed me off the damn catwalk, and I could have—I could have—"

"Shh." Guy shifted his grip on my arm and pulled me in for a hug, wrapping his arms around me. "Gail, it's not your fault."

A sob broke through, catching me off guard. I pushed my face into the rough fabric of Guy's uniform, letting the rest of the tears flood. This wasn't how it was supposed to go. We were supposed to defeat the bad guy, I was supposed to be the one on the bed, and everybody was supposed to be okay.

Not flatlining, not in a coma. Awake, healthy, maybe a little scarred from the experience, but overall fine.

When the tears had slowed to a trickle, Guy rubbed my back one last time and took a step back. "He'd be lapping up all this attention now," he said, and I laughed because there wasn't anything else I *could* do. "He's going to tease you forever when I tell him about this."

"Don't you dare," I said, wiping at my cheeks. "Do you mind if we . . ."

"Sure." Guy pulled over chairs for both of us. I immediately curled up in mine. It was foolish, but I felt like if I looked away from Jeremy for even one minute, he might slip away. "If the nurses try to kick us both out, I'll distract them and let you make a run for it."

"Isn't that defeating the point?" I asked.

He smiled and draped an arm across the back of my chair. "Shut up."

I don't know how I fell asleep again. I shouldn't have been able to, not with all the nurses coming in and out of Jeremy's room, but curled up in my chair, I caught a couple more naps. Sometimes when I opened my eyes, it was Vicki sitting in the chair, pretending to read a fashion magazine. Sometimes it was Guy, or Angélica, and even Kiki once. She gave me a sad, fearful look, like she wasn't sure what my reaction to her being there would be.

I closed my eyes and decided not to deal with any of it.

Finally, I woke up and I was on my own. Guy had likely gone off to sit by Sam's bedside, Kiki was gone, and Angélica, I imagined, probably was dealing with one of the hundreds of tasks required to get being legally declared dead overturned. I stretched and rose to my feet. Jeremy's face hadn't changed at all.

"You need to wake up soon," I said, squeezing his hand once. "You're seriously missing out on Vicki fawning over you."

There wasn't any change. I felt my lip tremble and ducked out of the room before I could start leaking again.

I went back to my own room and took a shower, standing under the too-hot spray for so long that I felt like boiling my skin off. Rather than changing into another hospital gown, I traced my steps back to the closet where I'd once hidden while breaking Naomi out of the same building, and helped myself to some scrubs. Feeling better about that and pretty much nothing else, I went back to my room

The man standing in the middle of it made me stop in my tracks.

"Ah, there you are," Eddie Davenport said as he turned. He wore a pressed suit with creases sharp enough to cut. "The nurses were unable to locate you, so I told them I'd just wait here for you."

If I had hackles, they would have risen at the mere sight of him. I wanted to fly at him and tear his eyes out, but I kept my cool, stepping inside and closing the door behind me. The stolen scrubs felt rough against my skin all of a sudden. The last time I'd seen this man, he'd been declaring me guilty of murder.

"What do you want?" I asked in a surprisingly calm voice.

"Miss Godwin." His smile had probably graced hundreds of gossip sites and *Forbes* magazine spreads. It only sent a cold chill through me. All I could see was him in that wood-paneled court chamber, lit by that weird yellow light. "I'm happy to see that you're well and not too injured by your recent experience with Dr. Cooper."

Tell that to my friend in the coma, you jackass, I thought.

"I'm here," Eddie went on, "to offer you an apology."

"You sent me to prison based on a bullshit trial," I said, folding my arms over my chest. "Would you like a diagram of where exactly you can shove that apology, or would me telling you straight up suffice?"

"A little anger is to be expected," Eddie said.

"A *little*? Your mother spent over a week beating me senseless because you couldn't be bothered with things like 'evidence,' your sister used me as bait for a sociopath, and you couldn't be bothered to listen to your own niece when she told you Cooper was bad news, a price that I and several of my friends paid for." My hands were in fists again, but I kept my arms tightly folded. If he so much as moved wrong, I was going to go for his throat. And I knew precisely where that would lead me.

Eddie's face twitched, but that was the only sign he gave of any guilt. "Be that as it may," he said in a voice I imagined he'd used in boardroom meetings over the years, "I am here to offer you a pardon for the charge of accessory to murder, seeing as Angélica Rocha is indeed alive and well."

"You don't care that you ruin lives, do you?" I said.

"Contrary to popular opinion, Miss Godwin, I care very much." Eddie inclined his head. "Davenport Industries is fully prepared to make full reparations for your pain and suffering. Should you ever need anything, you have only to ask, and, of course, you always have a place within the company if you wish to return to your training and transition. The Mobium—"

"I'll pass, thanks," I said in the coldest voice I'd ever

heard myself use. "I've had my fill with Davenport's particular brand of 'charity.'"

I could sense from his body language that Eddie was growing annoyed, but he only smiled.

It made my blood want to boil.

"No wonder Jessie likes you so much," Eddie said. "My offer still stands, whether or not you take it. If you choose not to, well, I wish you luck in all your future endeavors, Miss Godwin. And on behalf of Davenport Industries, my sincerest apologies about any mistreatment you've suffered at the hands of my family."

This time, I did tell him where he could shove that apology. His smile only tightened, the lines around his eyes and mouth growing whiter, but it never dropped away from his face. "I see," was all he said. He nodded like I'd made a compelling argument and headed for the door. "Good-bye, Miss Godwin."

"Here's to never meeting again," I said.

He inclined his head. At the door, he paused. "There's just one more thing," he said, turning back. "About your escape from Detmer . . ."

I was still shaking with rage twenty minutes later when Angélica found me sitting by Jeremy's bedside again. "Is it true?" she asked without preamble. "You told Eddie Davenport to have sex with a goat?"

"More or less," I said. "Davenport and I are done. The minute I'm discharged from this place, we have no official ties to each other."

"Without finishing your training?" she asked, raising an eyebrow.

Despite my fury, guilt did seep through the cracks. Angélica was as innocent in all of this as I was. I winced. "Yeah, I'm sorry, but I just don't think—"

"Gail, I'm messing with you." She bumped her shoulder against mine, smiling. "Even if you'd stayed, our training relationship would be over anyway."

"What do you mean? The Mobium, it's still evolving."

"Yeah, it is. But I handed in my resignation half an hour ago when I *also* told the CEO of Davenport Industries to have sex with a farm animal." Angélica gave me a proud look when I gawked at her. "I believe your boyfriend is in the middle of doing the same thing as we speak."

"Are you sure about this? I mean, it's fine for me to quit. I still have my job at Mirror Reality, which will *probably* handle my grocery bill if I don't worry about luxuries like paying the rent and electricity bills. But you, that was your entire life."

Angélica shrugged. "I'll figure something out."

"But you love training superheroes."

"Maybe I'll start a superhero gym."

I shook my head, boggling. For me to cut ties with Davenport was one thing: they'd screwed me over almost from the beginning. But Guy had found his community there, and Angélica, she'd been so entrenched in the very fabric of the place. And for them to just up and leave like that, it made my stomach sink.

"Hey," Angélica said, and I realized I hadn't hidden

my expression as well as I thought. "This is my choice. It has nothing to do with you and everything to do with my personal beliefs. You don't need to worry about me. I worry about *you*, that's the way it goes."

"You're not my trainer anymore," I said. "You can't tell me what to do."

She grinned and cuffed me on the shoulder. "Keep telling yourself that."

Impulsively, I hugged her, holding on for dear life. "Thank you," was all I said. "And if I didn't say it before, I'm glad you're not dead."

She hugged me back. "That makes two of us."

On the other side of the room, something made a loud buzzing noise and promptly exploded in a shower of sparks. Angélica and I broke apart. I looked around in confusion, but we hadn't been attacked. There was only us, Jeremy, and the smoking machine in the room.

"What the?" I asked, craning my neck as nurses raced in. Every machine was going crazy, screens blinking on and off. The beeping sounded like a chorus of angry alley cats. Jeremy's body arched up, which made both of us jump. "What's going on?"

"Stay back." Angélica yanked me out of the way of the incoming nurses.

"But . . ." My protest died on my lips as Jeremy's body suddenly sagged back onto the mattress. All beeping stopped. The machines returned to normal in the blink of an eye (except for the one that was still smoking). Nurses raced around, chattering at each other too fast for me to follow. "What just happened?"

"No idea. But we need to get out of here since we're underfoot."

"But Jeremy—" He hadn't woken. His face was still slack and ashen.

Angélica dragged me bodily out of the room and held on to my arm as we stood by the observation window. When Vicki raced up, out of breath and holding her mask, Angélica tilted her head. "What took you so long?"

"Has there been a change?"

"You owe me ten bucks," Angélica only said to Vicki.

"What are you talking about?"

"Look at his hands," she said. It took me a second for my brain to process what I was seeing. There, in the space between Jeremy's fingers, were tiny blue flickers of electricity. They weren't coming from the machines. They sparked onto the bedsheets, burning tiny holes in the fabric.

"Oh my god," I said. "Does that mean what I think it means?"

"It means he's going to be fine," Angélica said. Vicki, next to her, sagged against the wall and closed her eyes. It occurred to me that Jeremy's feelings might not be as unrequited as I'd suspected. I filed that away for later and continued to watch in fascination as waves of blue sparks rolled over his hands. The monitors keeping tabs on his brain activity never changed, though. "Looks like we're getting a new member to the powered team."

"Oh, he's going to love that," I said.

"I'll stay here." Vicki swallowed hard a few times. "Somebody needs to keep an eye on him and make sure—"

"He's going to be fine," Angélica said. "He's too vain to come back truly evil, and he wasn't dead that long."

I got the feeling they'd been through this kind of transition before. As for me, I was too busy reeling. Being electrocuted hadn't killed Jeremy.

It had given him superpowers.

He was going to completely lose his mind over that when he finally woke up.

Angélica cleared her throat and grabbed my shoulder, pulling me along. "C'mon, you can buy this newly unemployed friend of yours a chocolate milk in the cafeteria," she said.

My last glimpse of Vicki, as my ex-trainer pulled me away and around a corner, was of her discreetly brushing a tear away.

Guy joined us in the cafeteria, his tray holding considerably less food than either of ours. It was disgusting hospital food, which I definitely hadn't missed, but I dug in with gusto. We filled him in on the news while we ate.

"Sam's going to be okay, too," Guy said, pushing his brownie toward my plate. "So that's all of us. We're all fine—or going to be. For the most part."

"And Kiki is safe from Cooper, and hopefully Rita Detmer wants nothing else from me." I finished my first milk carton and reached for the second.

"So what now?" Angélica asked, snatching up the brownie before I could get to it. Guy gave her an aggrieved look, but she only shrugged.

I tried to hide my laughter at his expression. "I don't know about you," I said. "But I'm ready for that vacation now."

EPILOGUE

"This is your idea of a vacation?" Guy asked, landing out of sight of the front gate. "Gail, you realize that's a prison, right?"

"It's only a few days," I said.

"It's only a few days *in a prison*."

Davenport Industries might have granted me a pardon for the charge of working with Brook to kill Angélica, as the latter was definitely not dead, and I had never worked with the former. But that didn't mean I hadn't broken the law. So I was going back to prison . . . for breaking out of prison in the first place. And judging from the look on Guy's face as he set me down in the trees beyond Detmer's expansive lawns, he was ready to fight each and every member of Davenport on that issue.

"I know that," I said, rolling my shoulders. "The

only part that's going to suck is being separated from you, I promise. Besides, Rita owes me one. I'll be fine."

"Rita Detmer has Villain Syndrome. Her idea of 'owing you one' is probably to blow you up and put you out of your misery. You don't have to do this. I can get you a lawyer, or we can work something out—"

"Rita owes me," I said again. "I'll be okay."

"But why are you going back?" Guy looked distressed now.

"I told you. I need a vacation." I took pity on him and rose on my tiptoes to kiss him. The height difference was really going to give me a cramp in my neck, but I didn't care at the moment. Guy sighed when I pulled back. "Relax. Just a few days, then we're on for that dinner and a movie, right?"

"That'll be a nice change of pace. I'll visit you every day."

"Deal." I kissed him again. Before I could change my mind, I pushed away, gave him a little wave, and emerged from the trees. The guards at the front gate all snapped to attention as I approached. They weren't used to prisoners coming to them of their own volition, but after my first experience with a prison transport van, there was no way I was getting back in one of those. I walked up to the first guard and gave him a mocking little salute. "Gail Godwin, reporting for duty, sir."

He gave me a puzzled look. "Where are your handcuffs?"

I sighed and held out my wrists. Belatedly, they scrambled to slap me in a pair of manacles.

It had been two days since I'd been discharged from the hospital and from Davenport. Jeremy had yet to wake up, but there had been several weird power surges, and even Vicki felt confident enough to leave his side for more than twenty minutes. By all reports, Kiki was going through Davenport and undoing the damage that Cooper had done, and Davenport was launching a full-scale investigation into the Lodi Corporation to figure out if there were any more Mobium subjects.

I really hoped it was limited to Brook, Angélica, and me. The world didn't need manufactured superheroes. Especially since Mobium's creator had never been found. I personally suspected the Lodi Corporation had killed Dr. Mobius the night they'd come after him, the night we'd escaped from his false lab together. But—and I was never going to share this with Kiki—I also suspected there was a strong chance he'd been in the Lodi building that Raptor and I had destroyed.

I really wasn't sure how I felt about that.

The guards dragged me to processing, with Dr. Kehoe and her assistant (who visibly paled upon seeing me). "Please tell me you have no new scars," Dr. Kehoe said with a sigh, "and we can just skip that bit."

"Blame Cooper," I said as I peeled off my shirt to show off my brand-new scars from Cooper's incisions.

An hour later, I strolled out of processing, wearing the green tunic and pants one more time. I was already salivating at the thought of visiting the dining room, but I made Tabitha the Perky Guard take me straight to Raze, who tackled me with happiness. I escaped with only a couple of bruises by promising to meet her for dinner, and headed back toward my cell.

As I passed the glass wall of the gym, I felt something cold settle between my shoulder blades. I turned, and, just like that, Rita stood there.

I sighed at her. "You're not here to deliver another lesson, are you?"

She kept staring.

"Because honestly, I'm kind of done with all of your lessons, no offense. Experience might be a great teacher, but you're kind of a crappy one."

Rita made a noncommittal noise in the back of her throat. "You survived," she said.

"I did. It's really with no thanks to you," I said.

For a second, I thought I'd gone too far. Rita's face was still blank and unreadable, but it *felt* like there was a storm brewing beneath her skin. And I was under no illusions: if Rita wanted to take me out, I would go down, and I would go down hard.

But there was no reason I needed to let her know I feared her, so I pushed my shoulders back. "Kiki says hi. She's safe. We killed Cooper." I really wasn't sure how I felt about that still. It had woken me in the middle of the night with the taste of metal in my mouth. I could still see the sheet-covered stretcher being carried out of the factory in my mind, and the mirrored poses as the current had electrocuted both him and Jeremy. "So even though I know you're not going to say thank you, I will say this. You're welcome. Now if you could leave me alone, my life would be so much better, thanks."

She moved too fast for me to throw up anything but a very basic, shoddy block. I knocked her fist away from my rib cage, but the second punch still landed on the side of my head. I dropped to one knee, surprised that there weren't little cartoon birds flying around my head. When I looked up, Rita was already languidly strolling away.

I climbed to my feet and brushed my pants off. That answered that question. But right before Rita turned the corner, I saw her pause and swivel. I went tense, expecting another ambush attack.

The old woman inclined her head, just once. It looked like it took every effort in the world to do so.

Understanding struck: that was all she could do to thank me.

Before I could do anything more than gape, she'd ambled around the corner.

"Always a pleasure," I said under my breath as I brushed off the front of my shirt for good measure. Rita Detmer was finally done with me. After her insane Villain-Syndrome-fueled plot had completely altered my life in every way possible, she was done. A sense of real and beautiful freedom washed over me.

Of course, I was still standing in the middle of a supervillain prison, but life wasn't perfect.

Bolstered by that, I stuck my hands in my pockets and whistled all the way to the dining room. After my adventures, I really needed a five-star meal. I spotted

Lady Danger and Venus von Trapp across the room and waved to them both as I made my way over. Neither looked particularly surprised to see me back, but they were both bursting with news about what had happened with the new sushi chef (there was apparently a roll named in Lemuel Cooper's honor) and what had happened after my breakout. I let them gush as I proceeded to order everything on the menu.

When Raze came bouncing up, I made sure to pick the razor blades from my soup. I listened to my rather strange ex-nemeses with almost a sense of contentment. Jeremy was going to be okay, Guy and I were finally going to go on that date, Kiki was out of danger, Naomi had returned to her job at the Domino, and Angélica was *alive*. Everything in that moment felt crisply, sublimely perfect.

Or it did until an hour later, I made my way back to my new cell to catch up on some more sleep. The woman sitting on the top bunk looked up as I palmed the door open, and a slow, vicious smile spread across her face.

"Hello, roomie," Brooklyn Gianelli said.

ABOUT THE AUTHOR

LEXIE DUNNE is a woman of many masks, all of them stored neatly in a box under her bed. By day a mild-mannered technical writer and by night a novelist, she keeps life interesting by ignoring it completely and writing instead. She hails from St. Louis, home of the world's largest croquet piece, where she can be found reading comics and spoiling her dog. *Supervillains Anonymous* is her love letter to the caped evildoers of the world. She does not count herself among their company, no matter how many cliffhangers she writes.

www.dunnewriting.com

Discover great authors, exclusive offers, and more at hc.com.